Piper Jean

KOREA RISING

FALLING FOR KOREA BOOK 2

Vaniker Press

Published by Vaniker Press LLC, all rights reserved.

ISBN: 979-8-9864577-4-1 (eBook)
ISBN: 979-8-9864577-5-8 (Paperback)
ISBN: 979-8-9864577-6-5 (Audiobook)
ISBN: 979-8-9864577-7-2 (Hardback)
www.piperjean.com
www.vanikerpress.com

For Peter
You'll always be
my love story

1

JI-HEE

I checked my phone again, no texts, no missed calls, nothing. Forty-five minutes alone in the Los Angeles airport, and Grandfather wasn't responding. Not that I'd complain. I'd never complain another day of my life, because being here meant I was finally free from my London reform school. I wheeled my suitcase over to a hard plastic chair and dropped down with fatigue. I shouldn't worry. By this time tomorrow, I'd probably be eating Grandfather's favorite oxtail soup and watching Korean dramas.

But I couldn't help going over it again in my mind. Grandfather had called St. Austin's school and had me discharged. He'd sent a car to pick me up and take me to the airport. He'd bought me a direct flight to LAX and said he'd be waiting for me. So where was he?

After another lonely hour passed with no response, disappointment crept along the floor to hover around my seat. I leaned back and closed my eyes with my phone gripped in my hand. He had to call.

A small voice interrupted my thoughts. "Are you waiting for someone, too?"

I opened my eyes to see a young girl next to me. She couldn't have been more than twelve years old, and she'd spoken in my native language. That startled me almost more than the fact that I hadn't noticed her sitting down.

I responded back in Korean. "I'm waiting for my grandfather." I hadn't spoken it in so long but loved how my mouth wrapped around the words. They flowed, easy and comforting, like eating a bowl of steaming rice after a long day without food.

The girl wore her hair in a short blunt cut that accentuated her thin neck. In her lap, she gripped a blue backpack with frayed patches of bands sewn into the denim. I recognized one of the bands that JAYNE talent represented. It was the agency my family owned and what kept us in the top tier of Korean wealth. Not that she would know any of that. *I* wasn't an idol or a famous actress.

She stared at me with hopeful eyes, and I realized that maybe she'd come to sit by me because she was nervous in a large airport alone.

"Where are your parents?" I asked.

The girl shifted. "I'm traveling with my aunt, but she went to change the baby, so I'm watching our luggage." She looked down at the single gray suitcase at her feet.

"Where are you traveling to?" I asked.

"Home." She frowned. "Busan. My parents let me go to California for the summer with my aunt, but school starts soon." She rested her chin against her backpack and sighed with weariness.

I smiled down at her and held out a hand. "My name is Lee Ji-hee. What is yours?"

She shook my hand. "Choi Bora," she said with another sigh, even more dramatic than the first one.

"I bet you're kind of homesick if you've been gone all summer."

Bora shook her head. "No, I'm not homesick at all. I don't want to go home."

"Really, why not?"

"I love living with my aunt. She lets me do whatever I want. My mom makes me do all the dishes and both of my brothers are too busy to help." She glanced up at me with her bangs hanging in her eyes. "You wouldn't understand having a mean family. I bet you only have a sister and nice parents."

Without thinking, I reached out and smoothed her hair back so she could see. Then almost laughed at the irony of what she'd just said. I definitely did not have a nice family. "I have one brother," I said. "His name is Gun, and he bosses me around every chance he gets. Also, my mother hasn't let me eat sugar since I was four."

Bora looked at me and narrowed her eyes with disbelief. "Not even Crunky bars?"

I smiled. "I've never had a single one."

Her mouth dropped open. "That might be worse than dishes. I could never live without Crunky bars after school."

"See," I said. "Maybe your mom isn't so bad. She buys you treats."

But then Bora looked me up and down. Her eyes rested on the diamond tennis bracelet on my left wrist. "I wear hand-me-downs from my brothers." She stuck her feet out straight in front of her. "Even their shoes. I can tell by *your* shoes that you're not poor. You don't have to wear your brother's gross stuff so maybe that makes up for not having sugar."

I looked at her black Adidas and then at my own designer tennis shoes. Her shoes weren't terrible, and her clothes fit her well enough, but it was true that everything I wore was expensive. That was normal for me. My family was very wealthy, maybe not as disgustingly rich as most of the Elite, but we still swam in the same pool. I liked to think of us as guppies in a pond of over fed koi.

It could have been my imagination, but her lip seemed to curl up when she glanced at my leather Chanel purse next to me. "I bet you have an easy life," she said.

I crossed my arms and took a steadying breath. I didn't think some young know-it-all would understand that money wasn't everything. Maybe her mother made her do dishes, but mine had turned her back on me.

After hustling me off to London, I was pretty sure she covered up my disappearance from Korean society by making me into another case of boarding-school-banishment. Having a daughter go abroad for school was socially acceptable to the Elite—correctional schools were not. She saved face, but I'd lost all of my friends and my family in one day. I looked down at the girl's shoes again. "What size of shoe are you?"

"I'm a 241," she said. "Why?"

I was a size larger than her, but her feet were probably still growing. "Do you want to trade me shoes?"

"What? You'd do that?"

I shrugged. "I can buy another pair."

She leaned down, inspecting my shoes closely. "Wow," she whispered. "Are they real Jimmy Choo's?"

I slipped both off and handed them over. "Yep. They're real."

She immediately gave me her shoes, almost like she was afraid I'd change my mind. "Nari and Hana will be so jealous when they see these," she said, as she did up the laces. "I'm wearing them on the first day of school."

I wiggled my feet to fit into her shoes—very tight.

Bora caressed the gold on the canvass with reverence. "How do they look?"

"Perfect," I said.

She beamed at me then tilted her head. "Thank you."

"Of course," I said with a shrug.

"Are you going home too?" she asked. "When does your school start? Maybe we can hang out sometime."

"I'm attending a school here in California and living with my grandfather."

She sat up straighter. "You're going to school in the States? International?" She gave a laugh. "You really are rich then. What is the school like? Will there be kids of famous movie stars there?"

I frowned, thinking. I was shocked when the night guard woke me with Grandfather's phone call. He'd only spoken briefly, telling me the name of the new school—Marklem Academy—and that it wasn't a boarding school. But I hadn't cared about anything other than I was leaving London. No more stark rooms and cold bunk beds. I'd no longer suffer without a phone or computer, and there would be no mandatory exercise at 5:00 a.m. in the rain. Instead of identical blue polyester uniforms, I'd go back to my tailored shirts, designer dresses, and forget every bad day in London. I'd have my freedom again.

The night guard had retrieved my things from storage and rushed me from the still dark and sleeping school to a waiting car with barely time to change. After that I'd been more excited about charging the cell phone I hadn't held for three years than what my new school would be like. I cleared my throat. "I haven't toured it yet, but my grandfather thinks it's perfect for me."

"Is it better than Daeshim Academy?" she asked. "All the rich kids in Korea go there. Have you heard of it?"

I couldn't tell her I'd already attended Daeshim and blown my chances of ever going back, or that my family hid me in London, too embarrassed to own what had happened. I gave a little laugh. "I don't really care where I go to school, as long as I live with my grandfather."

Bora watched me closely. "Your grandfather must be nice."

I nodded. "He is."

"Do you know how lucky you are? You're rich and you're living in California without a nagging mother. If I only had my grandfather at home, I could hang out with friends all day," she said.

I tried to smile back and say how right she was, to be all cool about it. I was lucky to be here. But London was still too fresh. At first, I thought my family would regret their decision. Surely, they would miss me, realize their mistake, and bring me home. I didn't belong in reform school.

Only they never did.

I swallowed hard. "Yeah, it is going to be cool living in the States," I said softly.

"But what about your brother?" she asked. "Is he going to visit you?"

I shifted in my seat. "Maybe." He wouldn't. If he tried to, I'd refuse to see him.

Bora raised her eyebrows. "Mine would definitely visit."

I smiled but wished she'd stop asking so many questions. My

older brother, Gun, had been my idol right up until he helped ruin my life.

Our last day together had been an average day at Daeshim until he yanked me out of class early and drove me home.

Gun dropped his backpack down on the kitchen counter. "What were you thinking, Ji-hee? Someone took pictures of you with Chul. Kim Chul, the most popular boy at school."

I sunk down into a chair at the table. I'd never seen my brother this angry. "You told me to make friends at Daeshim."

Gun paced back and forth, fisting his hands at his side. "Are you really that stupid? We are nobodies there, and you're just a first year."

"Chul doesn't care about that," I said.

Gun scoffed. "Everyone cares. Most kids at our school own islands and we own a single yacht. It's expected that you know your place." He threw his hands in the air. "But then you go after the one boy Min has liked her whole life. Her family has more money than all the rest of them combined, and you ask Chul out right in front of her." He slammed a fist on the table and yelled. "Did you think nothing would happen?"

"Nothing did," I squeaked. "We went shopping. That was it."

Gun took a deep breath and closed his eyes. I wanted to cry. Gun never yelled at me. But worse than that, I could see he was terrified. I knew my brother. He was guarding his fear, hiding it under anger.

When he spoke next, it was with complete calm, but his words still echoed in my dark moments, wormed their way to the front of my mind and played on repeat.

"Someone took pictures of you in the dressing room, along with pictures of you modeling clothes in front of Chul. It looks like you gave him a private show."

My breath caught in my throat. "What do you mean? I would never—"

Gun's mouth formed a hard line. "It looks bad, Ji-hee. Do you have any idea what this will do to the company if those pictures get out?"

I'd cried myself to sleep, so afraid for school the next day. But the next day never came. My brother made sure I was on a plane to London eight hours later.

Gun might not have been the one to bury me, but he definitely passed out the shovels. My face must have betrayed emotion because Bora reached over and patted my hand. "I get it. Brothers suck," she said.

Someone I assumed was Bora's aunt wove through the throng of people near us with a wailing baby strapped into a front carrier. "I've got to go," Bora said, quickly. "Thanks for the shoes." And then she was wheeling the suitcase toward her aunt who looked relieved to see her.

My phone vibrated in my hand, and an instant smile pulled at the corners of my mouth.

Grandfather was here.

I pressed the phone to my ear with eagerness. "Hello, Grandfather. I'm so excited to see you." I rushed over my words, but the line remained silent. "Hello?"

I scanned the airport for Grandfather's balding little head. Maybe he wasn't inside yet. "Hello? Can you hear me?" It must be a bad connection. I grabbed the handle of my only luggage, a dark blue leather suitcase on wheels, and began walking toward the doors. But I stopped when my eye caught something that shouldn't be there. I blinked and looked again. That wasn't possible. But the beautiful man, walking next to an even more beautiful woman, continued in my direction.

The emptiness on the phone echoed, unrelenting in my ear.

I stared at the couple, the set of his shoulders, the line of his jaw. That couldn't be him. My high school crush, Chul, the reason I got banished from home. He couldn't be here in California. But then he saw me.

I froze.

Before I could run, or hide, or *die*, Chul waved at me. That part of my brain that tells your heart to beat and your lungs to expand stopped working. The only part of me still functioning were my eyes, which had become fixed and wide. Chul and his new wife quickly walked toward me. I gawked, stupefied, as Chul's arm wrapped around her hourglass waist.

"Hello, Ji-hee." Grandfather's leathery voice sounded strange as the call finally connected.

I gripped the phone, my breath coming in short, urgent gasps. I knew Chul had gotten married after his graduation. I even bothered to read the one letter Gun had mailed me along with the wedding invitation. He'd explained how Sydney Moore had attended Daeshim her senior year and how they had all become friends. Shocking, because last I knew, Gun and Chul were definitely not friends.

I wished Chul and Sydney well, and I even hoped my parents sent a nice gift to the happy couple. But I never wanted to see Chul again, like ever.

I harbored this horrific fear that Chul knew about the pictures, that maybe he had somehow become implicated too. I wouldn't put it past my stupid brother to lose his cool and corner Chul, demanding to know what happened. He could have blamed him. Or worst-case scenario, maybe Chul had seen the pictures. It was bad enough that I left school without explanation, but if he knew why . . . I squeezed my hands tighter around the phone. There was only so much humiliation a girl could take.

"Is that your grandfather?" Chul pointed to my phone, still pressed tightly to my ear. "Tell him we're here so he can stop worrying."

"We're so sorry we're late," Chul's wife said. "We didn't know you were coming today."

"Why *are* you here?" I asked.

Chul frowned. "Didn't he tell you?"

I shook my head. This had to be a horrible misunderstanding. Grandfather wouldn't do this to me. Not after everything else he knew I'd been through.

Sydney stepped closer, and a look of concern passed over her face.

"Ji-hee are you there?" Grandfather's voice rose on the line. I turned from them and walked a few steps away.

"I'm here. I can hear you," I said.

"Did Chul and Sydney meet you already?"

I licked my dry lips, not sure what to say to that. "Uh, yeah, but—"

"Are you surprised?"

I choked. "Very."

"I knew you would love it." He chuckled over the line. "I remembered you said he was one of your friends at Daeshim that—"

I cut him off. "Where are you? Are you close?"

Grandfather didn't speak for a heartbeat too long, letting an ominous quiet creep through the line. The air, alive and tense, crackled around me. Finally, he spoke. "I can't come."

"What do you mean, you can't come? Are you stuck in traffic?"

He cleared his throat. "No, that's not it. Don't be upset, but things haven't worked out. I'm not moving to California," he said.

Heat and pain pressed against my chest. Grandfather had been my last shred of something normal. "Am I not going to Marklem Academy then?" My voice cracked and I swallowed the lump in my throat.

"Marklem Academy doesn't exist," Grandfather said flatly.

"What did you say?"

Grandfather's voice took on an edge of anger. "Your mother wants everything perfect, so Gun made up a school so perfect and flawless that she agreed to let you leave London."

I stood in stunned silence, my mind trying to wrap around such a terrible lie. "Why am I here then?"

Grandfather sighed. "Maybe you can't go back to Daeshim, but you don't need a silly private school. At your age I went to public school with a lunchroom, and soccer teams, and meaner than tar teachers. It was a great education. If you can't be in Korea, then at least I'm giving you that."

I kept my voice calm. "You can't attend public school in the States without a guardian, or at the very least, a residence."

"Why do you think Chul and Sydney are there? They agreed to let you live with them and be your official guardians for the year."

My mouth dropped open. "Chul?"

"You start your first day at Bishop High tomorrow morning.

Everything is taken care of, enrollment forms, your Visa. Gun did all the paperwork. You only need to show up."

I gritted my teeth. Gun had forged signatures, made up some ridiculousness, and I was the one that would get punished when the ball dropped. I tried to speak, but only a strangled sound came out. I was going to kill Gun. "All Mother has to do is a search for Marklem Academy. She'll see it doesn't exist."

Grandfather laughed. "Gun made a fake website, along with emails. He's been corresponding with your mother as the principal of Marklem."

My voice rose. "She's going to find out."

Grandfather sighed. "She will, eventually. Then my daughter will do what she should have done long ago. She'll bring you home. You belong here with us."

I fought back tears. Grandfather meant well, but I no longer had a home.

2

HARRISON

The shove came from behind. I caught myself and turned to see Calvin grinning like an idiot. My friend wasn't small, but I outweighed him by at least forty pounds of muscle. If I returned the favor, we'd lose a few lockers. I kept walking down the hallway in no mood to talk, not even to Calvin.

He kept pace with me. "Harrison, where've you been?" He was breathing hard, which meant he'd run from the parking lot.

"I rode the bus."

Calvin wrinkled his nose and then laughed. "Really, why?"

"My dad grounded me."

"I thought you said he wasn't your dad."

I stopped at my locker to open it. "He's my dad enough to ground me."

Calvin sidled up next to me. "It's only the first day of school and you're already grounded? What'd you do?"

"I told him he wasn't my dad."

Calvin burst out laughing. "I thought you were just venting the other night. Were you really stupid enough to say all of that to him?"

I slanted a heavy glare in Calvin's direction.

He stopped. "Sorry, but I wish I could have been there to see the look on Jeff's face. Or are we back to calling him dad now? You can't seem to decide."

I could hear the disapproval in Calvin's voice. He was the only one I'd talked to about this, and he thought I was being lame. Maybe I was. Jeff's face when I'd yelled at him this morning wounded me more than the grounding. He wasn't my biological dad, but he'd raised me. I couldn't remember him *not* being around. Some of my first memories were of Jeff teaching me how to cut waffles, Jeff playing cars by the Christmas tree, Jeff tying my shoes. He'd always been good to me.

When I didn't answer, Calvin gave my shoulder a little bump. "You know it's not Jeff you're mad at, right?"

"No," I said. "I'm mad at him, 100 percent mad."

Calvin leaned his back against the lockers next to me and sighed dramatically. "He treats you the same as Ozzy and Becca, maybe even better. You never doubted Jeff until his parents moved here."

It was true. I'd never had a problem until last spring when Garrett and Gretchen announced they were moving to LA from New York. It was a big shock because they didn't say a word until they called Jeff right before boarding the plane. They wanted it to be a surprise that they bought a house right around the corner from ours. "*To be closer to our grandchildren.*"

It took me a long time to realize *I* wasn't considered part of their family. They'd call us every year at Thanksgiving. Ozzy and Becca would talk and laugh for an hour or more, but then when I got on, they always had to go right away. "*We can't let the turkey burn* or *we have guests coming, so we have to go now.*" I'd been too young and naive to notice how they never said *I love you* back. They sent Christmas presents and checks for birthdays. Mom said the birthday money was for college, so I never saw those supposed checks, but at Christmas, a giant box would arrive at our doorstep. We'd all be so excited, but Mom would promptly whisk it into her bedroom and lock the door. When she emerged, she would pass out gifts. Becca's always came with shiny wrapping and big bows, but mine and Ozzy's were never wrapped. One year I asked why. I still remember Mom kneeling in front of me with a soft smile and telling me that only girls care for fancy wrappings. My six-year-old brain never would have thought that she'd unwrapped Ozzy's presents to split them up. But why didn't I see it when I was older? "I'm allowed to be mad," I said to Calvin.

"Yes, full-on foaming-at-the-mouth mad. But not at Jeff. He's the real victim here. I bet you a hundred bucks he's dealt with their crap his whole life. Trust me, he knows."

I snorted. "What does he know?"

Calvin grinned. "That his parents are as worthless as scribbles on a bathroom wall."

I paused from stuffing junk into my locker. Jeff didn't know what happened between me and his parents over the summer, but he had to know they'd been snubbing me all these years. I think, in his own way, he'd been trying to make up for it. I had eight thousand dollars sitting in a college fund that didn't come from Garrett and Gretchen. I thought about the anniversary trip he and Mom canceled last year for no other reason than *Mom wasn't feeling up to it.*

He should have told me the truth and let me handle it. Knowing he'd sacrificed and worked harder to make up for them only made it hurt more. I closed my locker. "I'll see you in class," I said and turned to go.

"Wait, wait, wait." Calvin held up both hands to block me. "It's my turn. I've got a serious SOS."

I folded my arms. "What's up?"

Calvin's eyes went big, and his smile turned all gooey. "Tiffany said she'd go to homecoming with me this year."

"That's awesome, man." I slapped him on the shoulder, and he stumbled sideways. "I told you she'd say yes."

Calvin righted himself and stood up taller. "Except—" He looked away. "She said yes with one small condition."

I closed my eyes. "Don't say it."

Calvin softly banged his head against the lockers with a sigh. "It would be one night, Harrison. You can do one stupid date with Regan."

I glared at him. He should have banged his head harder. "No. Get someone from the soccer team. Any one of those guys would give their right foot to date Regan."

Calvin folded his arms and nodded, but his eyes went to steel. It was a bad sign. He was persistent when it came to girls, especially Tiffany. "Okay," he said. "I will give you my 2019 gently used Mazda with low miles if you will ask Regan to homecoming."

I scoffed. "Your mom would have kittens if you gave away your car."

"My mom wouldn't know." He placed a hand over his heart. "I promise to never tell her."

I still couldn't decide if Calvin was smart or if he had the brains of a goldfish cracker. One minute he'd be giving me insightful advice about my family that no normal high schooler had business understanding, but then he'd blow it by saying something like this. "She'd know when it was always parked at my house," I said. "Besides, I don't need a car. Jeff doesn't usually have a problem letting me drive his."

"I'll pay you then." Calvin squeezed his eyes shut, bracing. "Name your price."

"Not happening. See you in class." I walked away but with a sinking feeling. He wasn't ready to give up. I knew Calvin, and I knew Tiffany. We'd been going to the same school since fifth grade. By tomorrow, it would turn into tag team, alternating between bribes and subtle threats.

But I wouldn't touch Regan. We'd dated last year as juniors. She was funny, intelligent, pretty, and the meanest person I'd ever met. It didn't take me long to figure out that the barf feeling I had every time we hung out was because I didn't enjoy destroying people the way she did. And she was a master at hiding it. Bad things, terrible things that left girls in tears, would happen with Regan around. They would seem like a coincidence, or sometimes it just looked like Regan was trying to help. Only after I dated her for a while did I start to see how she'd set things up. She was the mean girl at our school, but no one else seemed to see it.

Over the summer I emailed my school counselor to make sure I didn't have any of the same classes with Regan. And yet, when I walked into calculus, Regan sat in the second row talking to the student body president, who I barely recognized because of her false eyelashes. They were so thick they looked like caterpillars crawling across her eyelids.

I didn't react but found a seat alone near the back. Both girls turned and gave me their first day of school little wave. I could almost hear their voices in my head. *"Oh my gosh, it's been so long, Harrison. We've missed you so much."* I ignored them both.

I noticed from the corner of my eye when Calvin and Tiffany entered hand in hand. He didn't need me to ask out Regan. She'd go with him. Half the girls in this school wanted to go with him.

The bell rang and Ms. Smars stood up. She walked to close the door, but a girl with long dark hair zipped past and into the room. She quickly scanned the class with a kind of resigned choose-your-poison look on her face until her eyes found mine.

I couldn't look away. She moved with purpose and the closer she came, the tighter my gut got. She took the seat in front of mine, dropped her bag on the floor, and immediately turned to face me.

"Hi, I'm Ji-hee." She held out a delicate hand and smiled.

I shifted and a strange sensation enveloped me, almost a feeling like I'd needed to brace to receive that smile. I took her hand too fast, which was warm and soft. I tried to smile back. Instead, I opened my mouth and something that sounded almost like a grunt came out.

She looked at me a little funny with one arched brow. "Are you okay?" she whispered. Not in a mean way, but more in a truly concerned that I was ill kind of way.

I nodded hard. Again, too fast. Not even a little cool.

She tilted her head like she was curious. Inky dark eyes gazed into my own. And there it was—in the space between one heartbeat and the next, she managed to yank on feelings I didn't know existed. Finally, I found my voice. "I'm Harrison Barrett." I still held her hand, and she didn't pull away.

"Nice to meet you, Harrison." The way she pronounced my name was different, like the syllables were unfamiliar, so I said my name again.

I knew I'd done the right thing when she smiled and tried a second time. "Harrison." She spoke it perfectly.

I was hyper aware that I still hadn't let go of her hand, but I couldn't make myself. Not yet. "Where are you from?" I asked, and then belatedly realized this might sound rude. "I mean. You're new here?"

She tipped her head to the side, and her hair moved against her neck. Super distracting. "I'm from Seoul," she said.

I grinned. "So, you're an exchange student from South Korea."

"No, not an exchange student." She pressed her lips into a line, and I watched, captivated.

Ms. Smars moved from her desk. "All right. I have a syllabus for everyone." She handed a stack of papers to each front row student for them to pass back.

I reluctantly let go of Ji-hee's hand, and she turned to face the front of the room, then passed me a syllabus as the pile shuffled our way. I stared at the line her shoulders made, then noticed how she sat unnaturally straight in her chair, not that it looked unnatural for her, it just wasn't how the rest of us sat.

Ms. Smars projected the class syllabus onto the Smart Board, but I couldn't seem to stop watching Ji-hee. Every little thing about her, from the curve of her neck as her head tilted down, to the sound of her pen as she scribbled notes, held my attention. I thought about tapping her on the shoulder. She'd turn around again, and this time, I'd say something clever.

I lifted my hand but stopped myself. My eyes flicked to Regan's long blonde hair done in soft curls. I didn't need to wonder if she had watched Ji-hee sit down in front of me and then turn to introduce herself, or the way I'd frozen-up and stammered. She'd watched. I couldn't do this, not with Ji-hee or any girl in this school.

Regan had been hovering in my background since we broke up. This new ploy of *Calvin can only go with Tiffany if Harrison takes Regan,* wasn't Tiffany's idea. This had Regan stamped all over it.

Yesterday I didn't care that Regan was a crazy jealous ex. I had zero plans to date anyone this school year. There wasn't a single girl at Bishop High that I was interested in. But yesterday I hadn't met Ji-hee. I could see Regan launching a full-out war against the new girl, complete with grenades, rockets, and nukes. I raised my hand.

Ms. Smars noticed me right away. "Yes, Harrison?"

"I think I'm in the wrong class." I was up and pulling my backpack onto both shoulders before Ms. Smars could respond.

She frowned and bent over her monitor as she moved the mouse. "I could have sworn I saw you on the roll."

I moved past Ji-hee without glancing down. "My counselor can work it out," I said. I didn't mean to. It wasn't a conscious decision. But before I could get to the door, I turned.

Regan was looking at me. I could feel her calculations, but her face blurred into the fringes as my eyes zeroed in on Ji-hee. She slowly flipped through the pages of her book, unaware that I couldn't take my eyes off her. My feet saved me by moving faster, and I was in the hall before my stupid heart could turn back for more.

3

JI-HEE

S eeing the only friendly face walk out of class left me feeling more lost than when I'd walked in, but I reminded myself that I had at least one friend here in LA.

Sydney.

I'd expected her to be guarded or even annoyed that I was living with them. But she surprised me by being gracious.

"Your room is here." She flipped on the light. A soft glow illuminated a queen-sized bed with a white quilt, a tufted velvet chair in the corner, and an old vintage armoire that smelled faintly like orange oil. The whole room was small but welcoming, especially the full-sized, walk-in closet. At least I could go shopping.

I let out the shuddering breath I didn't know had built up and pulled my suitcase next to me before sinking down on the edge of the bed.

Sydney moved and sat on the chair. "I take it that living here with us was a surprise." Her voice floated past me, feather-light to smooth over my frayed nerves.

I almost resented it. But instead of asking her to leave me alone in my misery, I started talking. It felt strange at first, like I was a rusty old bike that someone was dusting off and using again after years in a damp garage, but Sydney made everything easy. She asked me questions, and I kept answering her. The more we talked, the more my words poured out until it seemed like I'd told her the whole dismal story of my life right up to landing in California. She even asked me about the pictures taken in the dressing room, so I guess that cat was out of the bag. None of it seemed to bother her except for the fact that I'd had no idea I'd be going to Bishop High instead of Marklem Academy.

Sydney shook her head. "We thought you knew. Gun asked us if you could live here for the school year, and he was the one that flew out and enrolled you at Bishop High. Your grandfather called Chul after you landed and asked us to pick you up."

"I bet you were surprised."

Sydney smiled. "When we never heard back from Gun, we thought you weren't coming anymore. But I think he wasn't sure on the date he could get you released."

I lowered my head. I was pretty sure Grandfather put off calling me because he was ashamed. Gun had lied to get Mother to agree to let me go to California, and somehow he'd gotten tangled up in it. I don't know why I expected him to move. Maybe he'd thought he could at first, but Grandfather was old. Leaving Korea would be too hard for him. "Thanks for getting me on short notice," I said.

Sydney laughed "Don't thank me yet. Your first day of school is tomorrow."

I nodded. "I'm okay with that."

Sydney watched me closely before speaking. "Your situation is . . . complex."

I snorted. "If you mean I got sent away to a school for heroin addicts simply because I offended the wrong people among Korea's Elite, then, yes, it's complex."

She grimaced at this, like she really did get how bad it had been. "Gun didn't like the school."

I laughed bitterly. "He was the one that said I'd be safe there. But I guess he meant my family's reputation would be safe."

Sydney didn't disagree or try to defend it further. Instead, she asked the one question no one had bothered to ask me since the whole nightmare started. "How can I help?"

I licked my dry lips and decided to lay it all out for her. "Gun thinks he can fool our mother, but no one can. She's eventually going to catch up to me. It might be in a month, or it might be the whole school year, but I don't want to go back to Korea and definitely not London. I want to live in the States and have a shot at normal for my last year of high school."

Sydney smiled then. "I think Gun and Chul can help with your mother, and if normal is what you're after you'll do great at Bishop High."

Last night I'd told Sydney some of what I wanted, but not everything. Sure, I wanted to stay here, and it sounded wonderful to sit in a school lunchroom and talk about the movie coming out on Friday night or worry about a science test instead of my crazy family. But there were other things I *wouldn't* let myself want.

Like Harrison Barrett.

His wavy black hair, and wide mouth, the way he watched me from under thick lashes with dark intelligent eyes, he was exactly the kind of ticking-time-bomb I knew not to touch. I'd fall for a guy like Harrison. Despite this, I'd still wanted to follow him out that door.

Of course I hadn't.

I'd keep my rust-covered heart securely welded shut and focus on getting through my senior year.

So instead of a handsome boy with the promise of warmth, my gaze found the two girls in the second row. They both turned to openly watch me, then leaned close to whisper. A small snicker escaped from the beautiful one.

"Stupid," I mumbled to myself in Korean. I went back to my book but paused when from the corner of my eye I saw a flash at the window above the door. I let my eyes wander slowly up, so I wasn't staring.

Another face, a young man with dark hair and darker eyes, peered in. I didn't know him, but he looked decidedly out of place. I felt his focus land on me, and I turned my face down toward my desk. I didn't know who this guy was, but I was sure he was Korean.

HARRISON

"Harrison, I don't think I can move you." Mrs. Jensen, the school counselor, peered at me over her wide-framed glasses and then back at her computer. The wrinkles around her eyes deepened. "I know you requested to not have any classes with a certain individual, and mostly we've avoided that. But first period is the only calculus class. You both want to take it, so can you just buck-up and ignore her?"

I raked my hand across my face. I'd already explained this, but it wasn't sinking in.

Mrs. Jensen typed on her computer and paused. "It looks like you have the same lunch and she's in PE with you too. I can't switch PE because it's the only one not full."

"At least take me out of calculus," I said.

Mrs. Jensen sighed. "You have enough math credits to drop it, but it won't look as good on your transcript for college." She peered at me over her monitor. "There's not much left that isn't full. Do you want to take another art class? You've never done ceramics, and we have a beginning class first period."

"Yeah, sure. I don't really care," I mumbled.

A knock sounded, and then the door to Mrs. Jensen's office opened slowly. The school's principal, Mr. Young, poked his head in. "We have a new student." Mr. Young stood aside. "This is—" he held up a sheet of paper and slowly pronounced the name. "Han-bae Yun. He's from Seoul." Mr. Young beamed as a student behind him stepped past and entered the already cramped office.

The new guy met my eyes cooly, then turned and spoke to Mrs. Jensen. "My assistant emailed you my preferred schedule," he said. "If you can confirm this, I would like to go to class right away." Han-bae spoke near perfect English and moved with exactness, reminding me of Calvin's karate coach. I stood up straighter. He was close to Calvin's height and didn't look scrawny, but it was hard to tell because he wore a full suit with vest and jacket. He even had a collar pin across the knot of his tie. Who was this guy?

Mrs. Jensen bit her lip and looked back at her computer. "I saw nothing about a new student."

"Han-bae's mother called me this morning," Mr. Young said with a little too much eagerness. "I assured her we would accommodate him."

Mrs. Jensen frowned but didn't lift her eyes from her screen, not seeming as impressed by Han-bae as her boss was. "His parents will need to fill out the paperwork and provide immunization records to the nurse before I can—"

Mr. Young cut her off. "Yes, all of that will be taken care of Jensen. Just find the email from his assistant."

Her eyes flashed, and she frowned at Mr. Young. They had a silent stand-off with him shifting from foot to foot before she sighed and looked back at her screen. "I don't know how someone not employed in our district would have access to our school's scheduling, but I do see a schedule in this email, if this is what you are referring to."

Mr. Young flushed. "Well, yes, yes. Don't worry about the how. Let's print up that schedule and get this smart young man started."

Mrs. Jensen stood as the printer behind her whined and slid out a single sheet. She took the paper and turned back to Han-bae. "How surprising that you have an assistant at such a young age."

He took the schedule from her without a response. "Is Lee Ji-hee in this first period?" Han-bae asked.

I tensed. This guy knew Ji-hee?

"Is she a friend of yours?" Mr. Young asked, all smiles.

Mrs. Jensen glanced uncomfortably at her idiot boss. "We can't give out other student's personal information. You understand, I'm sure," she said pointedly to Han-bae.

Han-bae narrowed his eyes at her, and his words became clipped. "Is she, or is she not?"

Mr. Young barked with nervous laughter. "She's probably his sister," he said looking at Mrs. Jensen.

I watched Han-bae's reaction to this. He didn't act like he was asking after a sister, but I couldn't discount it. They were both from Seoul and both new students. It would be weird if it was just a coincidence.

Mrs. Jensen reached for Han-bae's schedule, but he pulled it up and back before she could touch it. "I'm going to first period now."

Mr. Young clapped Han-bae on the shoulder. "Perfect. Do you want me to show you the way?"

Han-bae rolled his shoulder away from Mr. Young. "Don't touch me."

I filed away his frosty behavior without comment, but that was the moment I knew I was going to stay in calculus.

Jensen's face went a shade darker. She opened her mouth to argue, but I could see that Young, for whatever reason, wanted Han-bae here. It was all wrong, but this guy was in, and nothing Jensen said would change that.

I spoke up. "No changes for me today, Mrs. Jensen. Thanks for your time. I'll take Han-bae back and show him the way." Until I knew what was up, I wasn't leaving Ji-hee alone with this self-absorbed loser.

Mr. Young beamed, still with his big stupid smile. "Harrison is an excellent student. He can show you the ropes."

I walked out of the office and without stopping, called back. "Let's go."

Han-bae followed but managed to look annoyed, or disgusted, or both, which bugged me more than it should have. His clothes, shoes, hair, and especially the expensive looking watch on his wrist translated to the type of perfection that only comes with funds to burn. I wondered how well that would sit here. Most guys at Bishop rolled out of bed. "So, when did you get here?" I asked.

"This morning."

I whistled. "I'd still be sleeping off the jetlag. Are you really excited to start school or what?"

Han-bae glanced from his paper to the numbers above each door as we passed. "I have work here."

I almost laughed out loud. "What kind of work?"

"The kind that someone like you will never be involved in," he said.

I laughed. "Let me give you some advice that you probably won't take. But you should. This school has a lot of cool students. If you want people to play nice, consider dialing the pretentious-jerk-mode down." I stopped at the classroom door for calculus. Class was almost over, with less than five minutes to the bell. I glanced through the window. Ji-hee was still there.

Han-bae stepped closer to me so he could see into the classroom. He scanned the room and then his eyes stopped when they reached Ji-hee.

Something primal twitched in me, and I got the same feeling I would have if say a lion suddenly showed up for a stroll through Bishop High's halls. It was part shock, and part panic, but mostly anger. Who was this guy and what was he doing at my school? He knew Ji-hee's name, and now he was ogling her. "Who are you staring at?"

Han-bae turned from the door with a sneer but didn't answer me. "Thanks for the advice," he said. "I'll worry less now that I know the secret code at your school. Do you have a secret handshake too?"

I scoffed.

"No?" He mocked with wide eyes. "That's too bad. I was hoping we'd be friends."

The intercom speakers in the hall crackled with life, and the rumbly laugh of one of the seniors on the party committee echoed in the hallway. "Hey Arrows. Welcome back. This year is going to be awesome."

His voice droned on while yells and whoops echoed from the classrooms with the deep bass of the boys starting in with a chant of *GO ARROWS! GO ARROWS!*

The bell rang. I hung back and let myself blend into the fray of bodies filling the hallway. Han-be moved to the side, He watched as students left, and he waited. I really hoped this guy didn't turn out to be Ji-hee's dirtbag brother. But then again, him being her brother would be way better than a stalker.

Ji-hee was the last to leave. She carried her bag on her slim shoulder, and I got an even better look at her perfect legs as she walked by.

One thing was clear. Dirtbag wasn't her brother. She didn't stop and greet him or even notice the hungry way he watched her walk away.

I noticed.

4

HARRISON

Yelling echoed through my bedroom door, followed by a single bang. "Get up, before I dump a glass of water down your neck." Ozzy's voice hadn't deepened all the way and came out with a squeak, making the threat laughable.

I rolled over with a groan and fished for my phone on my nightstand, then stared bleary-eyed at the screen—6:07 a.m. I stuffed it under my pillow, ready to go back to sleep. I didn't have to be at school until 8:30 a.m.

The banging sounded louder, and I cracked one eye open to see my doorknob rattle as Ozzy began picking the lock. The door swung inward, and the lean form of my brother stood outlined in the hallway light. He'd almost filled out. Now that he was a freshman his arms and legs had more muscle, and the last of that middle school awkwardness disappeared. I wished, not for the first time, that he could go to my school.

He stomped to my bedside and pulled the blanket away. "Why are you still in bed? Mom made eggs."

"I'm sleeping," I growled.

"You'll be late."

"My school starts at eight-thirty, you idiot."

"I have practice. Come eat with us."

"No," I mumbled, hoping he'd stop talking long enough for me to fall back asleep.

Ozzy sat down on the edge of my bed. I could feel his silent brooding as he inched closer. Ever since our parents decided that he wouldn't attend Bishop High with me, Ozzy had been a constant riptide of hurt and resentment. As if I'd had any say in the matter. Garrett and Gretchen had been the ones that gave the real push with the offer to pay for private tutors, and Mom had been the one to agree to it. He should be mad at her not me.

Garrett and Gretchen hadn't even offered to buy *me* mechanical pencils. But then I wasn't an ice skating protégé with two Swedish trainers, both warring over who would sign me. Mom had every right to want this for Ozzy, and public school wouldn't work for the kind of schedule he would need to keep. Still, I was bugged that Ozzy blamed me. Or maybe he just didn't want things to change between us. I sat up. "Is it really that important that I eat with you?"

Ozzy nodded and looked genuinely sad. "I never see you anymore."

"Because you're always at the rink playing Olympic champion," I said.

Ozzy tried to snort, but it came out no more than a delicate scoff. "I'm not in the Olympics."

"Not yet," I said and swung my legs out of bed. I grabbed a pair of mostly clean jeans off the floor and a tee shirt from the closet before following Ozzy out to the kitchen.

Becca sat at the table dipping toast with the crust neatly trimmed off into the yolk of her sunny-side-up egg. "Harrison, do you want a dippin' egg too?" she asked sweetly. Her two front teeth had fallen out last week, giving her a slight lisp.

I ruffled her hair and grabbed a glass from the counter, then sat down next to her and poured myself some juice. "Sounds good," I said with a wink.

"My teacher said eggs have protein." She spoke around a small Becca-sized bite.

"I used the last of the eggs," Mom said. Her shoulders seemed to hunch where she was standing at the sink, rinsing grapes for our lunches. "You're never up this early, so I didn't think you'd want to eat with us." She began wiping her hands on a towel. "Let me run to the store real quick and buy some more."

Ozzy, who'd been shoveling in eggs, froze, looking from me to Mom's back. He picked up his plate and tried to hand it to me, but I stood and walked to the cupboard. I grabbed a bowl and patted the top of Mom's head softly. "I'd choose Captain Crunch over eggs any day. Don't sweat it."

Mom smiled in that exhausted way that had become her signature. She opened the pantry and pulled out Life cereal.

I hated Life cereal.

"We're out of everything but this." She put the box in my hand.

Life was Ozzy's favorite, but I reminded myself that Ozzy was constantly training and there was always some tense try-out for the next level of skating. Mom's way of dealing was to feed him. I put my bowl back before sitting down to eat a dry handful from the box.

"Mom, can Harrison drive me today?" Ozzy asked. "Dad's working from home, so he won't need the car."

Becca stopped chewing her toast and looked at me. Even as a five-year-old she knew I'd have to ask Jeff if I drove Ozzy.

Mom sat down next to Becca with one of her protein shakes. "No, Harrison will just make you late. Grandpa said he was driving you this morning."

I raised my eyebrows. "I've never made Ozzy late."

Mom cleared her throat. "You can't get to the rink and back before school starts."

"I can if we leave right now."

Ozzy jumped up and grabbed his backpack from the floor and his lunch from the counter. "I'm ready," he announced.

I wondered if he minded getting a ride with Garrett. I hated Garrett, but I had reason to. Ozzy, on the other hand, was the golden boy.

Mom's eyes followed Ozzy's. Was she thinking the same thing I was, that Ozzy didn't want to be around him? Ozzy stood there almost panting with eagerness when she turned to me with a funny smile, like she'd tricked me. "Ask your dad if you can borrow the car first."

I hadn't spoken to Jeff since yesterday with my big first-day-of-school blow up. I shrugged as if to say: *I don't have a problem, he's the one avoiding me.* But it was all bluff. My stomach did flip-flops on the way to his office.

I knocked softly on the door before giving it a little push. I'd only meant to crack it open, but I pulled my hand back, embarrassed when it swung clear to the wall. I wasn't trying to barge in. To make it all worse, Jeff was on a video call.

I started to retreat, but he motioned me forward. "Come in, Harrison. I've got the call on mute."

I stepped inside but now that I was actually standing here, I panicked. What was I supposed to say after acting like an idiot? I'd basically told him yesterday that he wasn't my dad. I ran my hand through my hair. "Uh, Ozzy wanted me to drive him to the rink before I go to school."

Jeff nodded. "Okay, you can take the car for the day. It's probably not cool to take the bus as a senior."

I let out a breath, glad he didn't make it awkward. "Thanks," I mumbled and turned to go.

Jeff spoke before I could leave. "Harrison."

I turned back.

"Can your dad get a hug before you go?" He asked quietly.

The word, *dad,* wasn't lost on me. Jeff was making a point. He loved me and I'd been a jerk. We both knew it. Stupid tears pricked at my eyes. I swallowed hard before any emotion showed. "I'm a little old for hugs," I said.

"But you'll give your dad one anyway, right?" I knew he'd been out late last night, working his second job at the warehouse, the job he had so the rest of us could have more comforts. Jeff stood up and moved away from his computer. I towered over his five foot eleven frame, exactly the same as Ozzy. Standing next to them made me feel a little like Shrek, but Jeff easily pulled me down for a hug and thumped my back the same way he'd done my whole life. It made my chest burn and constrict. Maybe Jeff and I didn't share DNA, but we shared other things. I still didn't think I could start calling him dad again. Not with Garrett and Gretchen hanging around. They were at my house more than I was now.

After I dropped Ozzy at the rink, I ran back home to shower, brush my teeth and even put gel in my hair. I left in plenty of time to get to school and maybe even find a parking spot. I backed out slowly but then saw something in my rearview mirror that made me brake so hard the car jerked.

Our neighborhood bus-stop was at the end of my street, two houses down. The normal crowd, mostly freshman and a few sophomores stood around looking bored. Burke was there, a whiney little freshman that bullied my brother, the twin girls that moved to our street last year and mostly stuck to themselves, and Hudson, Ozzy's only friend in the neighborhood. But off on her own, all long legs and silky hair, stood Ji-hee.

I sat for five whole minutes, idling in the drive. I tried to think of a smooth way to offer her a ride, but the bus came and picked them all up before I got up the nerve. I shook my head and finally backed out, driving in the opposite direction of the bus in case she sat in the back and saw me. Not that it would matter. Why would it matter? That left me driving out of our neighborhood the long way, and there was the morning commute traffic, which put me to school too late to get a spot anywhere but off campus on one of the side streets.

I ran, but still only made it to calculus after the bell rang. Ms. Smars hadn't started class yet, so maybe I wouldn't get a tardy. Ji-hee sat in the exact same seat as yesterday. Han-bae sat on the front row. So, I took the seat right behind Ji-hee again. I didn't miss that Regan was two rows ahead to my left. If she turned even a little, she had a clear view of not only me, but Ji-hee.

Ms. Smars stood up and said, "Today we are having a pop quiz." She tilted her head to the side. "It's really more of a placement test so work hard."

We had the whole period, but I finished in under thirty. Ji-hee never stopped working. The bend of her spine as she leaned over her desk made it seem like math was the only thing that mattered, like this test was the most important thing in the room. I wanted to rank high enough that she'd at least notice me, but the girl was one hundred percent focused. She didn't turn around once.

I, on the other hand, was plenty distracted. Today she wore a white button up shirt with a little rounded collar and a pale blue pleated skirt. Overdressed for Bishop High, but I liked it. I wondered if I would like her in sweats and a tee shirt. I definitely would.

She straightened with a sigh and flipped her paper face down. Her long black hair brushed the top of my desk and shimmered like sunshine reflecting off water. I froze and watched as she rolled her neck in slow circles back and forth. If I moved my fingers forward just a few inches, her hair would sweep across my hand. I wondered if it made me a creep that I wanted to touch her hair so bad. Maybe. But then Ji-hee placed both hands on the back of her neck, sliding them up, scooping and gathering her hair. She pulled a black band from her wrist to wrap it in a knot on the top of her head. Fine wispy strands cascaded down and a subtle flowery scent with just a hint of vanilla reached out to me. It was all I could do to not lean forward and inhale.

I glanced up. Ms. Smars sat at her desk on her phone and seemed distracted enough that I could talk to Ji-hee, maybe even get her number before class ended. I started to lean forward again when something pricked along my skin. I raised my eyes. Regan had turned in her seat and watched me. Then her eyes flicked to Ji-hee. Just for a moment they narrowed. When she looked back at her test, a coolness hissed off her. You couldn't see it. Nothing in her posture ever changed, but I could always feel when Regan was mad. If Regan didn't like someone, she'd find ways to hurt them. It was as natural as breathing for her, and now, she'd just caught me staring at the new girl. I did the only thing I could think of. I was out of my seat and sitting behind her before the rational part of my brain could put on the bad-idea-brakes. And this was definitely a bad idea. "Hey Regan."

I placed my hand on her shoulder and leaned forward to whisper in her ear.

She raised her head. "What are you doing? I'm not done with my test. Ms. Smars—"

"She's busy. Just keep working and she won't notice us," I said.

"What do you want? I have to finish," she said.

I knew Regan. She was trying to sound indifferent, but curt words couldn't cover up that she seemed to lean into my hand. "Calvin said you wanted to go to homecoming," I whispered.

She stiffened and I kicked myself. "What I mean is." I cleared my throat. "I wanted to ask you. Calvin said you might go with me if I asked."

Regan turned in her seat and her blue eyes searched mine. Her smile was slow to start, but then she was glowing and nodding yes.

This was a kamikaze move if I'd ever made one. I'd just lied to Regan and asked her out, basically sacrificing myself to protect a girl I didn't even know. But I really, really wanted to know Ji-hee.

5

JI-HEE

Regan McAllister was as broken as she was beautiful. And I knew beauty, but I also knew that being able to turn heads often came at a heavy cost. Mother always drilled into me that my looks were my greatest asset, and my father was quick to pat my head and say how pretty I was if I dared ask about the family business. It was Grandfather who taught me never to confuse beauty with worth. At Grandfather's house I could trade my bows for dusty fishing hats. He'd take me to play chess in the park and for hikes in the full sun. If I scrapped my knee, instead of scolding me about how no one likes a girl with scars, Grandfather would help me up and say, "Walk it off, Ji-hee. You're tougher than the road." And I was. Somewhere along the line, I learned that resiliency was better than beauty.

But Regan didn't have a cool grandfather, or if she did, she didn't get that lesson. She was one hundred percent aware of her looks, and all of her beauty had one aim.

Harrison.

In an almost greedy kind of way she guarded him, measured and saved his every word, every look—like even the air he breathed was a prize. She had it bad for Harrison.

The guy I couldn't like.

I should have been happy that someone else wanted his attention. But I wasn't. She wanted too much of him. Regan wanted Harrison with so much hunger that it only made me notice him more. Every move she'd made while sitting diagonally, just ahead of me, had been to get his attention. She'd flipped her hair, sighed dramatically and even tugged at sandy brown boy shorts, so thin and tight, a spray tan could have covered more.

Whatever she was doing must have worked, because Harrison got up and changed seats to sit in the one behind her. I couldn't hear what they were saying, and I didn't want to. Or if I was being honest with myself, I didn't *want* to want to.

She let out a soft squeal and whispered louder, "Tell me you're getting a limo."

Calvin perked up and turned from where he was sitting in the front row. "Did you ask her?"

Ms. Smars dropped her phone on her desk and stood, walking to Calvin. "Is there a problem?"

Calvin grinned. "Not anymore. I'm going to homecoming."

"Wonderful. I'm glad your dating future is secure, but can you please maintain quiet so the rest of the class can finish their test?"

Calvin looked down at his desk with a stupid grin, and I snuck another glance at Harrison. Regan's stare intercepted my own. She narrowed her eyes. It was like she was some kind of flirt-zone goalie, and I couldn't even look at Harrison without her jumping in front of me. I leaned back in my seat. Even if I wanted to compete with her, I wouldn't. Harrison and any boy I could possibly fall for was off limits. Mother had made sure of that.

The class quieted down, and Regan returned to her test, but Harrison stayed where he was. I wasn't going to look at him . . . was he looking at me? I didn't believe in psychic powers or any of the old superstitions my grandfather kept. Only this guy made me unsure. It had to be all in my head, classic overthinking. I bit my lip. He wasn't looking at me.

But I could feel his pull, his desire for me to lift my gaze and glance over just a fraction. My eyes flicked up and locked with Harrison's. That's all it took. He held me just as steady and sure as if he'd been holding my hand. A smile, nothing mocking or playful, but a determined I'm-not-going-anywhere smile settled across his lips.

Regan started to turn her head from her test, almost like she could sense our connection, but before her all-knowing glance could reach me, Harrison's hand shot out and settled on her shoulder. It was a gentle touch, the kind that I could imagine would come from him. She froze and then seemed to lean back, closer to him.

I looked away then laid my head down on my desk and closed my eyes. It bothered me that he touched her. I wanted it to be me, but I had too many of my mother's secret hooks in my life. A future with me would be like trying to save water in a paper cup. The cup looked solid, but give it a few days, the water would turn stale and soak through the bottom. I kept my head on my desk and waited long minutes after the bell rang. I could tell when he left. The room weighed less.

I walked from the classroom down two hallways and turned right. My locker was in the L wing. I pulled out my phone and opened my email from the school that had my schedule and locker info. It was locker number L-426. I was so focused on memorizing my combination that I walked into another student.

"Hey," Calvin reached out to steady me as I stumbled backward. "You okay?"

I looked up stupidly, but it wasn't Calvin that I noticed. Harrison stood at his open locker just a meter away.

"Oh, I'm good. Sorry, I wasn't looking," I said.

"That's okay. You're Ji-hee, right?" Calvin grinned encouragingly. "Are you an exchange student?"

I shook my head, but then he just stood there as if he expected an explanation. *My grandfather sent me here with a host family that are really just my former crush and his new wife to hide from my scheming mother probably wouldn't work.* I let out a nervous laugh. "I'm here with some family friends. I wanted to go to school in the States for a year." I shrugged. "You know, try new things."

"That's super cool," Calvin said. "We should show you around and—" His eyes lit up. "I have the best idea. Do you want to go to our school dance?"

Harrison's head snapped up. He pushed off his locker and moved closer. "We both have dates. Who are you thinking of?"

"Astor," Calvin said.

Harrison frowned.

"Uh . . ." I swallowed and tried to think of what to say. Maybe I shouldn't go, but I kind of wanted to. My don't-lose-your-heart rule would be easy if Harrison wasn't my date. And he already had one. I tried not to scrunch up my nose when thinking about who.

"Not Astor," Harrison said.

Calvin turned to Harrison. "Are you crazy? His dad owns a limo service. That makes the ride free." Calvin took my hand in his. "Trust me, you're going to have the best time. homecoming is awesome."

With a firm swipe, Harrison pushed Calvin's hand off mine and replaced it with his own. Then he stepped between us. "We can get you a date, but not Astor."

"What's your problem?" Calvin said, hotly. His face softened as he pointed to me. "Say you'll go."

At this point, I was aware of only one thing. Harrison was holding my hand. I tried to breathe normally. "Sure, sounds fun," I said. It might have been my imagination, but Harrison seemed to pull me closer.

"This is perfect," Calvin said. "Now we can all go." He glanced at Harrison who was now gripping my hand in his. "Uh, Harrison, let the poor girl go. She's not even your date." He cast an anxious glance down the hall, and I wondered if he was worried Regan would see.

I laughed to lighten the mood and gently removed my hand, then turned so my back was to Harrison. I smiled at Calvin. "Thanks for inviting me."

"Can I get your number?" Calvin pointed to the phone still in my other hand. "I'll send it to Astor, and he'll text you."

Before I could respond Harrison reached from behind and slipped the phone from my hand. I spun around in surprise. He typed on my screen quickly before checking his own and handing mine back. "I have your number now. I'll get you the details."

I grabbed it but leveled a look at Harrison. "Don't take my phone again."

Harrison returned my gaze and dropped his voice low. "I'm sorry," he said.

I wondered if he just didn't want Astor to have my number. But why would he care? I tried to think of a comeback. Some kind of burn that would keep him in check.

Before I could respond, Harrison strode forward and threw an arm around Calvin's shoulder. He turned back to me. "I'll text you." Calvin tried to protest and say something, but then Harrison locked his arm around Calvin's neck, basically dragging him away.

I'd just agreed to go to an American homecoming with a guy that I didn't know, and if Harrison had anything to do with it, the guy wouldn't be Astor. Whoever he was.

I found my locker but the mystery boy who was in calculus stood next to it with another girl and the principal, Mr. Young. I hung back and watched. Yesterday, after class I'd walked right past this guy without a glance, but I wouldn't have missed another Korean, even if he hadn't stood out in his hand tailored suit and tie.

The girl was pulling stuff from the locker and dumping it into her open backpack. "I don't know why *he* has to have this locker," she snapped. "We all got locker assignments two weeks ago."

Mr. Young stared the girl down. "Han-bae isn't used to our school. I was hoping you could be gracious and not make such a big deal about switching lockers."

Han-bae wasn't a name I recognized, but it was common enough. I was sure he was top money back home. He just had that look. Which was weird, because I should know him, unless he was new money, a family that made it into the Korean Elite while I'd been rotting away in exile.

The girl at the locker ripped a little magnetic mirror off the inside of the door and chucked it into her bag, then zipped it up angrily. "I'm all about being welcoming but kicking me out of my locker because this jerk couldn't walk a few halls over is ridiculous and you know it, Mr. Young." She stood and swung the bag onto her shoulder before stomping off.

Mr. Young looked at Han-bae apologetically and then motioned to the now empty locker before walking away.

Han-bae unzipped a black backpack and took out a laptop as well as a tablet that he set on the top shelf. I approached and spun the dial on my locker next to his, focusing on the combination.

He turned to me, and I had no choice but to glance up. His eyes widened and then a slow smile crept across his face. "Long time no see," he said.

He spoke in Korean, but I answered him in English. "Do I know you?"

"You don't remember?" He searched my face.

I shook my head but smiled to cover my unease. I would remember him if we'd met. He was well groomed, average height and build—nothing stood out. But I'd remember his eyes. I'd noticed in the hallway yesterday after simply walking past. He'd watched the world around him with something more than curiosity. Calculation maybe.

He laughed. "I'm joking. But he waited a second too long—a second that maybe said I *should* know him—before adding. "Of course you don't know me. I'm Han-bae, and my surname is Yun." He held out his hand, and I shook it.

"Lee Ji-hee," I said. His skin was warm and his easy smile almost reassuring. But if there was anything I'd learned from the Elite, it was that nothing in our world was easy.

HARRISON

"I still don't get it," Calvin said. "Why not Astor? If he goes in our group, it will—" He shrugged. "You know, like elevate our status, like getting bigger chips at a better poker table. He's student body president at Taylor High."

"Why does it matter?" I asked.

Calvin grabbed his hair in frustration. "This is high school, Harrison. Why can't you just take an insecure minute like the rest of us and care what people think? He's friends with half the city."

"He's not friends with us," I said. "We haven't talked to him since middle school."

"But he asked me to set him up for homecoming."

I kept walking along the front of the school. I wanted to catch Ji-hee and offer her a ride home, but I hadn't seen her once since PE, our last period together. "If he's so cool, he won't have trouble getting his own date," I said.

"But," Calvin growled, clearly frustrated. "You know he doesn't go to our school. The only reason he would even go with our group is that he has this bet that he can go to every homecoming in the valley. He needs a date from our school, and if we don't set him up, someone else will."

I glanced East to the parking lot. Ji-hee had to be gone. I turned back to Calvin. "You know Astor is a jerk."

Calvin looked down at his shoes, but he couldn't argue with me because we both remembered middle school. Astor and I ended seventh grade still boys with gangly arms and legs that made it obvious our muscle to bone ratio was off. That summer I ate with a fierceness that had Mom running to the grocery store every few days. Stacks of pizzas, whole roasted chickens, gallons of milk, I couldn't get full. By the time eighth grade started I was walking the halls in a man's body. It had been embarrassing at first, all the attention from students and even teachers did double takes. I'd felt relieved when I walked into gym that first day of class to see Astor there looking much the same as I did. We both towered over the rest of the school. But where I'd been self-conscious with the attention, Astor had reveled in the thunder of it all. He bragged that he could beat any guy at wrestling, and me showing up as his twin only made him more competitive. He'd been trying to pick a fight with me ever since.

"You know Tiff wants to do the limo thing. She's begging me, and I'm not going to say I can't afford one," Calvin grumbled. "Everyone's a jerk in middle school. I'm sure Astor has changed."

"We don't need a limo," I said. "Save it for prom."

"Dude, you sound just like my mom. I seriously want to punch you in the face right now."

I gave Calvin a sidelong look that said go ahead.

Calvin glared, even more mad. "Don't rub it in."

"Rub what in?"

I could practically hear Calvin grinding his teeth. "That you're all muscle. I'd probably hurt my hand."

I laughed. "Come on Cal."

Calvin's voice rose with anger. "You come on."

I stopped walking. Calvin was my best friend. and he almost never got mad. "Okay." I spoke calmly. "You know more than anyone how much I don't want to go with Regan."

Calvin nodded but his cheeks were still bright red.

"I'm doing this as a favor, and it's not without huge risk. I don't want Regan starting her full-on tantrums all over again."

"But that's just it," Calvin said. "If you're already going to suffer then you won't even notice Astor."

"I'll notice him." I paused, searching for the right words. "*I* want to go with Ji-hee, and now I'm going with Regan. I don't want that kind of guy on a date with the one girl I'm interested in."

"You were interested in Regan at one point," Cal said. "Maybe you could be interested again."

"That's not happening," I said.

Calvin frowned and we both started walking again. "I could tell you were into Ji-hee, but do you like her that much? You don't even know her."

"I want to get to know her. After homecoming is over, I'm going to ask her out."

Calvin gave me a sidelong look of pity. "Let's not get ahead of ourselves. Did you forget the hand holding in the hall? Totally weird.

Most girls will think you're a creepoid after that. You might as well buy a big rusty perv van and tint the windows black."

"She doesn't think I'm a creep," I huffed.

"Sure," Calvin nodded with mock enthusiasm. "She's super interested. That's why she glared at you and told you not to take her phone."

"We keep staring at each other." I said.

Calvin stifled a laugh. "You think staring brings a girl in?"

"It's not like that," I said. "She stared at me too. And when she did —I just knew."

Calvin scoffed. "Knew what?"

I sighed. "That she'll be the one. The person I click with."

"All of this because you want to *click*?" Calvin shook his head. "You're such a girl."

I grinned. "Yeah, but I can still break your hand with my face."

Calvin returned my volley with a spike. "True. But can you find a guy for Ji-hee that you won't want to break?" He reached up and clamped a hand on my shoulder. "Good luck."

6

JI-HEE

Gun's emails started coming the day after I got here from London. Dear sister, Blah, blah, blah, blah. But I was still too mad at Gun to do anything but delete them. I'd had six so far. But this one tonight, I sat on my bed and considered opening it. The subject line was what gave me pause.

Agree to Mother's email.

The last time I'd heard from Mother had been in London, the day she dropped a bomb on my life that had me scurrying for cover. Only there was no duck and cover for something that big. The best I could do was keep it secret. It was the reason I couldn't like a boy, and it was something that no one at Bishop High could ever know about.

I was engaged.

I'd been sitting in science class when the school counselor came to get me. Counselor Amy had been kind since I'd arrived, one of the only ones. As we walked to her office, she was tense and didn't talk. I knew whatever waited was bad news. But bad news in a place like this was just average news, something that happened every day. You looked at the teacher wrong and you lost basic necessities, like being able to shower, or go outside for sunshine, or even have a single blanket at night. So, her bad news vibe seemed unimportant. I'd already given up on most comforts, and if more punishment was to come, I'd figure it out. I was taking it one day at a time in here.

"You have a phone call from your mother," she said, as we approached her office.

My head jerked up. "What?" I asked stupidly.

"Your mother is on the phone. She wants to speak with you in private. I will just wait out in the hall until you are done. Take your time."

Mother hadn't called, not once since I'd arrived. My throat got hot and tight. "Am I going home?" I whispered.

The counselor's eyes looked sad. "No, Ji-hee. I think the people who run this school have different plans for you." She immediately straightened and folded her hands together. "What I mean is," her voice sounded panicked. "You're not ready to go home." She wrung both hands together and then said, "Talk with your mother, and I'll be here when you finish."

I walked into her office and closed the door. A black corded phone lay face down on the empty desk. I sat and took a breath before picking it up. If Mother wasn't calling to tell me she'd pull me out of this hellish place, then whatever she said wouldn't matter.

Only it had mattered. It had mattered more than any decision I would ever make, and Mother made it for me. I had been abandoned, only for my family to turn around and trade my life for stocks and influence. JAYNE industries was doing well, but it would do even better with the money the Bitgaram family could invest. All I had to do was marry a boy I'd never met. A boy I didn't love.

So now Mother was emailing me. After no other communication, she was simply going to act like nothing ever happened. I skipped Gun's email and scrolled until I found hers. I stared at my mother's name: *Lee Sari*. The line seemed darker than the rest, and an involuntary shiver ran down my spine. Could she have already figured out that Marklem Academy was a sham? I opened it.

Ji-hee,

. . .

The importance of pleasing your future in-laws is paramount to our family business. Myang Bitgaram wasn't keen on the idea of you leaving St. Austin's, and the only reason I indulged my father's desire for you to attend Marklem Academy instead was because I thought you might do better with less restrictions. Don't waste your time brooding now. You can see how accommodating I'm being by sending you to California. In return, I expect you to embrace the Bitgarams. When they reach out to you, and I'm sure they will soon, I want you to impress them with manners and politeness. I've taught you how to behave. Mrs. Bitgaram needs to understand what a smart and talented girl you are. Once she sees that you are thriving in California, she will agree with me that you are better off there. Also, remember to stay out of the sun. The Bitgarams won't want you if you mar your skin.

I am coming to visit next week. I will arrive Saturday at 1:00 p.m. Arrange to give me a personal tour of Marklem Academy, on Monday, and then I plan to speak to the school nurse about some new diet restrictions. Myang has asked that you lose two kilograms. The sooner you start the better.

Best,

Mother

I lay on my bed with my arm draped over my eyes, like not seeing the lit screen of my laptop would somehow erase every horrible word I'd just read.

I was so cooked.

There was no way out of it now. I wondered how long Mother's driver would search for the fake address Gun had given her before she realized there was no such school as Marklem Academy. This whole crazy plan to hide in plain sight hinged on the fact that my mother was notoriously neglectful.

And losing 2 kg was insane. I'd always been on the thin side, hovering somewhere around 49 kg. If I lost two more, I wouldn't have breasts. I gritted my teeth and sat up to grab my laptop again. I scrolled back to Gun's email. Whatever that liar had to say better contain miracles.

Dear Sister,

Look, I get it. You're mad. And you have every right to be. I screwed it up worse for you than it already was, but you've got it wrong. We were tricked and you paid the biggest price. But now the stakes are higher. Mother went and signed an agreement with the Bitgaram family. You're engaged. I think you already know this, but Mother hid it from me for a long time. I can't tell you the whole plan yet, but Chul and I are working together now, like we should have done in the beginning of all this mess.

Step one of the plan: respond to the email Mother just sent you. Don't ask how I was able to read it before you did. I've got something in the works that will prevent her from leaving Korea, but I need your help on a little reverse psychology. Gush and go on about how excited you are for her to visit. Then take it one step further with a big thumbs up on her silly diet. Tell her you've been wanting to lose a few anyway. If problems in the business are boiling over, and she thinks you're already happily starving yourself, she'll skip the trip altogether.

I know you've ignored all my other emails, but I need you to respond to this one. Let me know if you're willing to play ball, otherwise I need a different plan.

I do love you, and I'm sorry. So sorry for everything.

Gun

I bunched the quilt in my hands and gnashed my teeth into the pillow. I didn't want to hear his excuses. But now, this plan was my only shot at staying here where things were normal, or as normal as you can get if you're me. I knew Mother and if trouble came up at the company, she wouldn't trust anyone but herself to fix it. The plan was solid.

My fingers hovered over my keyboard. If I swallowed some of my anger—just enough to work with my idiot brother, I had a chance. I replied to Gun's email with one word.

Sure.

Then I took my laptop to my desk and sat down for some serious work. Playing dumb with mother and lacing lies with truth was dangerous. Like bad for your health, dangerous. She could smell deceit, even through email. Gun knew this, but he also knew I could pull it off.

By the time I finished, the only thing I wanted was a hot bath, but someone knocked on my door. I considered not answering until Sydney's voice came through. She sounded worried. "Are you awake, Ji-hee?"

I opened the door and summoned a smile. "Hi, Sydney."

She wore an apron and smelled like burned oil but spoke softly. "Chul said that you got some bad news today. I just wondered if you're okay."

My mind scrambled. Could she be talking about my emails? Gun said he and Chul were working together. "What do you mean?" I asked.

Sydney met my eyes. "Gun found something. Something bad and now Chul is trying to help. He was worried because I guess your mom sent you an email that was kind of harsh. I understand if you don't want to talk about it, but if you need anything . . . I was just worried."

I folded my arms. "I'm okay. You don't need to worry. But how did Gun get my mother's email?"

Sydney folded her hands. "Chul has a talent, or some might think of it as a flaw, but sometimes if the situation is really extreme—and yours is—he can find things online. Like look at someone's personal information."

I gasped. "He hacked my mother's accounts."

Sydney winced. "Don't be mad."

"I'm not mad, I just—where is he?"

Sydney's face fell. "He won't show you, Ji-hee. He hasn't shown me either."

"Why?"

"Gun thinks whatever they found is dangerous."

"But—"

"Look," Sydney said. "I trust Chul. If there's a problem, he's going to fix it."

I wouldn't say a word, but I really wanted to tell Sydney that the last time I'd had a problem and Chul was involved, it essentially ruined my life.

HARRISON

Last night I texted Ji-hee twice, and she still hadn't responded.

**I have a guy lined up for your Homecoming date.
He's a cool guy.**

I considered sending more. A meme? A stupid question? I wasn't ready to give up, and if she wasn't going to answer me then intercepting the bus was my next move. I pulled out of my driveway just as Ji-hee walked out her front door. I had both windows down and called out, "Hey, Ji-hee," all while looking surprised to see her. I wasn't. I'd planned this to the minute. I pulled the car to the curb and hopped out. "You live here?" I pointed across the street to my house. "This is me."

Ji-hee froze in her tracks—like a kid seeing her teacher at the grocery store. Your brain takes a minute to process that person actually exists outside of school. I jogged across the street, all while trying to keep my shoulders loose.

Ji-hee looked up at me when I stopped in front of her and took a step back. I rubbed the back of my neck feeling self-conscious. "We're neighbors," I said, lamely. Was I always this stupid? I pointed down the street. "Do you see the yellow house with the blue shutters?"

Ji-hee nodded.

"That's Calvin's house."

She smiled but still seemed uneasy, like she'd rather be anywhere than here talking to me. Maybe it was the fact that I could lift Ji-hee with one arm. Sometimes people feel anxious just from my size. I tried to look like your average boy-next-door and not like I could wrestle alligators. I rolled my shoulders and did my best to keep my voice relaxed. "Do you want a ride to school?" As soon as the words left my mouth, I knew it was a mistake. If she turned me down, I was in a corner. There was no saving face after ghosting me on text and then rejecting a ride. I could see the excuses forming in her head. She was trying to think of a polite way to say *pass*.

"Before you decide, I should warn you that this bus driver has six DUI's."

She paused with the unspoken *no* on her lips and frowned. "What's a DUI?"

"You know, driving under the influence. The driver, he's always drunk."

She laughed. "He isn't."

Her laugh was killer. A single chime of flawless joy, and all I could think was I wanted to hear it again. Like if there was a perfect sound in all the world, it would be Ji-hee's laugh. "You're right. He's just an energy drink junkie. But you still shouldn't ride the bus."

"Why not?" she asked.

My brain spun like one of those wheels where you land on a prize, but I knew what I had to do before the wheel even stopped. *Be honest.* Jeff had drilled this into me so I hoped it would work. "I want a chance," I said.

"A chance to do what?" she asked. "Show me your driving expertise?"

I laughed, all nerves. "No. I want to hang out with you and be like —you know—friends."

She gave me a look that said she didn't buy this.

I cocked my head toward my car. "Come on. Say yes. It's just a ride to school."

She smiled. "Friends is okay."

I let out a sigh and followed her to my car. We both got in and I pulled slowly off the curb. Had I just friend-zoned myself? "So, you live with the Kim family? I've seen them a few times. When did you move here?"

"Just a few days ago," she said. "Right before school started."

"Have you ever been to the US before now?"

"Nope, not even to Hawaii and everyone's been there."

I didn't tell her that she was off-base. I hadn't been to Hawaii and most of my school hadn't. Maybe the top 10 percent—the rich kids—had, but no more than that. I'd gotten the impression yesterday that she came from money. "What do you think so far?" I asked.

She smiled. "I like it."

"What do you like?"

She swept her hand out the window. "The sun, the freedom." Her eyes took on a determination, like she was holding onto something important.

I nodded and made a mental note that she mentioned freedom.

She turned back to me. "I'm sorry I haven't answered your texts yet."

I tried to shrug like I didn't care but didn't completely pull it off.

"You texted that you had a date for me, but you didn't say who," she said. "I was trying to think of a polite way to ask why you are so against Astor."

"The date is my little brother, Ozzy. And if you'll say yes, he will be a hundred times better. Astor and I have a history, and I just want to avoid him if I can. He's actually a jerk."

Ji-hee nodded. "Okay, I don't mind if my date is your brother. Can you tell me about him?"

We pulled into the school parking lot, and I cruised slowly through the aisles. "Ozzy is a freshman. He is a champion figure skater and because of this he's schooled with private tutors so he can train. Oh, and this will be his first date so go easy on him."

"He sounds like a cool kid." She frowned. "What do you mean by *go easy on him*? Is that like an American saying?"

"It means don't be so cute because your beauty will leave him in ruins, but honestly there's no way for you to be less cute. Maybe just don't smile or even talk. You should consider wearing a ski mask."

Ji-hee laughed and the sound wrapped around me again, making my heart buzz. I concentrated on finding a parking space and not on the perfection sitting next to me. I saw one, swung in, and killed the engine.

I'd been so focused on smooth driving that her next statement caught me off guard.

"You and Regan seem to be a couple." She said it like a question. I wanted to give her an answer, but how could I explain without sounding like a loser?

"No. I asked her to homecoming because we're all friends, and Calvin wanted me to go in their group. I used to date her, but we broke up."

She nodded but I could tell she was disappointed. I wasn't sure if it was that I'd told her we used to date or something else. I wanted to be honest with Ji-hee. I just couldn't think how to explain that I asked Regan to protect her and not sound like a complete psycho.

She lowered her eyes and turned from me to open the door. I quickly got out of the car and walked to her side. But I could feel she was already pulling away.

"Thanks for the ride." Ji-hee tossed her hair over her shoulder while swinging her backpack into place. She took one step away from me when someone yelled from a few cars over.

"Hey, Ji-hee. Ji-hee, over here."

I scanned the parking lot and found who I feared. Han-bae strode toward us. He didn't pause, or hesitate, or even notice me. Where I lacked confidence, he was sure of himself. He stopped directly in front of Ji-hee and grinned wearing another stupid suit. "I was waiting for you. Can I walk with you to class?"

7

JI-HEE

Han-bae wore an Armani gray pinstripe suit from the new fall collection. I'd seen the previews online with Sydney, but until now, hadn't the pleasure of seeing it in person. He did it justice, but Bishop High wouldn't. I wondered again how I didn't know this guy if he was both Korean and rich. Whether I liked it or not, that was my crowd. I'd searched through all of my social media for a picture, a whisper of Han-bae. He had to be a friend of a friend at least. But this guy didn't exist outside of his real self.

"You look fine today in Armani," I said. I hoped he would be flustered or maybe even give me a clue to who he was, but Han-bae stepped closer, so close I could feel heat from his body.

He grinned. "You should come shopping with me next time." He eyed my Target jeans.

I'd been so proud when I got them because of the blending-in factor, but I knew someone like Han-bae wouldn't appreciate them. I took a step back and turned to Harrison who was busy locking his car with a scowl.

Harrison's eyes flicked between Han-bae and me darkly. "I need to find Calvin," he said.

If Harrison was jealous—he wasn't jealous—but if he was, he

shouldn't be. "Okay, I'll see you later, then," I said, trying not to feel disappointed.

He only nodded and walked away with his head down.

Han-bae matched my own stride as we made our way to class. He even reached out for my backpack, but I clutched the straps tightly. I wasn't going to let him touch my bag. It had my laptop inside with all my secrets. "I've got it," I said.

"What's wrong with me carrying it? Our lockers are side-by-side," he said.

A small twitch of alarm made me momentarily stop. I thought of the girl he'd displaced to get the locker he wanted. The locker right next to mine. He was also in every single one of my classes, which meant he was either manipulating things, or Cupid had some stupid new hire field-testing serendipity. "But I'm not going to my locker," I said as I shifted my pack to my other shoulder, farther away, and started walking again.

He shrugged. "Okay, I'm planning to follow you anyway."

I glanced up at him with my best *what the heck* look.

He immediately laughed. "That sounded weird. I just don't know how you move around this school so easily. I'm feeling lost."

"I don't think you're lost," I said with a skeptical shake of my head.

Han-bae held up both hands. "I'm good with English, so I thought the States would be easy. But I hate it here. I do feel lost, and a friend would be nice."

Han-bae was the second guy to ask for friendship today. "That's fair." I nodded and smiled pleasantly the way I'd been taught by a solid decade of nannies, but I wasn't sure friendship was what he really wanted. And Han-bae did want something. "Okay, so as a friend can I ask two questions?"

"Shoot," he said.

"Why are you here?"

"Business. My mother is investing in a company in California, and I'm supposed to help run it, but I need to graduate so . . . I agreed to finish high school here and get my diploma."

I bit my lip. He'd answered quickly, almost too quickly, like he was reading a script. Maybe he was just nervous around me. I did feel a tad sorry for him. "And where do you live? You can't be here alone."

"My dad sent one of his assistants. He's half American and grew up in a house just around the block from here." Han-bae grimaced. "The poor guy's been demoted to babysitter, but he jumped at the chance to go home for a while."

All of this might sound far-fetched unless you were a Korean chaebol. Children of very rich conglomerates are groomed young to take over. Sending your kid halfway around the world to learn the family business while they are still in high school wouldn't be off the menu. What did sound fishy was sending him to Bishop High. His mother would have sent not only a personal assistant but a private tutor. Kids in Armani didn't go to public school.

"Okay, last question," I said.

"But that was your last," He tilted his head to the side with a grin. "You said two."

"Give me a freebie, then."

Han-bae stroked his chin. "Hmm, I don't know. Nothing's free anymore."

"But we're friends now."

Han-bae looked down at me and his eyes turned serious. "Then I'll give you a hundred more. Ask away."

"Why aren't you on social media?"

Han-bae grinned. "You checked me out." He looked a little too pleased at the idea that I'd searched for him.

"I tried to. But your social-metrics score is zero."

"I like privacy."

"That much?" I asked, skeptical.

He shrugged. "I keep my circle tight for a reason."

I rolled my eyes but kept walking. When we entered class, I noticed Harrison already in his normal seat with the spot in front of him, my spot, wide open. I avoided his gaze and sat in the very front row which let Han-bae take the desk next to mine.

Part of me twinged with guilt over Harrison, but it was small. I had bigger problems with my mother and her possible visit. Harrison was better off not getting involved in my drama.

HARRISON

What did I expect Ji-hee to do? Growl at Han-bae and tell him to get lost? *Yes, yes I did.* But that was the stupid part of my brain talking. Girls like Ji-hee don't growl.

JI-HEE

That night Mother emailed me back. I sat on my bed for five whole minutes, closing and reopening my laptop until I worked up the guts to read it.

Ji-hee,

I am glad that you are already working on your diet. Don't go overboard or you will lose too much, and that's not attractive either. I got an email from your school nurse, and she is eager to help you. Of course she is. I offered her a bonus. Since things are well in hand, I'm going to stay in Korea. I have important work that keeps piling up at the office. I trust that you will do what it takes to please the Bitgaram family.

Best-

Mother

I grabbed my phone to text Gun. This was a home run. Mother bought whatever nonsense he and Chul had cooked up to keep her at the company. She even believed my lies about being excited to "slim down." I didn't know who sent the fake nurse email, but I didn't care as long as it kept her in Korea. I texted Gun.

Mother's not coming. She emailed to break our date and

give a head pat over my pretend diet—I might just Door-
Dash a devil's food cake and eat the whole thing myself in
defiance. Keep your word this time and let me know what
the plan is moving forward.

He texted me right back.

**Good job, Sis. I almost have plans set but searching for one
last piece.**

One last piece? I knew there was something big brewing, something really bad that he didn't want to tell me. We'd tricked Mother.
But what about next time or the time after that. She wouldn't stop,
and when one of us tripped up, she'd uproot my life or level it.

I woke in a cold sweat. It had been a nightmare of course but my
arms and legs still tingled with remembered pain. I had stood atop an
impossibly high skyscraper. Grandfather appeared at my side, all
crinkly smiles and whispered something I couldn't hear. He kept
repeating himself as he walked backward to the edge of the building.
I moved closer, alarmed and trying to hear his voice. He took one last
step off and tipped backward, still speaking the silent words. I
reached for him with a scream, but he hadn't fallen. He bobbed along
in midair as if it was water and motioned me forward. As I got closer
his words came in staccato bursts. I watched and listened until I
could hear. "Take back what you don't have."

"What don't I have?" I asked.

"You don't have you."

"I'm here though. I'm me."

But he motioned to my chest and when I looked down, I could see
my own heart fluttering. It was no longer under protective ribs and
muscles but attached outside of my body. It beat weakly and strained
against a thin golden thread that sliced through its center with each
pulse. As I stood there helpless, more threads slid up from the
building and wrapped my heart, layering upon themselves like wrap-

pings on a mummy. Soon I could barely see the strained movement of each beat.

I looked back to Grandfather terrified, but he only watched me with pity and finally motioned me forward. I stepped hesitantly to the edge of the building. The rough cement scraped along the soles of my feet, but when I inched my toes off, the air felt cool and welcoming. The sun at my back turned to a soft warmth, and I stepped into the nothingness. Instead of bobbing on unseen currents like Grandfather, I fell, plummeting down. I jerked to a stop, tethered to the building by the threads binding my heart. Needles of pain burned as it began ripping away from my body. "No," I screamed.

I sat up in my bed, clutching at my chest. It was just a dream. I gulped in air, covered in sweat and fear. Before the sun began to rise, I got up and got myself ready for school. I had freedoms here, but not enough to get attached. This was just a place to bide my time until I was a legal adult. And I didn't need a stupid dream to know that trying to make it anything else wasn't a good idea.

8

HARRISON

The front door to our house stood propped wide open with a brick when I pulled up. I idled in Jeff's car and checked my texts. There were three from Mom that came in succession.

Dad and I need a favor.
Don't worry It's not a big favor.
Your grandparents are coming over after school.

Garrett and Gretchen were not my grandparents. They'd gone out of their way to make that perfectly clear more than once, and spending time with them was closer to abdominal surgery without anesthesia than a favor.

When I got out of the car, Garrett came out the front door carrying Mom's big blue suitcase in one hand and a shoulder bag in another. Awesome. He walked past me with no more than a disgruntled glance in my direction and then hefted the suitcase inside his car. That wasn't a promising sign.

I slowly went inside and stood in the great room. Mom rummaged through the refrigerator before she closed the door and turned to her mother-in-law who sat serenely at the island looking like an old-time movie star. Gretchen kept her white hair in smooth waves to her chin and always wore tailored monochromatic suits in shades of gray, black, or sometimes navy. Some combination of plastic surgery and makeup kept her skin looking closer to my mom's age than a retiree.

"I honestly can't believe you're doing this for us, Gretchen," Mom said. "I feel like it's too much."

Gretchen raised her chin and sniffed. "You and Jeff haven't been anywhere alone together in much too long."

Mom sighed into a smile. "It will be so nice to get away." She turned back to the fridge. "I don't have extra meals prepped, but everything is all cleaned out now. The least I can do is not leave you with moldy mashed potatoes on the back shelf."

"We won't have trouble. There is always delivery, and Garrett hired a private cook last week. She can come and feed the children."

Mom's eyes went big at this, but she didn't say anything. None of us had gotten used to the way Garrett and Gretchen spent money. Jeff didn't seem to even blink at it, but then, he was born with a sliver spoon in his mouth or maybe it was gold. Mom said Jeff grew up in New York and went to private school. But to us, he was just this average down-to-earth dad all about using leftovers and not leaving lights on. He did his own ironing, and he had Mom cut his hair to save money. Trying to imagine him ever living the way Garrett and Gretchen did kind of blew my mind.

Becca bounded in the kitchen and her eyes lit up. "Nanna. You're here," she squealed and climbed up onto the stool next to her for a hug.

Gretchen's features softened as she held my sister. Whenever Ozzy or Becca were around, some small part of Gretchen that seemed actually nice seeped out. It made her half human instead of a card-board cut-out prop at the theater.

"Are you and Grandfather really staying two weeks?" Becca asked.

"Yes, love, and we are going to have buckets of fun. Tomorrow after school I'm going to take you and your brother shopping for new clothes."

I noticed that she said *brother* and not *brothers*. Mom didn't. She moved to the pantry and hastily organized the mac n'cheese boxes. Gretchen's kitchen was probably more sterile than an operating room. Ours was lived in. Mom shouldn't have cared, but Gretchen was good at making people feel uncomfortable in their own homes.

Thinking back to our Fourth of July BBQ still left me sick with humiliation.

We'd all waited for Dad to come home, but he'd called to say he had to work late at his second job, so I fired up the grill. I'd seen him do in a hundred times. How hard could it be?

"Are you sure you know what you're doing?" Mom yelled out to me on the patio while she pulled potato salad out of the fridge.

I speared a steak and placed it gingerly on the hot grill. "I've got this, Mom." I noticed Gretchen and Garrett didn't move from their spots on the outdoor swing to help. I loaded four of the eight steaks onto the grill and made sure the temperature was at the highest setting before shutting the lid, then went in to help mom carry out the rest of the food. I was lugging the second cooler of ice and drinks to the backyard when I heard Mom scream. I dropped the cooler and ran, but Garrett got there first. The grill was on fire. He calmly turned off the burners and unscrewed the lid to the salt, dumping the whole thing over the flames. Then turned to me. "You didn't clean the grill before you started," Garrett snapped. "There were pools of grease."

Mom laughed nervously as big blooms of black smoke wafted around the patio. "Jeff always forgets to do that."

I moved toward the grill, but Garrett stepped in front of me. "You've ruined most of the meat. I'll finish the rest."

His words stung, but I told myself he was just one of those old crotchety guys that couldn't handle stress. I put both my hands up and pinched my lips together to keep any smart comments from coming out.

"Harrison, why don't you grab the napkins," Mom said. The lines around her eyes had deepened as she gave me a pleading look. I could almost hear her voice in my head. "Be a peacemaker, son."

I nodded and went to the kitchen, giving myself extra time with deep breaths and counting to ten—twice.

When I came back Garrett was scraping the grill and the charred steaks were in the trashcan next to him. Gretchen stood close by and whispered in his ear. I was glad Mom didn't notice. She was setting up lawn chairs on the grass.

"Come here, Harrison," Garrett said. "I want to talk to you."

Maybe he was going to say sorry for being a jerk.

He sighed. "Tonight, I want you to tell your mom and our son that you can't go on the trip."

I frowned, confused. "The trip that's in two weeks?"

"Yes, the Australia trip," he said. "You should be working instead of playing. You said yourself that college is going to be expensive."

"Yeah, but I'm applying for scholarships, and two weeks won't make that big of a—"

Gretchen interrupted. "We don't want to burden your mother by talking to her about this." She gave me a pointed look. "Do the right thing and tell them that you don't want to go."

I snorted. "But I do want to go." I couldn't believe they were actually suggesting I not go on the family vacation. "Dad and I love spear fishing, and Australia has some of the best places."

Gretchen's eyes went to ice, but her voice remained calm. "We know you're not a bad kid." She spoke deliberately, like I was slow and needed things spelled out. "However, you do need to remember whose kid you are and are not."

My breath caught in my throat, burned there like a hot coal. How dare she imply that Dad wasn't my dad. But she continued, like her judgments were somehow deserved, as if my very presence was an insult and she was being the patient one. "It's not our son's responsibility to sacrifice the life he planned so you can have what you want. Who do you think will be paying for your trip?"

"They're paying for Ozzy and Becca. They'd pay for me too."

Gretchen let out her signature singsong laugh. The one that had made her famous on Broadway. "You're so naive, dear."

I shook my head. "Why would you say any of this to me?" Suspicions stirred in my brain. So far, I'd kept any dangerous thoughts buried under a thick layer of denial. But the truths I wanted to be lies were rising up, demanding to be heard. Those little voices that wondered why my name wasn't included on the official Christmas letter Garrett and Gretchen sent to all their friends in New York. Three years ago, I'd stumbled onto one of their cards by accident. Dad had it stashed in the back of his desk drawer under a pile of bills. They spoke of Ozzy and Becca by name but never mentioned me. The rejection I got when I tried to pick them up from the airport. I'd been so proud to have my driver's license in time to get them when they flew in for a visit. Mom had seemed so nervous when I left and insisted I change my shirt and add gel to my hair. Then something about the dismissive way they followed me to baggage claim, the scornful look on Gretchen's face as I asked how their flight was. Garrett called a limo instead of accepting my ride. I'd made excuses and pretended that next time would be different. But truths that ugly don't just go away.

I shook my head. Maybe Gretchen and Garrett didn't love me, but my parents wouldn't have planned this trip if they could only take two of their three children. "I'm not naive," I spat. "My dad loves me. He would be happy to pay for me."

"Call him Jeff. He's not your dad and he's not paying for this trip," Gretchen said.

My brain skidded to a halt.

Gretchen let her words hang in the air, almost like she savored my pain, before she continued. "My son assumed we would take you too, but to be frank, you were never invited. We told Jeff that we'd like to take our grand-children on a trip. You're not ours, Harrison, and we don't owe you anything. We never booked your ticket. There is no bed for you in the hotel and every event we paid for is reserved for six people, a nice round number, not seven."

"Dad—"

Gretchen held up a hand. "Not Dad."

I glared at her and stammered. "He wouldn't—it's not—not like—" I shook my head.

"What is it like then?" Garrett asked as he flipped steaks next to me with deft movements, his meat perfectly seared. When I didn't answer, he

spoke, his voice sounding wise next to my struggling words. "You're not a kid anymore. Jeff is killing himself working two jobs so he can pay for your upcoming college, and now, you want him to pay for a trip too. Don't you think it's time to do the right thing?"

Suddenly I was unsure. What was the right thing? Was I really the reason he had been working so much? I watched Mom spread a blanket in the grass. The fourth had always been a happy time, but tonight Mom's face was stiff as she worked. Becca immediately plopped down on the blanket with pillows.

"Mommy, I'm hungry," Becca said. "When is the food going to be ready?"

Mom looked over her shoulder with a frown.

I winced inwardly, Mom shouldn't be in a bad mood because her husband was late again, and I'd burned the steaks. She should be laughing at lame dad jokes and eating Jello.

I grabbed the hotdogs out of the cooler and ripped the bag open, dumping the whole package, juice and all, on the sizzling grill. Garrett sighed and pushed them aside with his spatula as if cheap hotdogs would contaminate his remaining steaks.

"Becca," I called over my shoulder, ignoring him. "I'm making your hotdog right now."

Gretchen jumped up. "You can eat that garbage, but my family will not." She grabbed the spatula from Garrett, scooped up the hotdogs, and dropped them into the garbage can. They tumbled in on top of the burnt steaks with a wet thud.

I ground my teeth. Becca loved hotdogs, but I knew better than to argue with Gretchen. I turned on my heel and walked into the kitchen then straight to the front door. My hand grabbed the handle just as dad opened it. He looked tired but smiled when he saw me. "Did you save me some steak?"

I made my face relax. "Garrett's still grilling, but they're almost done." I knew just how to put my shoulders back and pretend I was okay. I wasn't.

That same night after Gretchen and Garrett left, I lied. I told my parents that I couldn't get work off. Then I threw in that if I didn't miss a day over the summer, I could get an extra bonus. I argued my point with dollar signs and in the end, they agreed to go without me.

The memory of that terrible night wasn't even two months old, and now my parents were leaving me with these freaks. "Uh, Mom, can I talk to you a minute?" I asked.

She stuck her head out of the pantry. "What do you need?"

I pursed my lips. "In private. Can we talk in private?"

She glanced at Gretchen, still giggling right along with Becca and walked quickly to the office. I followed and she shut the door. "What's wrong?"

"Nothing, it's just . . . um are you and Jeff going somewhere?"

She beamed and clasped both hands together. "Your Nana and Grandfather bought us a trip to Hawaii. We're staying in their timeshare."

"That's . . . cool."

"I can't believe they did this for us. Your dad mentioned how we missed our anniversary and the next thing you know they're texting us tickets to this posh resort."

I ran my hand through my hair and let out a sigh. "When do you leave?"

"Tonight." Mom's eyes shined and she started bouncing on the balls of her feet, clearly excited.

"Can I stay at Calvin's?"

She blinked. "Why?" she asked, looking a little deflated.

My eye caught on the stain in the carpet from when I spilled my model car paint. I'd been fourteen, old enough to be more careful. Jeff hadn't even gotten mad, just blotted it up and told me it was only carpet. I shrugged. "I just feel like I'd be in the way."

Mom sighed. "Your Nana and Grandfather don't know much about how the house is run. They're going to need you, and this will help everyone to finally . . . bond."

I didn't point out that they weren't my grandparents, or that if they were, we wouldn't need help *bonding*. "Yeah, I get that, but I can come back if they need me."

"No, I'm counting on you to stay and help."

I nodded. I didn't want to ruin the one break Mom and Jeff were getting, even if it was being paid for by demon spawn.

She smiled like she believed in me. Jeff had that same smile. I wondered if the good parents in the universe took some secret class on how to love teenagers. "Are you okay?" she asked.

I kept my face blank and nodded. "Yeah, you can count on me to help."

9

JI-HEE

The last few days I'd kept my distance from everyone—Han-bae, Regan, Harrison. I even walked the other way when I saw Calvin in the hall. It was just easier. But as I changed in the locker room, I knew there'd be no avoiding Harrison in PE. He'd find ways to catch my eye and smile or make little thoughtful gestures. Monday, after our fitness test he'd handed me an ice-cold sports drink, and yesterday he ran over to help me fold and put away the mats when it was my turn.

Mrs. Liv blew her whistle and asked everyone to break into groups for drills. Han-bae gave me a questioning look, but I shook my head. Harrison dared to take a step in my direction prompting Regan to immediately tug his arm. "Harrison, can you be on my team?" Her voice turned breathy as she pulled him back toward the pack of girls on the right side of the gym.

I walked to the bleachers and sat a few feet from two other girls that also hadn't been picked for a team. Harrison watched me in between each shot. I shouldn't have but I watched him right back, not caring that Regan gave me death glares.

Just this little bit of attention from him was like trying to stop myself from going down a waterslide. It was easy if I stayed up at the top, but if I started the slide there was no stopping gravity. And no other guy had as much gravity as Harrison—not Han-bae, not Calvin who was better looking, and not any boy I'd ever met. For me, Harrison was just that guy.

Ms. Liv blew her whistle again and pointed at me. "Go get a ball and you three form up. You can shoot baskets over there." She gestured in a careless manner to the sad looking portable basketball hoop in the far corner of the gym. It leaned to one side like it would topple if you hit the backboard too hard. Clearly Ms. Liv didn't care if we could shoot or dribble, she just wanted us to look busy.

"Where are the balls?" I asked the girl next to me. She wore two plain homely braids on each side of her face, and a long dress with closed-toed sandals over bunchy athletic socks. Definitely not great fashion sense, but when she spoke, kindness radiated off her. She was the kind of girl you could imagine selflessly diving into freezing water to save a single cat, or the girl who would help an old lady carry groceries.

She pointed to a door at the back of the gym that was slightly ajar. "The extras are in the storage closet. Do you want me to get one?"

I stood. "That's okay. Ms. Liv asked me." I turned back to her. "What's your name?"

"Diana," she said, shyly.

The other girl on the bleachers looked up when I spoke. She had flawless skin and an uneven haircut. I couldn't decide if that was on purpose, or if she'd just cut it herself and messed up. Either way, it looked cool, and the girl was pretty enough to be a model. "I'm Harmony," she offered. "I'm new this year."

Diana turned to her. "Where did you move from?"

"Boston," Harmony said, proudly.

I heard Diana giggle as I moved down the bleachers. "I like your accent," Diana said. "I have an aunt in Boston."

Their voices faded as I walked past Regan's mob and watched from the corner of my eye as Harrison did another layup. Harrison called my name, but I pretended not to hear.

The storage door groaned as I pushed it open and flipped on the sputtering fluorescent light. The closet was big enough to be a room and filled with more junk than anything. I wrinkled my nose as I walked past equipment that smelled like sweat, oil and rubber. Torn mats were haphazardly stacked in the corner along with an overflowing bin of jumbled bats and bent golf clubs. Next to that a broken tetherball pole leaned forlornly against the wall. I found a tall rack of basketballs in the very back of the room. The only three left on the bottom were flat with no air pump in sight, but there was one on the top that looked promising. It was a different color than the rest, neon yellow and black. I reached and stretched, going up on tiptoe, but my fingers barely brushed its edge. I reached farther and jumped up to tap it hard, hoping the ball would roll forward. Instead, it ricocheted off the back wall and fell straight down ready to pummel my upturned face. Before I could react, a large hand shot out from behind me and gripped the ball in the air just inches from my nose. Warmth pressed at my back and Harrison's deep voice spoke close to my ear. "You almost got hurt." Somewhere in the confusion his other hand had wrapped around my waist to steady me, and heat spread out from his touch. We both stood frozen for the length of one heartbeat, two, three. I wanted to lean back and let him hold me.

He broke first and let go. I didn't turn around but listened to him walk out and then the thud as he bounced the ball in the court. When I exited the storage room Diana and Harmony were shooting hoops with a yellow and black basketball.

HARRISON

I waited outside the school for Ji-hee, hoping she'd ride home with me. Instead, she walked right past without making eye contact, straight toward the bus. She barely even blinked. But she did slow and stop when she saw Burke, the snot-nosed bully from our neighborhood. He stood under a tree outside the bus crying. Actually crying.

Ji-hee watched for only a moment and then carefully walked forward. "Hey, your name is Burke, right? We both get off at the same stop."

Burke straightened, embarrassed to be caught crying. What did he expect? But it was doubly bad to have a girl as hot as Ji-hee notice. He quickly wiped away tears. "Yeah, I'm Burke, What's it to you?" he snapped.

I expected Ji-hee to back off, but she tilted her head to the side and said, "It's alright. Whatever it is, it's okay." Her voice had gone honey smooth, and she looked at him like he was some kind of cherished friend. She reached out a hand and placed it on Burke's shoulder. "Do you want to tell me about it on the ride home?"

Burke's chin quivered and he nodded. "My cat died," he said. Then absentmindedly let his backpack slide from his shoulder. Ji-hee caught it before it hit the ground. She gently took it from him. "Come on, let's get on."

Burke followed closely, becoming her personal shadow. I continued to watch them as they climbed the stairs and then sat near the front on the same row.

This kid didn't deserve to breathe the same air as Ji-hee, but she was saying all the right things to help him. I wondered if she would have been as understanding if she knew that he teased my little brother to death every chance he got. But I already knew the answer. Ji-hee was nice to everyone, maybe not warm and fuzzy to Regan, but that was just self-preservation. To the rest of the school, even Hanbae, she was all kindness.

I turned on my heel and headed to the parking lot. Burke didn't have a decent bone in his body. He was mean to pretty much everyone, but Ji-hee had managed to bring out something soft in him. If the Big Guy upstairs was keeping score, Ji-hee was beating us all.

When I walked in the front door our house smelled like lavender candles and very faintly like bleach. Ozzy and Becca were at the bar staring at sushi in little black trays. A maid was packing up a portable cart. That explained the bleach smell.

Gretchen ran her fingers over the top shelf of the open refrigerator. "There is still something sticky in here. She turned back with a half sneer and walked to the sink to wash her hands and delicately dry them on a white, crisply folded towel that I knew she'd purchased just so she didn't have to touch our stained ones. "I can pay you less or you can redo it," Gretchen had left the fridge open, and the maid rolled her eyes as she pulled a rag back out of her cart.

"Harrison," she said, moving on to me. "I was hoping you had some kind of after school club. Why are you here?" Her voice projected like she was back on a Broadway stage.

"Oh, I came home as fast as I could so I could help you and Grandfather." I let the sarcasm spill into every word. "Thank you for staying here and taking care of us. We would have never survived without you."

Ozzy snickered but Becca's eyes shot up and locked with mine. "We wouldn't have to eat slimy fish if Grandmother wasn't here."

"I told you darling. You must call me Nana." She picked up Becca's discarded chopsticks and placed them in her small hands. "If you will practice with these then you won't need to touch your food."

"I like forks, and I hate fish," Becca said, trying to put the chopsticks down while Gretchen kept shoving them into her hand.

"Nonsense. Fish is full of omega-3. You need to eat clean."

"I want peanut butter and jelly," Becca said.

Ozzy winced and took a bite of his fish. Our parents loved sushi, but they'd never forced us to eat it. I walked to the pantry and opened it. Our normal system of shove-it-in-and-close-the-door had been sanitized into something darn near military grade organization. All the food was now stacked neatly in small clear plastic bins. Most of the junk, I noted, had been replaced with whatever weird gerbil food Gretchen ate. Luckily there was still Skippy and a loaf of white bread. I grabbed what I needed and spread out on the table—as far from Gretchen as I could get—and made six PB&J's. Three for me, two for Ozzy, and one for Becca, even though she'd barely eat half.

Garrett came in from the back yard wearing his normal starched tan chinos and white collared shirt.

"Garrett, can you pay the help?" Gretchen asked. "She was sub-par, so not the full amount."

I watched the woman at the fridge tense and bunch her shoulders before taking a deep breath. She softly closed the door and walked to where Garrett was. He tapped on his phone and then nodded to hers as she pulled it out to check the balance. She glared at him before turning on her heel and marching out, grabbing her stuff without a goodbye.

Gretchen sighed like she had been the one slighted. "Can you call the agency and have them send someone else?"

"Already on it," Garrett said. He eyed me as I carried a stack of sandwiches over to my siblings and passed them out. Becca eagerly snatched her sandwich and took a bite. Ozzy set both of his sandwiches neatly next to him and stared at his fish.

Gretchen curled her lip up at me. "How kind of you to care for Ozzy and Becca. They really don't need your interference, though."

"What does interference mean?" Becca asked around a mouthful of sandwich.

"It means I gave you what Mom would have." I ruffled her hair as I carried sandwiches to my room.

Garrett stopped me with a hand on my arm. I was a full head taller than the guy, so I was a little surprised he did so. I shouldn't have been. It was the kind of challenge that said *I'm still bigger than you in all the ways you're not.* Garrett believed he owned the world because he had money. I met his cool gaze and finally faced the dark corner in my mind I'd been avoiding since the Fourth of July cookout. "Garrett, did you need something?"

"If you let Gretchen do her thing, she'll go easier on you," he spoke quietly so no one else heard us. In fact, if you want to go stay somewhere else while your mom is gone it might help."

"I'm not leaving my house, the house my parents bought," I said. "And I'm not leaving my brother and sister with a sadistic narcissist."

Garrett gripped my arm harder. "I made the down payment on

this house," he said. "Even paid the taxes for the last five years when things have been tight for my son." Then he leaned in closer and whispered in my ear. "And just so you're clear on who's the narcissist —Gretchen's actually a kitten. I, on the other hand, am not."

I smiled calmly at Garrett. "*My dad* loves me more than your money."

Garrett took a step back looking like I'd just punched him in the gut. "That's one thing we can agree on, Harrison. Jeff has never loved money. But he shouldn't work two jobs so you can play."

10

JI-HEE

"Pull out your laptops," Mr. Buchanan said. He clasped both hands and rubbed them together. Finance was, by far, my most boring class, maybe like learning your times tables when you'd already taken Statistics. Only today, Mr. Buchanan rubbed both of his hands together with enthusiasm. "I have a new assignment," he said. "I think—no, I'm positive that it will be enlightening for all of us. It's called Life Path Budgeting."

Anna, the overachiever of the class, already had her computer out and her hand up.

"Yes, Anna."

"This assignment isn't in the syllabus. How is it weighed for our final grade?" she asked.

"This is a new simulation that I added last minute," Mr. Buchanan said. "A certain student of mine shared it with me." His gaze slid over to Han-bae. "And I'm weighing it the same as a test. Don't slack off or you won't pass."

Han-bae kept his eyes glued to his computer screen.

"You will be randomly assigned a life path *and* a partner." When Mr. Buchanan said the word partner he looked right at me. "It doesn't matter if you have different preferences," he continued. "For the purpose of this assignment I've paired you up so you can simply learn financial planning with another person." Mr. Buchanan paced at the front of the class as he spoke. "If you wish it to be something romantic." He shrugged. "That's up to you. I've assigned everyone a path where you are gainfully employed or in college, grad, or trade school. Together with your partner you must create a five-year financial plan based on decisions you both make."

Anna raised her hand again.

"Yes, Anna," Mr. Buchanan said.

She frowned. "You have me married to Kimball and living in his parents' basement. I want a divorce."

Mr. Buchanan snickered. "All of the conditions were random. I assigned spouses based on who you usually sit by, because we generally tend to marry who we associate with."

I scoffed loud enough for everyone to hear.

"But I don't want to get married," Anna said.

Mr. Buchanan smiled. "Indeed Anna, in real life you will never be forced to marry, but for the purpose of this simulation I want you to see how working with someone can have both pros and cons on a long-term financial plan. You and Kimball can choose to drop out of school, take out more student loans, seek higher education, or get different jobs."

Anna started to argue, but Mr. Buchanan held up his hand. "I have some wrinkles thrown into each of these models. I'm going to call them surprises. Some of you will have a child within five years. A few of you will suffer either an accident or a debilitating illness. One of you will inherit a large amount of money, and one of you will die, leaving the other partner to proceed alone. I've also thrown in some lay-offs and promotions."

"This isn't fair," Anna said staring at her computer in disbelief. "I would never agree to work as a waitress while supporting Kimball through med school. I should be the one in med school."

Mr. Buchanan nodded. "Exactly, life is unfair. It's what choices you make while it's busy being unfair that make or break you. If you want to go to med school too, figure it out and go."

Anna huffed while Kimball scooted his desk closer to hers. "You go work at Denny's," she said. "I'm going to be a surgeon."

I scrolled through the assignments from Mr. Buchanan until I found mine. It definitely wasn't random.

Ji-hee Lee
Spouse: Han-bae Yun
Housing: Estate in Canada
Employment: Family money/Self employed
Surprise: Child, year three

Han-bae picked up his chair and placed it in front of my desk, so we were facing each other. He had his laptop open and spoke over the top of it. "Hey wifey," he said.

I raised my eyebrows at him. "You're the mystery student that suggested this assignment." I tapped my screen. "And you have our future all planned out?"

He grinned back at me. "And what if I do? Are you actually surprised that I made class fun for the day?"

"This is fun for you?" I asked.

"No," he said, suddenly serious. "But I had to do something. His lectures were killing me." Han-bae shrugged. "It's not a bad way to spend the hour and not so different from the lives we will have after we leave here."

I pressed my lips together. Han-bae kept trying to trip me up, but I wasn't going to let down my defenses around him.

He laced his fingers together and leaned forward. "Okay, What's our five-year plan in this scenario?"

I sighed. "Fine. I'm going to work in journalism. I'll pick Columbia for my undergrad, and maybe one summer I can save enough to go on a trip."

Han-bae surprised me as he reached out and took my hand. "We'll summer in Bora Bora and Saint Barthelemy. You can go to school wherever and whenever you want. I'll always take care of you, Ji-hee."

Han-bae holding my hand felt wrong, and I snatched it back right away. But for some reason his words and gestures made me think of Harrison. I tried pushing him far from my mind, but there was no fighting it. For the rest of the day the image of Harrison and myself walking along my favorite beach in Bora Bora stayed with me.

HARRISON

Ji-hee sat in the cafeteria a few tables over from me with the two girls from gym. I was glad. It was getting pathetic watching her sit by herself every day at lunch. Han-bae never came in here, probably too good for burgers and fries, but that was one less worry.

"Harrison, will you open my drink?" Regan held a Diet Pepsi across the lunch table toward me with a fake pouty look. "I don't want to ruin my manicure."

Her nails were wicked long. I was surprised she could even hold the can. I grabbed it and popped the top before handing it back. She took it gingerly and sipped, but her eyes kept darting over to Ji-hee's table. "It's a relief that she finally found her people," she said.

I grimaced. "Ji-hee has people?"

Regan's face distorted. "You know what I mean. She's found friends to eat with instead of us."

"But she's never eaten with us. I invited her. She said no." I looked away. Regan wasn't waging a war against Ji-hee. I should have been satisfied with that. But I wasn't. "Maybe if you'd invited her, she would have said yes."

Regan chewed her lip, something she never used to do. "I like you, and I don't want anyone else pushing in on that. Why does it matter if I invite her?" She raised her eyes to mine without anger, but there was something there. A flicker of regret maybe.

"To be nice." I shrugged. "Can't you be okay with that?"

"I think I have to be," she said. "But I'd like it if you could pay attention to me instead of her. I'm the one you asked out."

"I'm sitting here with you, aren't I?"

"That's true." The corner of her mouth turned up in an almost smile.

"So how about we let go of the drama and get along until homecoming." As soon as I said the words I realized how unfair they were. Regan wasn't being dramatic, at least not in this minute. If this conversation happened last year, she would have thrown a fit and stormed out of the cafeteria.

But Regan only studied me, and I wondered if she knew. Did Regan finally get that she'd been a monster? Was she sorry?

"Okay. No drama," she said softly. "But I have a rule of my own."

I folded my arms and tried to keep my features calm. "What?"

Regan leaned forward. "For homecoming, I'm your date. If another girl—even if it's Ji-hee—ends up being a damsel in distress, you let *her* date handle it."

I raised my eyebrows. Regan had me dialed in on this one. She knew I couldn't help but play the hero. And with Ji-hee the urge to swoop in and protect was strong. Maybe Regan couldn't see how much I liked Ji-hee, but she could see that I wanted to help her. "Deal. You don't take shots at Ji-hee, and I'll leave her to her own date." I glanced over at Ji-hee. She was laughing at something one of her friends said. Ozzy would take good care of her. I was sure of it.

11

HARRISON

J i-hee waited for me after lunch. She leaned against the wall in front of my chemistry class and motioned me over as I approached. My heart raced, but I tried to keep my walking even and steady. Is this what it felt like to walk a straight line in front of an officer when you were drunk? I felt weird. But it was Ji-hee and she was standing there all gorgeous and smiling at me. I was lucky to be upright.

"Hey," I said as I got closer. That was the most I dared say. She'd been hardcore ignoring me. I was afraid to open my mouth and mess it up.

"Can I get a ride after school?" She had her hands clasped tightly in front of her, and I could tell she was as nervous as I was.

"Yes," I said immediately. I'd never say no to her.

"Okay," she pushed off the wall and walked away without looking back. My whole chest expanded with something wonderful. Ji-hee wanted me to drive her home.

JI-HEE

Han-bae sat in his usual seat when I got to finance. I was late after getting up the nerve to talk to Harrison. It was a small thing to ask for a ride, and maybe I shouldn't have. I probably shouldn't have. But I'd decided that completely ignoring him was more work than just being friends. That's all this was. Friends.

Mr. Buchanan stood in front of the class lecturing as I took my seat. He was fanning himself with a stack of papers. The school had turned off the air conditioner for some reason. Maybe because it was September now. The weather was still sweltering, and Han-bae was melting in his Brioni gray wool suit.

Sweat beaded at his temples and he leaned over to whisper, "Are you ready for the test?" He loosened his tie and rolled his neck but didn't take his suit jacket off.

"What test?" I whispered back.

"Tomorrow's test on principal and interest, of course." His voice took on an almost mocking tone. "We can't be too careful with what little money we have as young adults."

I waved him off and stared out the window, wishing someone would open it. I wasn't in any mood for Han-bae's weirdness. "I don't need to study," I said. If the students in this class could peek into my bank accounts, they'd fall off their chairs, and I was pretty sure Han-bae's bank account was at least as big as mine. I was also more than sure Han-bae had learned the deep intricacies of finance right along with his Korean alphabet. Most parents focus on making sure their young children eat enough. But in Elite families, the ability to manage and increase wealth trumped getting enough rice.

"I don't have to study either," Han-bae said. "Do you want to know why?"

"Not really." I sighed. "This class is just easy."

Han-bae looked up at Mr. Buchanan to make sure he was still ignoring us, then lowered his voice to a whisper. "Aren't you a little curious about me? You can see that I have money. Money like yours."

"You mean that, like me, you have the cash to order the large fry at McDonalds?" I gave him a thumbs up. "Good job." As a member of Korea's Elite, Han-bae could probably buy every McDonalds franchise in LA. But admitting that I was part of the Elite crowd would be the same as dropping my disguise at the masquerade ball. I wasn't going to do that with him. Ever. What I really wanted was to figure out who this guy actually was.

"You're telling me you don't want to know my net worth?" he asked.

"Nope." He'd probably been sent by my brother to babysit me, maybe a friend from overseas. Maybe he'd been living in Monaco where it's easy to hide between the gilded cracks. This was the only place that made sense. His family could have lived abroad for the last decade either to grow a particular part of their business, or maybe it was even something shameful. A secret that his family wanted to hide.

Han-bae huffed, clearly frustrated. "Really, Ji-hee? You're not even a little curious about me?"

I leveled Han-bae with a bored look. "Not really. I mean you're going to Bishop High. Maybe you've managed to lose all your money." I laughed at him. "Don't worry, I can spot you at McDonalds."

Han-bae smiled. "I could bleed money and still not run out."

I scoffed. "If you really have that much then it must be new." Why was he bragging like this? "And I'm not really sure, but don't they say new money bleeds the fastest?" Having wealth, real wealth, came with consequences and talking about it, especially publicly was in the never-ever rule book. It was like in the top ten, right up there with never touch the principle.

Han-bae smirked like he'd caught me. "Just the fact that you're talking about whether my money is new or not betrays you."

I laughed. "More like betrays that I watch too many Korean dramas."

Han-bae's eyes flashed. "For the record, my family is not new. My de facto aristocracy is more established than most."

I smiled innocently and let my own eyes widen. "Wow. I'm so impressed."

He quirked one eyebrow. "Come on, Ji-hee."

The determined set of his shoulders said he wasn't going to let this go, but I wasn't giving in.

"When we first met you acted like you didn't know me and now —" I folded my arms. "You think you know how much I have in my measly bank account."

He snorted. "Your accounts are too padded for you to stay here. Bishop High doesn't deserve you." He leaned one elbow against his desk and rested his hand in his palm. "Why are you hiding, Ji-hee? What does this dumb high school in middle-class suburbia hold for you?" He studied my face, but I shut it all down, my thoughts, my feelings. It was all sealed tight in that dark dead part of my heart that no longer beat but would keep my secrets. I smiled wide at Han-bae. "Well, I had no idea I was floating around in a bunch of cash."

He lowered his eyes. "I like you Ji-hee. If you leave with me, I'll buy you anything you want."

An average teen, the kind that checked their bank balance on their phone before buying lunch, would be tempted by his offer. I was none of that, and even if I had been, my moral compass would have bucked the idea of letting some guy I barely knew shell out cash. It felt cheap and wrong. Still, I needed to play along. "Anything is a lot. What if I asked for a car?"

"I'll buy you a Maserati after school. Or are you a Lamborghini kind of girl?"

This wasn't going the way I wanted. I rolled my eyes. "My parents would definitely say no."

"Your parents aren't even here. You're staying with guardians, just like me."

I pressed my mouth into a hard line. He shouldn't know this much about me. "That doesn't mean they won't find out."

"Ji-hee." Mr. Buchanan called my name sharply and I raised my head. "Can you explain to us what embezzlement means?"

I sat ramrod straight as he approached my desk. Being called on was a clear reprimand for talking during his lecture. Normally I wouldn't have cared, but Han-bae already had me backed into a corner. When I opened my mouth the lessons that had been drilled into me since early childhood came pouring out. "Misappropriation of funds is usually committed by unvetted financial advisers. In substantive companies, embezzlement is dealt with privately and kept out of the courts, although it still regularly occurs, thus the grave importance of employing a loyal financial adviser."

Mr. Buchanan whistled, and the class laughed. I shifted in my seat uncomfortably and realized my mistake. My huge mistake. Great. If Han-bae wasn't sure before, he was now. The guy was a freaking Geiger counter, and I'd just lit up the room with radioactive glow. I laughed right along with the class and tossed my hair. "That's the textbook definition at least."

Mr. Buchanan eyed me with curiosity. "Can you tell us more, Ji-hee?" he asked.

I smiled sweetly, putting my mask firmly back in place. "Don't steal money. It's bad." There, the prefect Bishop High answer.

Mr. Buchanan nodded but wasn't satisfied with just targeting me. He turned to Han-bae. "What about you? Can you give me another example of embezzlement?"

Han-bae only glared back at him. Usually he was distant, but this open hostility was new. "Embezzlement can be an undeserved label," Han-bae said. "People are good at misconstruing the facts. Some-times you aren't given what was agreed upon at the onset, so you are left with no other choice than to take what is yours. That's not stealing."

A hush settled over the room and Mr. Buchanan took a step back. "I'm sensing a story here. Do enlighten us."

Han-bae shook his head once, a curt denial of letting anyone past his steel doors of privacy. Mr. Buchanan had no choice but to move on. He walked back to the front of the class and resumed his lecture.

I laid down on my desk letting my dark hair sweep over my face. Han-bae's eyes drifted to me. I could feel the weight of his stare. My head was propped on my arm, and I shifted so I could see him. He couldn't see my face, not clearly anyway, but I could see him. To anyone watching, it looked like I'd given up on class and decided to sleep. Han-bae's gaze became dark and unyielding, matching his clenched jaw and fisted hands. I shifted a tiny bit to see his eyes better. I expected to see rejection there, but his gaze showed only anger, almost rage. Not normal.

I reached up, flipped my hair free of my face, and sat up. His unguarded moment was there and gone, replaced with an eccentric harmless teenager in a full suit and tie. Han-bae was definitely not harmless. He'd closed off the darkness, pushed back on his demons, but I couldn't unsee who this guy really was. I had problems, big ones, but whatever haunted Han-bae made my issues with Mother and Gun seem like marshmallow fluff in comparison.

HARRISON

It wasn't dark yet, but the lights already glowed a dirty yellow across Bishop High's tennis courts. Across the net Calvin tossed the ball high into the air. The setting sun gleamed off his racket as he arched back and drove into a powerful serve. The ball landed with a pop and skimmed the ground making me lunge to just barely catch it with the edge of my racket. I sent it back to him with a looping topspin.

Tennis was the only sport that Calvin could beat me at. I had good foot work and fast-twitch reaction, but Calvin was a pro, and he freaking loved tennis. He also loved beating me.

He drove a shot cross-court, just out of reach. The ball kissed the line before skipping away. Calvin was all grins and back in position before I even moved to retrieve the ball. As I bent down to pick it up my eyes caught a guy sitting on one of the rusted-out picnic tables outside the court. Han-bae.

"Hey, Cal," I said as I jogged back. "I want to talk with him." I jerked my thumb over my shoulder in Han-bae's direction. Calvin leaned sideways to see him. "You mind heading home? I'll walk."

"Why do I have to go home now?" he asked. "Just invite him to play with us. We can rotate out."

"I need to talk to him alone, though. I'm gonna tell him to stop following Ji-hee everywhere. He's creepy as ever."

Calvin eyed me suspiciously. "Do you mean he's doing exactly what you do and following Ji-hee around the school? Did you ever stop to think that maybe he's just into her too?"

My face reddened and I looked down at my shoes. "I'm just friendly and invite her to do stuff."

Calvin's brows knitted together. "If I leave, you'll get into it with him. Do you really think that will help anything?"

"I'll just tell him to stop stalking her."

Calvin blew out a breath.

I held up both hands. "I won't do anything to him."

"Look, man," Calvin sighed. "I get that you're gone over this girl, but let's not get paranoid. Han-bae isn't stalking anyone."

"I've seen him, Cal. He follows her all the time and I've seen him going through her locker."

"Because you follow her too." He clapped me on the shoulder.

"I drove her home today, Cal. It's not the same thing."

Calvin shook his head. "You're on your own then, big guy. I've gotta get." Calvin grabbed his racket and took the ball out of my hand before heading to his car. He had to walk past Han-bae to get there, but they ignored each other.

I waved Han-bae over, but he stayed exactly where he was and waited. Fine. I exited the court and walked to the picnic tables. He studied me as I approached. Han-bae was a healthy guy, angular and built like he knew the inside of the gym. He probably owned one. As I got closer the smirk on his face twisted with cruelty. My hands twitched, restless as I sat down across from him on the picnic table and folded my arms.

Before I could say anything, Han-bae spoke. "Ji-hee's already taken. You should stop chasing her around."

I shook my head. "Ji-hee can choose who she likes, and you're definitely not her boyfriend." I laughed. "You're nothing to Ji-hee."

"I mean more to Ji-hee than you realize." Han-bae leaned close to me with a dangerous look. "And a girl like her would never consider scum like you."

I reared back.

"I have two very powerful parents that will do anything to insure my future. You have a stepdad with a lot of credit card debt, and apparently, he never bothered to adopt you."

I wanted to hit him. I wanted to knock him down so hard that he never got up again.

Han-bae's mouth twitched with amusement.

I clenched my hands into fists. *Don't do it Harrison. That's exactly what he wants.* Jeff's words surfaced quickly in my mind. He'd drilled it into me. *Never take the first swing. Never fight unless you must.*

Jeff had told me when I was six that my biological father died before I was born and offered to adopt me. I'd been the one to say no. Not because I didn't love Jeff, but my dad died saving someone. He was a hero, and the least I could do was keep his last name. I took a breath, even managed a tight smile before I spoke. "That's strange that you would dig around in personal records. Stuff like that isn't public."

Han-bae leaned back and shrugged. "For someone like me, it's public if I want it to be."

All the words I'd planned out, all the threats and convincing ways I'd thought of to tell this guy that he was out of line died. It was time for me to go. I stood up. This wasn't just a dumb cocky kid I was dealing with. This was someone who firmly knew his place in the world.

I used to know my place, or thought I did, until Garrett and Gretchen showed up baring their teeth. I pushed all my insecurities back and focused on what I did know. The problem might not be simple, but the solution was. I would do everything in my power to keep Han-bae far from Ji-hee, and right now that meant walking away.

12

JI-HEE

School hadn't started yet, but I already had two problems. One—tomorrow was homecoming, and I still didn't have a dress. This problem felt about as high school as I could get so I didn't actually mind it. Two—I was sitting in the school counselor's office before my first period and Mrs. Jensen seemed very worried.

She tilted her head as she stared at me from across her desk, then scooted closer with a play of emotions—mostly pity—flitting across her face. "So you're saying Han-bae hasn't been following you?" she asked for the third time. "I've gotten a report from another student that he's exhibiting stalking behavior."

I sighed. This had to be Harrison's doing. I wanted to be mad. I should have been mad. But the fact that Han-bae bothered Harrison enough for him to go so far as to report it, was at the very least, flattering. And honestly to anyone normal Han-bae's behavior was more than a little off. Still, I wasn't going to let Mrs. Jensen in on any of this. "He waits for me in the mornings," I said. "But I think he's just trying to make friends. We're both from South Korea so I think he feels safe with me."

Mrs. Jensen frowned. "I checked our security cameras, and I saw him opening your locker. Did you give him your combination?"

I bit my lip. "You're sure it was *my* locker? His is right next to mine." Mrs. Jensen knew the rules at Bishop High very well. However, she didn't know the rules of Korea's Elite. Getting into someone else's locker or having the exact same schedule, for that matter, would barely be bending rules. I'd already guessed that Han-bae had managed to worm his way into my shadow by passing along "gifts" for Mr. Young. He acted like an eager puppy around Han-bae and bribing is standard practice in my world. What I needed was more information, and to get that, I needed time. If Mrs. Jensen stayed out of it, he'd make a mistake sooner or later, and then I would know what he was actually doing here.

"It was your locker." Mrs. Jensen's kind eyes searched my face. "I could see the number clearly."

I smacked my forehead with my hand. "I forgot. I did give him my locker combo. I told him he could use it since I wasn't going to."

Mrs. Jensen looked skeptical. "Ji-hee, if he is bothering you, you can tell me. We won't allow it. I'm going to email your guardians." She tapped on her screen. "Chul and Sydney Kim?" She glanced at me. "Is that correct?"

I nodded. "You can email them, but honestly, Mrs. Jensen, if you do, they'll insist on coming in and will make a big deal out of this. Then Han-bae and I can never be friends. It will be awkward." I reached my hand out and touched her sleeve. "Truthfully, I could use more friends in this school."

Mrs. Jensen studied my face, watching for signs that I knew how to keep well hidden. With the Elite, lying to cover up someone else's lie, so you could catch them in a bigger lie was grade school stuff. Mrs. Jensen probably went home to a loving husband and a golden retriever. She would never get my world.

I smiled. "If I felt threatened at all I would tell you. Really, I would."

Mrs. Jensen nodded. "Alright. I'm going to let this go then, but only if you promise me to come straight here if anything strange happens or if you feel like he's bothering you."

"I promise."

. . .

Mrs. Jensen was a complete liar. My phone buzzed halfway through Calculus. Three texts came one after another. The first two were from Sydney.

Is everything okay? Your counselor called me and said that another student was harassing you.

Then.

I'm going to come and pick you up.

The final text was from Chul.

I'm going to reach out to Gun and give him this update.

This answered one of my questions. Han-bae wasn't sent here by Gun to watch me. If he was, then at the very least Chul would have known about it.

The last ten minutes of class my name got called over the school's intercom. *Ms. Smars can you please send Ji-hee Lee to the front office for dismissal.* The overloud tinny voice interrupted and everyone looked my direction. Han-bae turned around in his seat and tried to catch my eye, but I ignored him, jumping up and moving to the door.

Ms. Smars turned from the board where she was highlighting formulas. She handed me a quiz sheet. "It's open book so you can do it at home and turn it in tomorrow," she said.

I took the paper and nodded, but before I opened the door Harrison's voice rumbled behind me. "Ms. Smars, can I go to the nurse?"

I didn't wait to hear the answer but walked out into the hallway.

"Hey, wait up," Harrison called out to me.

I slowed and turned to watch his easy jog as he closed the distance. Guys like Harrison jog, and it makes all kinds of things spark in my brain. When I jog—and I don't jog—my long limbs make me look like a frog trying to walk. Whatever, I tried not to stare.

"Hey," I said, and pushed down the flood of emotion that washed over me with his nearness. He'd matched my stride and our hands brushed against each other sending an electric shock straight up my arm. One of my guilty pleasures was sneaking glances at Harrison, but he looked twice as nice smiling down at me as he did just sitting in class looking bored. I licked my lips and tried to think of something to say. "Uh, are you heading to the nurse?"

He snorted. "No, I just wanted to walk you to the office."

"Oh, that's nice of you." If he had been someone else, I would have added: *You didn't need to do that.* But the truth was I was glad he was walking with me. Glad that stupid butterflies were dancing around my insides, and glad that I could hear his deep baritone voice even if it was just for a few minutes.

"Are you excited for the dance tomorrow?" he asked.

I smiled. "Yeah. They don't have homecoming in Korea so it will be cool."

"I'm glad that you're coming." He hesitated. "Even though I'm not your date." His cheeks turned pink. "What I mean is, I'm glad we can all hang out."

I nodded. "I think it will be fun. Is your brother excited?" We were almost to the office, and I could see Sydney through the windows. She looked worried.

"Ozzy?" Harrison grinned. "Sure, he's excited. But don't expect much. He's not cool and not attractive. Not at all." He paused and quickly added. "Not like me."

I laughed but it came out nervous and weird.

Harrison cleared his throat. "Uh, I was going to offer to drive you home again and maybe hang out. Why are you leaving early?"

I gestured toward the office where Sydney still stood with a frown creasing her brow. "That's Chul's wife, Sydney."

Harrison glanced her way and nodded. "Your host family. I've met Chul but not his wife." He looked slightly worried, or maybe it was guilt. I considered calling him out over the interrogation Mrs. Jensen had given me. He was the only one that would have reported Han-bae, and part of me wanted to make him admit it. But somehow, seeing Harrison's discomfort felt like it was right up there with skipping dessert or waking up early when you didn't have to. Instead, I said, "Sydney's taking me dress shopping for tomorrow." It wasn't a lie. Sydney thought she was here to save me from some stalker, but Han-bae wasn't anything I couldn't handle. Once I told her the only help I needed was shopping therapy, we'd be prowling the mall together. She'd taken me once already, and walking through a store and buying exactly what I liked, instead of a color or cut my mother and stylist agreed on, was the best feeling.

He leaned closer. "Will you dance with me tomorrow? A slow dance. My brother won't mind. He'll probably want to be in the mosh pit half the time."

I willed myself to wave off. I needed to laugh and take a step back, joke around instead of promising trouble. That was the smart thing to do here. On the liking Harrison 1 to10 scale I had to stay below a five. Anything above that and the risk was too high when Mother came marching back into my life. But I didn't laugh or step back. I looked down at Harrison's hand. It was large and his nails were trimmed short and neat. I wanted to hold that hand. I wanted to dance with him the entire night. I wanted Regan to go away and Ozzy to find a different date. "Sure, we can do a dance." I spoke casually and then turned to go, my hand raised to wave a goodbye. I stopped. Movement and a dark shadow flitted around the corner. Han-bae.

I waited a moment, but he was gone. Harrison started to turn to see what I was staring at, but I caught his arm, so he stayed facing me. "Sydney is waiting, but I'm really looking forward to tomorrow."

My hand still rested on his arm, and a wave of heat shot between us. His voice was velvet when he spoke. "I wish I was your date tomorrow."

I opened my mouth to say something, but he backed up with a smile and spoke loud enough for anyone in the hall to hear. "We've got lots of time, Ji-hee."

I made myself turn around to walk into the office. We really didn't, though.

13

HARRISON

Ozzy knocked on my door just before five, when I should have been getting ready for the dance. I was lying on my bed playing a stupid phone game in an effort to simmer down from Gretchen's earlier accusation of me scratching their car while taking out the garbage cans. "Come in," I called without getting off my bed. I knew it was Ozzy because Becca was at her dance class, and I doubted Garrett or Gretchen would want to dirty their knuckles by getting anywhere near *my* door.

Ozzy opened the door and poked his head in. I looked up from my phone. "What's up?"

"I can't go."

"Go where?" I asked.

"On that date with the girl. You know, that one that you keep pretending not to like."

I gritted my teeth. "Why not?" I asked, trying not to sound mad.

If Ozzy didn't go, then Astor would. He'd already whined at Calvin, who then, in turn, whined at me after I sent the text saying Ji-hee was going with my brother.

Ozzy moved to sit on my bed and laced his long fingers together over his elegantly crossed legs. He sat perfectly straight, all muscle and grace. I wondered—not for the first time—how we could be even partially related. His voice held that fluid patience that he usually saved for Mom when she was mad. "I have another commitment," he said.

"Homecoming is tonight. It's too late to back out now." I looked back at my game and tapped my screen blowing up more alien ships.

"It's not going to work, Harrison."

I was quiet for a whole round and Ozzy waited. Finally, when I knew I wouldn't blow a gasket, I asked the question that I was already pretty sure I knew the answer to. "Why can't you go?"

"Garrett and Gretchen said no."

I didn't miss that he didn't call them Grandpa and Nana. Normally I would have questioned that but not now. Not when my night was about to be ruined. I narrowed my eyes at Ozzy. "Mom and Dad said you could."

"They didn't actually," Ozzy said. "We never asked them."

"So ask. Or I can." I closed my game and started a text.

Ozzy shifted. "I already did." His voice took on a leaden tone, like the words were too heavy to say. "They said to follow what Garrett and Gretchen want."

I took a deep breath and tossed my phone down. "Why don't they want you to go? Because you'd be with me?"

Ozzy looked away. He was the only other one that could see through their shows of perfect grandparents. Jeff could probably see some of it, but he turned a blind eye. And Mom saw what she wanted to. Ozzy had always been different though. He was like that contestant on a game show that somehow magically knew what was on the other side of each door, making all the rest of us wonder who was tipping him off. But there was no one on a hidden mic feeding him insider information. Ozzy could just smell lies and insincerity on people, even people he barely knew. Garrett and Gretchen were no match for him. "They said I'm too young to date."

I snorted. "You're old enough to skate in the adult league, but you can't go to a high school homecoming?" I jumped up and strode to the door, covering the space in two strides. But Ozzy moved faster and sprawled in front, both arms out to block me from passing. As if he could.

He shook his head. "Don't. It's not worth fighting with them, and I already tried. Gretchen is still mad."

I did a fake lunge, but he only winced and stood his ground. I wouldn't have plowed through him, and we both knew it.

Despite the trust Ozzy had for me, a vein throbbed in his neck, and he let out a shaky breath like it'd been a close call. "Why do you want me to go so bad anyway?" He cocked an eyebrow. "Aren't you afraid she'll like me instead of you?"

I ran my hands through my messy hair. "If you don't take her then this kid Astor will."

"Let me guess," he said. "Astor's a bonehead."

"The worst kind."

Ozzy grinned. "That's actually better then. If I went with Ji-hee she'd fall for me."

I snorted. "That's not happening."

Ozzy grinned. "But it could. Then what would you do?"

"You wouldn't do that to me."

Ozzy nodded. "You're right. I wouldn't but aren't you that much better off sending the girl you like off with a loser than with your very awesome brother?"

I let out a breath and laughed. Maybe Ozzy was right, but I still worried. "What if he's a jerk all night? He used to always try and pick fights with me."

"Just don't rise to any of his bait. If you do that the night will be fine." Ozzy rolled his shoulders like he was about to start one of his warm-ups. "I on the other hand have to go skate and pretend I don't care that I have no social life."

I hadn't considered that Ozzy would be more disappointed than I was. Mom wanted him to be good at skating, but Garrett and Gretchen wanted him in the Olympics. They were driving his career and at the same time ruining his teenage years. "I'm a selfish jerk," I said. "I'm sorry you can't go."

Ozzy shrugged. "I think next year I'm going to rebel and go to

Bishop High. You won't be there anymore, but I'm going to go and get a hot girlfriend."

I laughed. "I need to see Garrett and Gretchen's faces when you tell them that."

Ozzy opened the door to go but paused and turned back to me. "I need a promise that you won't challenge the Evil G's."

I frowned. "Who?"

"You know—the shameless duo that pretend to be grandparents —Garrett and Gretchen."

I smiled at him. "Evil G's. I like it."

JI-HEE

I leaned over the bathroom sink and close to the mirror before applying eyeliner. Despite my shaking hands, I had the line close to my lashes and flipped up evenly on both sides. Perfect.

"The dark brown was a good choice," Sydney said. "It matches your eyes."

I stood back and blinked, examining myself. I'd gone with minimal makeup. Just a little concealer, mascara and eyeliner. "What about lipstick?" I asked.

"I thought you didn't like lipstick," Sydney said.

"I don't. I hate it, but I don't want to look dowdy."

Sydney laughed. "Not a chance of that. If you don't want lipstick, then don't wear it."

"I like clear lip gloss."

"Perfect," Sydney said.

I rummaged through the drawer until I found the one I wanted. It wasn't sticky with just a subtle sheen. Before I could put it on, my phone pinged and I grabbed for it. I was nervous, so nervous.

It was Harrison.

My brother can't go to homecoming with you. He's really

sorry but has to do a special practice for skating. Astor Picket is going to be your date. I will be in the group, so you won't be alone.

I pursed my lips and turned to Sydney. "I can't believe these guys. Harrison has made such a fuss about me going with his brother and not this Astor kid, and now an hour before we're supposed to leave, he tells me I'm going with Astor." I sighed. "Maybe I shouldn't go."

"What?" Sydney squeaked. "You're not going to waste all this." She waved her hand at my hair that she had spent the better part of an hour curling and pinning into an updo. Plus, I had a gorgeous dress with matching heels that we'd found. It would be a shame to not go anywhere tonight.

"Are you worried about Astor?" she asked.

"No." I said. Whoever this Astor kid was, I could handle it. The only worry I had was dancing with Harrison.

"Then why not go?" Sydney asked.

I shrugged. "I guess I'd regret not going." I texted back.

Tell your brother that I understand. Is the time still the same? You're picking me up at six?

Harrison responded right away.

Yes, we will be there in about an hour.

I bit my lip and smiled at Sydney. "They'll be here soon."

14

HARRISON

I planned to remind Regan that this date was a one-time thing, that none of it meant we were together again. I'd told her as much at school, more than once. She clearly had other ideas when she opened the door in a tight silver beaded dress that dipped off each shoulder and pulled me inside with a breathless smile. Her arms wrapped around me tight, and I felt a little caught as she looked up at my face adoringly. That's when I realized coming up with the emotional currency to unwind her thinking tonight might break the bank.

I'd already thought of the perfect words to say: *Remember this date is just for Cal and Tiff, right?* Or maybe, *I'm glad we can still be friends even though we aren't dating anymore.*

But her comebacks flooded my brain before I even got a line drawn in the sand. *What do you mean we aren't dating anymore? What do you call going to homecoming?* Or, *what do Calvin and Tiffany have to do with anything? Calvin isn't the one who's going to be kissing me goodnight.*

I kept quiet.

"This is so perfect," she said. "Now everything is going to be the way it should this year." She craned her neck to look up at me and her heavily made-up eyes said even more than her words had. *Tonight was important to her. I was important to her.*

I gently untangled her hands from my waist and stepped back with the excuse of giving her the head-to-toe admiring look she expected. I even paired it with the words she wanted. "You look beautiful."

They hung empty in the air between us, but Regan giggled and did a mock curtsey. "Of course I do. I always look hot."

She didn't mention that I looked nice or ask me where I got the new tie but held her wrist out to me. I opened the box with her corsage inside and helped her slip the delicate white rose she'd requested onto her wrist. She'd changed her nails to dark red and for some stupid reason the flashy manicure with the extra-long, nearly sharp tips made me think of a Halloween horror house I'd been to as a kid. I couldn't stop staring.

Her dad finally came in and did a double take when he saw me. "Harrison, I haven't seen you around here for a while. Where have you been hiding yourself?"

Before I could answer Regan spoke up. "Daddy, where's Mom? She said she'd take pictures for me."

Regan's dad set his mouth into a hard line. "You're Mom decided to go boating with her friends."

A tightness formed around Regan's eyes. "Oh, that's okay." She reached forward and handed her phone to him, giving his hand a gentle squeeze. "Can you take a picture, Daddy?"

"Sure can, Sweetheart." He held the phone up and waved it around. "Okay, you two smile big."

Regan took my hand, and I followed her lead to stand in front of their giant fireplace. It was almost as tall as I was. Their mom had it imported from an old castle in Ireland and then refinished just enough to be modern but still hold onto old-world class. It was the exact kind of cool to catch the right person's attention, so of course Architectural Digest featured a single shot of the McAllister family sitting in front of their historic fireplace and a small article on how to *spend big to spend small*. Whatever that meant. But her mom lived for those moments. Brandi McAllister was born into money, so you'd think she'd just take that for granted. But as long as I'd known Regan, her mom's driving force had always been for people to *notice* their money. If enough eyes could see it, price tags didn't matter.

My theory was this kind of behavior bled into Regan. Brandi couldn't impress people enough. She was rich and her need to scream that to the world eclipsed all common sense. Regan was the same way, but with guys. She couldn't get enough attention from the man she loved. She needed to not just be noticed by her man but obsessed over. Her level of commitment expectations rivaled fairy-tales. Every guy wants to be the girl's hero and swoop in to save the day, but we have homework, and jobs, and even demons of our own. The final straw with Regan happened when she threw a fit over me not skipping my ACT prep class. *Because she missed me.* She couldn't stand that I was focusing on something other than herself. That combined with her methodically bullying other girls who she looked at as her competition was the nail in the coffin.

Her dad started to snap pictures while Regan overdid the closeness and drape of her body. She wanted a fan-boy more than she wanted a boyfriend. I smiled and held up two fingers in the peace sign. Tomorrow I would draw a line in the sand. I'd fill it with gasoline and light it on fire if I had to, but tonight, I'd just survive.

JI-HEE

I was nervous. For the entirety of my high school career, I'd been on a total of three dates. That wasn't really my fault. If I'd continued at Daeshim, I'm sure I would have had a normal or semi-normal dating experience. But reform school didn't really give me a chance to date, and now I felt broken, or backward, or something. I just didn't want to embarrass myself in front of Harrison, and I hated that I even cared. I shouldn't have cared.

The doorbell rang and I moved to answer it, but Chul placed a hand against the wood to stop me. "Hang on." He opened his phone and tapped his screen. I heard the call pick up and too late, realized he'd called my brother—not just a voice call—but video.

Chul held the screen up so I could see Gun's smiling face. "You look nice baby sister. Almost all grown up."

I rolled my eyes. "Can I open the door now?"

Chul stepped back but held the screen aimed at me so every awkward moment would be witnessed by my brother or maybe so my brother could grill Astor.

I opened the door to a full-grown man that literally took my breath away. His soft blue eyes said boy, but the rest of him was just as big as Harrison. At first glance he was better looking than Harrison with honey blonde hair, a deep tan, and perfectly balanced features. But then he smiled, and I felt it, that unease in the pit of your gut when something isn't right. It didn't help that his teeth were so unnaturally white that he reminded me of a Ken doll.

He raised both eyebrows in a question. "Ji-hee?"

Nope. Maybe all the beautiful perfection marked with that slightly predatory feeling he gave off flashing his big smile was what did it, but I wanted to close the door. Instead, I took a deep breath and stepped back to open it wider. "Yes, nice to meet you, Astor. Please come in and meet my host family."

Astor strode inside the Kim residence just as Sydney came from the kitchen holding a camera. She'd already warned me, but it felt more like a threat that she wanted to take pictures.

Chul extended his hand and shook Astor's, not in the least intimidated that Astor was twice his size. He introduced himself, then he handed him the phone without telling him that my brother was on a video call.

So weird.

I moved closer to Astor until I could see my brother. He sat at a desk in a dark blue suit and didn't smile. I pointed at the screen. "This is my brother, Gun. He just wanted to say a *quick* hello to us before we go."

"Make sure you take care of my sister," Gun said. "Her curfew is midnight and no drinking."

I mouthed the word *sorry* to Astor, but he shrugged and laughed. "Uh, yeah, sure."

Chul stepped forward "You don't sound sure."

Astor laughed again. He needed to stop laughing if he didn't want to lose to intimidation tag team. Who knew Gun and Chul would be this scary as friends?

"Are you sure or not?" Chul asked, all serious.

Astor finally shut his mouth and nodded. "I can get her home, and I don't plan on boozing it up."

We all heard Gun's response. "That's hardly reassuring."

I almost screamed, but Sydney saved it.

"Astor," she said, sweetly and took the phone from him, which she firmly placed back in her husband's hand. "Ji-hee has a boutonniere for you." She handed me the box and didn't comment that he didn't have a corsage for me. "Do you mind if I take a few pictures before you go?" This gave us something to do while Sydney clicked away and Chul stood by with the video-phone conference. I could practically hear their judgment as Astor rushed me out the door.

I followed Astor toward a stretch Hummer while he grumbled about my weird brothers. He didn't know the half of it. The Hummer door opened, and Harrison's towering form climbed out. He wore a black suit with a black skinny tie and a white shirt. Sydney had taken me shopping and bought me a dark pink sheath dress that hugged just enough to flatter, but not enough to make the night all about the dress. I skipped the normal diamonds I would have worn and instead went with a single sapphire on a gold chain. It wasn't fake but everyone would assume it was. Harrison's mouth curved into a deep smile, and then he whistled softly, too soft for Regan to hear. I was sure it was her screeching laughter echoing from inside. He watched me walking closer and something about it felt oddly comforting, like no matter what happened with Astor it wouldn't matter because Harrison was here.

Astor shoulder checked Harrison as we passed, but Harrison didn't react or take his eyes off me. I gave myself a mental shake. I had too much chemistry with this guy to get any closer than we already were. Harrison needed to stay in the five-feet-away zone.

15

HARRISON

Astor *had* changed, only not for the better. I thought nothing could be worse than an obnoxious guy that always had to be the center of attention. But I was wrong. When a narcissist evolves, the next step is almost always to sadist. And a sadist isn't satisfied to be the life of the party. No, they look to put the spotlight on someone else and then proceed to humiliate them. And what better target than the quiet girl from another country.

"So, what kind of name is Ji-hee?" Astor asked. His eyes gleamed wickedly as he glanced around for the others to get his joke. "Jeeeee-heeee. It sounds like some kind of redneck mating call."

Regan and Tiffany ignored him, but Calvin shifted and cast a nervous glance in my direction.

Ji-hee frowned. "It's Korean. I thought that was kind of obvious."

Astor's eyes widened with delight. "Touchy. I was just asking."

She paused with a thoughtful look. "What kind of name is Astor?"

Astor stiffened. "What do you mean? It's just a name. A lot better name than Jeeee-heeee."

Ji-hee shrugged. "I just wondered. You brought up mine, so I thought you wanted to talk names. Yours is kind of . . ." Ji-hee tipped her head to one side. "Space-age."

My lips twitched at this. Everyone used to call Astor *Comet* when we were in grade school. Someone started saying it because he was crazy fast at tag. No one knew why but he'd hated it, and for fifth graders that's like blood in the water. Two guys in another class even made up a song about it. Things got so bad at recess one day that he'd flipped out during tag football and gave Steven Trubar a bloody nose. After that, no one dared call him Comet.

Ji-hee didn't know it, but she'd just picked at a sore spot. I knew we all remembered, but Calvin and Tiffany weren't meeting his eyes, and Regan was trying to smooth it over with drinks from the mini fridge. "Does anyone want a Pepsi?" she asked.

I cleared my throat. "That's funny you should mention space-age, Ji-hee. I think the name Astor is from the word Asteroid. Speaking of which, wasn't Comet your nickname in like fifth grade?"

Astor's face hardened. "Shut it, Harrison," he growled.

I leaned forward with my elbows on my knees, getting in his space. "Like Ji-hee said." I flipped both hands in the air. "You brought it up."

"There's also Sprite, and Mountain Dew," Regan said.

"I'll take a Sprite," Ji-hee said.

"Yeah, me too," Calvin chimed in. "Tiff, you want a Pepsi?"

Tiffany's eyes had gone a little wider as she looked between me and Astor, but she nodded yes to Calvin and soon everyone was quietly sipping their drink. "Do you guys want to open the sunroof?" Tiffany asked and tapped the top of the Hummer.

Regan wiggled over to press the button to open it, and both girls stood in the center with their upper torsos in the wind. They threw their arms up and yelled as the car drove through the streets. Calvin joined them after a minute and motioned for me to follow, but I shook my head. They didn't invite Ji-hee so I stayed where I was. She didn't seem to care, just leaned back in her seat and pulled out her phone. That left Astor and me to glare at each other for the rest of the ride. Yeah, homecoming was going to be freaking fun.

JI-HEE

Astor was a terrible person, but he wouldn't have qualified to even bring up the *rear* with the jerk-parade that existed in private schools. He had the petty insecure boy thing down but in a purely unsophisticated way. Making fun of someone's name is child's play. In private school, harassment has one end—to force someone out. And every year there is a line of kids leaving, dejected and broken. At Daeshim Academy I'd been one of those kids. I didn't last a single semester. Someone older, richer and way more popular felt threatened. Min had wanted me gone, and that's all it took. Astor could do his worst. I'd barely notice.

The car stopped near a pier, and we all piled out. The sea air was cool and fresh with the sun taking its time in an unhurried descent, as if daylight still had plenty to do.

Regan glanced around at the only building close by, a bait and tackle shop. "Is this where we're eating?" she asked, clearly disappointed.

"Look over there." Calvin pointed out to the pier. A table had been set up complete with music playing on a portable speaker.

Tiffany and Regan clutched at each other's arms and ran toward the table with squeals. "It's so beautiful."

I could hear Calvin behind me laugh and then whistle. "You sure are, babe," he yelled as he ran to catch up to them.

Harrison didn't hurry. I could feel him walking behind me. Astor stayed just ahead, looking out at the ocean with clear disdain, like not even the perfect view and fresh air was going to save his sour mood. It was pretty clear he'd weighed my worth the moment I opened the door, and apparently, he'd ranked me somewhere between long lines and cracking the screen on your new phone. Me needling him over his name didn't help, but I had no regrets there. If I had to choose between talking with Regan or Astor for a solid hour, I'd choose Regan. But wait, lucky me, I was going to get both.

"Harrison," Regan called. Calvin was already holding a chair out for Tiffany, and Regan stood with both hands on her hips and a what-about-me pout on her red lips. It gave me a little thrill that Harrison didn't hurry his steps but continued to match my pace, staying just behind me. I slowed down, and then, so did he. Finally, Regan sat down on her own next to Tiffany with a huff.

For one insane moment I wondered what Harrison would do if I turned and grabbed his hand. I'd rise up on tiptoes and speak in his ear. "Let's run away together." Then I'd pull him after me. We wouldn't go to the dance but race down to the beach and walk all night hand in hand.

I wouldn't do it of course, but part of me wanted to.

Astor turned back to me. "Are you coming or not?"

I sighed. This was going to be a long night. "Yeah, sure," I said and then muttered under my breath. "Wouldn't miss it."

Harrison chuckled behind me, and I jumped, not realizing he was as close as he was. He moved next to me and matched my stride. "The food will be good, even if your date isn't."

My eyes flicked ahead to Astor, but he'd already left us and was seating himself next to Regan. It was weird because he should have left that spot for Harrison. It almost felt like a challenge, but Harrison didn't even blink. That left two open spots, one directly next to Astor and one on the end. As I approached to sit next to Astor, Harrison took my elbow and steered me away from him to sit on the end. Then he took the one next to Astor.

As soon as we were all seated, two adults showed up. I think it might have been Calvin's parents. They began opening insulated boxes and passed out paper bags stamped with the In-N-Out logo along with cans of soda.

Tiffany laughed. "Good choice, Cal," she said with a genuine smile.

"Have you ever eaten here?" Harrison asked me.

I shook my head.

"Do you like cheeseburgers?"

"I like hamburgers, but I don't usually eat cheese."

"Here," he said and took my bag as Calvin's mother placed it in front of me. He pulled out the cheeseburger and unwrapped it. "Do you have a knife or anything to get the cheese off, Janet?" Calvin's mom handed him a plastic spoon, and he scraped my cheese off before putting it back together and setting the food down in front of me.

Calvin's parents made sure everyone was set and then strolled hand in hand back to the beachfront shops, leaving us alone.

Astor leaned close to Harrison. "She can feed herself, you know," he growled.

Regan had watched the whole exchange with the burger but didn't speak a word. Her eyes flashed angrily at Harrison. He ignored her and spoke to Astor.

"Just being a gentleman to all the girls since you're not going to."

Calvin immediately cleared his throat. "Ji-hee, what do you think of LA?" He seemed more interested in diffusing a situation between Astor and Harrison than in my answer. I answered him rather dryly. "I love it."

"Really?" Tiffany brightened. "What do you like about it?"

I should have just said something nice, or at the very least something to not encourage the fight between Astor and Harrison. Instead, I stirred the pot. "The people. Everyone here in LA is really, really nice." I glanced over at Astor. "Astor, you're my favorite so far." I clutched my hands to my chest with an exaggerated gush. "You're my dream date."

Harrison barked with laughter and Astor began to rise but then soda shot out of Calvin's nose, and everyone started laughing at him instead.

Astor sat back down, gritting his teeth and glared at me. I winked back and took a bite of my burger.

Astor looked away.

Tiffany giggled nervously, "Seriously though, it must be strange living here," she said stealing glances at Astor. His face was crimson now.

I swallowed and wiped my mouth before I spoke. "Not really. I lived in London before I lived here so it's just like another big city." I shrugged. "There are benefits to living abroad."

"So did you go to dances in London?" Regan asked.

I shook my head. "This is my first dance."

Tiffany beamed. "You're going to love it. The music at our school is always awesome, and everyone dances in big groups."

Astor scoffed.

Regan gave him a look and asked me, "Why were you in London?"

"I went to boarding school there but came here for my senior year to be with family friends." It was far from the real truth but still truth enough for Regan.

"Chul and Sydney Kim, right?" Calvin asked. He nodded to himself. "Those guys are loaded. Chul has like all these cars. I even saw him in a Lamborghini. Are you as rich as they are?"

Regan's eyes slanted down, but I knew she was studying me closely. I chuckled. "No one is as rich as the Kims."

"Why do they live in our neighborhood then?" Calvin's eyes were big with curiosity. "Is he hiding? Is it like Korea's version of witness protection?"

I laughed. "No, Sydney is finishing her undergraduate and then they'll go back to South Korea where they own a very nice home. She's from California and didn't grow up with money like Chul. And I think she just loves that house."

Harrison's voice took on a defensive tone. "It's not a bad house."

"Dude, it doesn't even have a pool," Calvin said.

"Mine doesn't either," Harrison shot back.

"Yeah, because none of our parents can afford one," Calvin said. "But Chul is rolling in it." Harrison scowled but Calvin kept on. "Chul should totally buy a mansion with a pool the size of the moon. His wife will get over it." He lifted both hands. "Tell me I'm not right, Ji-hee. Wouldn't you love it if they had a swanky house?"

I almost laughed thinking about how Chul owned two yachts with pools. But Harrison's stare stopped me. What I thought of money seemed to really matter to him, like if I thought living in a house like Sydney's was slumming it, he'd see me differently and not in a good way. Everyone went quiet waiting for my response.

Chul was next level. His portfolio quadrupled most of Korea's Elite, but his little house in that cookie-cutter neighborhood existed completely outside of my mother's influence. I wasn't sure I could put a price tag on that. Living there had given me a level of peace I'd never felt before. I looked right at Harrison when I answered. "What makes a house a home isn't the size or having a pool in the back yard. None of that matters to me."

16

HARRISON

Astor disappeared. The second his feet hit the dance floor he melted into the crowd and was gone. I knew Ji-hee wasn't his type. She was smart and naturally beautiful, not the spray tan, heavy makeup kind of look he usually went for.

Regan and Tiffany hadn't noticed yet, they were busy giggling and admiring other girls' dresses. Ji-hee noticed, she definitely noticed. Her eyes had followed Astor as he strode away from her without so much as a backward glance. She remained silent with a stoney-eyed stare. Her shoulders tightened, but she managed to stand a little straighter.

Every part of me wanted to go find Astor and teach him a lesson, but I knew better. Frustration bound me like barbed wire. If I moved, it would only tighten and hurt more.

Calvin stopped next to me. "Dude, did Astor split?" He was back from the soda machine and waved at Tiffany.

I nodded. "Yeah, he hasn't changed."

"I wonder why he didn't like Ji-hee," Calvin said.

I shook my head. "He's too superficial to appreciate a girl like her. The guy's a pig."

Calvin blew out his breath, and we both glanced to where Ji-hee stood. She had her delicate hands folded neatly in front of her, but I could feel the embarrassment rolling off. And who wouldn't feel that way. Astor had just dumped her in the middle of the dance without any explanation. He knew she didn't know anyone in this school. She barely knew us.

Ji-hee looked around the room as if contemplating her escape. She unzipped the little purse hanging from her wrist and checked her phone, then put it back and turned around. She was going to leave. I could see it in the determined set to her jaw. I started for her, my mind raced for the right thing to say. I moved and then Han-bae appeared out of nowhere, stepping right in front of her.

"Hey, Ji-hee." He flashed his brilliant smile.

Ji-hee titled her chin up to him. "I didn't know you were coming tonight," she said.

A bitter spark of jealousy flared as I rushed to their side. "Hey, glad you're here, man." It was probably the most insincere thing I'd ever said in my life, but if there was anyone worse than Astor as Ji-hee's date it had to be Han-bae.

"I've never been to something like this." He shrugged. "But I came alone, so kinda awkward." He looked down at Ji-hee's face. "Dance with me?"

And then as if on cue, a slow dance started. I cursed the DJ in my head.

Regan and Tiffany turned in unison and made their way to Calvin and me. Regan passed Ji-hee as Han-bae wrapped his stupid arms around her waist. Regan didn't even glance at them, and I realized she must have known Astor would ditch Ji-hee all along.

She approached me with a seductive smile and held out her hand. I took it and tried not to grimace as we walked out to the center of the room. I positioned us so I was close enough to Ji-hee to watch but did my best not to be obvious about it. I kept my eyes firmly on Regan and Ji-hee in my peripheral.

"You lied to me," Regan said, sweetly.

I frowned down at her. "When?"

"You promised that if I was nice to Ji-hee you wouldn't play knight-in-shining armor. You'd let Astor handle things. But all through this date you've stuck by her. You even scraped the cheese off her burger."

I scoffed. "The cheeseburger? That's what made you mad?"

She pulled her hands down to my shoulders and gripped them harder. "Do you know that I hate pickles?"

"I mean . . . no. I've never thought about it. But what does that have to do with anything?"

"That's my point. You've never noticed. I've picked them off every sandwich you've ordered for me and not once have you checked or asked." She pulled back a little and her eyes studied mine. "But with Ji-hee you're different. You're attentive."

I sighed, guilt settling deep in my gut like something rancid. "I didn't mean to lie to you. I just wasn't expecting Astor to be . . ."

"To be such a jerk," Regan offered.

I laughed at her candid remark. "Well, yeah."

"None of us did." Regan sighed. "I think we all hoped he would have grown up over the last few years, but he didn't. Too bad for Ji-hee, but you still aren't holding up your end of the bargain." Her voice held a subtle threat.

"You're right. I'm trying though. Can you still be nice to her?" I asked. "I'm your date and I'll do better."

Regan just stared at me. "Before I answer that, I have a question."

"Sure," I said.

"Why did you ask me to homecoming?"

I rubbed the back of my neck. "Tiff and Calvin really wanted me to."

Regan scoffed. "Since when did you do what people want? You always do exactly what you want and don't care what people think."

I studied Regan. She'd never been this open before. I wondered what changed. Maybe we both had over the summer. "Okay," I nodded to her. "The honest answer is I thought you'd notice I liked Ji-hee and be mean to her." I let that sink in for a minute.

"I haven't done a thing to her," she said.

"And I'm grateful."

She gestured over at Ji-hee and Han-bae. He was holding her much too close as they both swayed to the music. "She has that Asian kid now and they're perfect for each other. Let's end tonight right." She pulled my neck down hard, bringing me closer. "Focus on me."

"Just because they're both Asian doesn't mean they're perfect for each other," I snapped.

"I didn't mean it that way."

"Yes, you did," I said.

"Okay, maybe I did, but regardless, why can't you just forget her and be my boyfriend again?"

Maybe it was the mention of being her boyfriend, or maybe it was watching Han-bae's hands practically caressing Ji-hee's back, but something gave way in my brain and all the words I'd been afraid to say came tumbling out. "I broke up with you because you're always so freaking mean."

"I was never mean to you," she said quietly, much quieter than I had been. A few couples close to us had turned to look.

I took a deep breath and tried for calm. Why was I so worked up? "You were awful to everyone else. You always looked for someone weaker than yourself to pick on." I watched her face for some form of acceptance. She had to own at least part of this. I continued but gentled my voice. "Look, you're popular, and beautiful, and smart."

"If I'm all those things, why don't you love me?"

I answered as honestly as I could. "Because if another girl even looked in my direction, you got mean, and you acted like I couldn't have anything in my life that didn't revolve around you."

We both stopped when the music faded. Neither one of us spoke and then Regan's eyes filled with tears. "I'm not like that anymore. I don't know why I was that way before. I think I was just trying to deal —everything with my parents is so messed up, and instead of facing it, I lashed out."

I nodded. Not many people knew how bad things were with Regan's mom and dad. They both put on a front. But I knew. I'd seen their screaming matches firsthand. That's why it had been so hard for me to break up with her. She was already hurting, and I didn't want to add to it. "I'm sorry." It was the only comforting thing I could say to Regan.

"Are you sorry enough to be my boyfriend again?" she asked.

I shook my head no. "Regan, this was a mistake. We shouldn't be here together."

Regan stepped away and smiled up at me as she wiped away her tears. "You might be right, Harrison. We could have worked, but I hurt you for too long. I think I already knew that, but I was hoping I hadn't completely ruined what we had."

I hated seeing her cry. And these were real tears, not the fake crying and tantrums she used to pull. She was different now. But I still couldn't be with her. "Maybe we don't work, but I want to be your friend. I mean that."

Regan nodded up at me. "I expect you to stick around, maybe even be slightly jealous when I get a new guy." She smiled then and I felt some of her pain fall away. "But Harrison that's why you're perfect. Even after all the torture I threw at you, you're not afraid to be my friend." The slow song had ended and ArenaZ began blasting around us as people started stomping to the beat. She moved close again, and there was no bitterness as she placed her hands on both sides of my face. She pulled me down, turning my head so she could speak in my ear. "I'll be a better friend to you than I was a girlfriend."

JI-HEE

Reform schools, with all their brutality, have a common denominator with Elite schools. You have allies, nothing more, and they are only allies if you have the social credit to afford them. This was just as true in London as it was in Daeshim. No weaknesses are allowed, no flaws, no chinks in your armor, just walls and defenses disguised with insincere smiles and social graces.

Only I'd left that all behind. Here, I could have a real life, friends, people I cared about. Only watching Regan dance with Harrison didn't feel like I was a friend. I definitely cared but not like a friend.

The slow dance ended and I pulled back. I should have been thankful that Han-bae was here. He'd saved me from complete humiliation, but now, more than ever, I just wanted to leave. "Thanks for the dance," I said and moved to walk away but his hand shot out, and he grabbed my arm, a little too hard. I don't know why, but instead of yelling at Han-bae to let go, I looked at Harrison. Regan had her hands wrapped around his face. She'd pulled him down to her level and spoke in his ear. It was the gentle look on his face that made me stop and go rigid.

"Where are you going?"

I blinked. It was Han-bae. All of me came back into focus, I looked up at him and narrowed my eyes. "Let go," I said, putting steel behind my voice.

He held on for a second more, and then let go, throwing both hands up like I was the one being aggressive. "I'm just wondering where you're running off to."

I pushed down all my annoyance. "I need to use the restroom."

He stepped aside, and I moved past the crush of bodies to head to the side doors. I passed Astor on the way. He was laughing with a group of girls. I tried not to roll my eyes as I continued out to the hall and finally the bathroom. It was mostly empty. Two girls I didn't know were touching up lipstick. I closed myself in the last stall, leaned against the wall, and pulled out my phone.

There were two texts. The first was from Sydney.

Everything good?

The second text was from Gun.

How's the date? That kid, Astor, treating you okay?

I sighed and responded with a thumb's up emoji to both of them, then dug down into the bottom of my clutch until my fingers wrapped around cool metal. I pulled out Grandmother's wedding ring, a simple circle of gold with an engraving that said *yeonin* on the inner band. In English the closest translation would be *one's love*. Grandfather gave it to me after she passed away four years ago. Something about having it on my person made me feel protected, as if she stayed by my side. I'd hid it in reform school and then slept with it on my finger every night, clutching at the token that tied me to my grandparents. Now that I was out and could actually wear jewelry I kept it on a gold chain around my neck under my shirt. I didn't want anyone to see it. I knew it was irrational, but it felt almost like eyes could tarnish or steal away its importance. Tonight, I had taken it off the chain and put it in my purse. I rubbed my fingers over the smooth metal, feeling more grounded already. It was slightly dented on one side and worth no more than a few hundred Korean Won, but it was absolutely my favorite possession. I dropped the ring back in my clutch before zipping it securely inside and exited the bathroom.

The song changed, and the deep bass of a ballad beckoned me forward down the hallway. I squared my shoulders. I'd stay. I'd go find Han-bae and dance with him. I didn't trust him, but I felt safe enough in the public space. It was better than skulking off with my tail between my legs.

As soon as I passed the stage Harrison stepped into my path. He mouthed something, but I couldn't hear so I touched my ear and shook my head. "I can't hear."

He bent down and leaned closer. His warm breath tickled my neck as he spoke low in my ear. "Do you want to dance now?"

I nodded yes.

We were surrounded by strangers and this moment felt stolen with no one to stop us. Harrison and I could never be, but I could have this one dance. I'd file this away under the *lost chances* chapter of my life. Later I could take it out and study it, remember how perfect Harrison was this night. I didn't think, just did what seemed natural as Harrison laced our fingers together. His hand was large and warm and then he was leading me to the dance floor. The swaying bodies around us merged like a shield. I was always being watched, inspected, but not now. Not here. Right now, it was only Harrison. The song seemed to slow down as he pulled me close into an embrace that made my heart stumble and then pick up. The energy around us built, like the whole universe had been waiting for just this one moment when we would finally come together.

Harrison moved his hands to settle lower on my waist and then he lifted until my feet left the floor. It all seemed so effortless, and he leaned his forehead against my own. I glanced at his mouth wondering what it would be like if we kissed. The song wound around us as I floated in his arms.

The music trailed off before I was ready. Harrison set me down and I opened my eyes to see him smiling softly at me. "Let's keep dancing," he said.

I couldn't stop my return grin which only encouraged what happened next. He kept his arms around me as another song started.

HARRISON

It was easy to forget with Ji-hee. The whole time we danced there were no other people, we weren't in my school's stupid gym decorated with shabby posters and flowery streamers. It was just us, and this girl was like coming up for air.

I hated when guys said they loved a girl. We were in high school. Guys in high school don't have a clue what love is. But I did know this: I felt a pull from the first moment I saw her walk into my class. After tonight, I couldn't look at her any other way than with this feeling, and there was only one word for it—love. Her laugh and smile, her smell, her perfect legs, and her skin that seemed to glow. It all drew me in. And that was only the superficial stuff. There was something more, something that maybe I couldn't define yet. Ji-hee had a depth to her. She was kind, and that seemed like the most important trait, something I shouldn't let go of.

I wrapped my arms a little tighter around her, like I could hold and protect her forever. I wanted her to be mine.

And then Astor appeared.

I saw him before he saw me. He scanned the sea of people around us, then zeroed in. I pulled Ji-hee even closer, but he was already closing the distance. His angry stride made every nerve go taut as we locked eyes. He stopped when he was close enough to touch. I realized then that this is what he'd wanted from the beginning. He abandoned Ji-hee knowing I'd step in, and that was enough of a reason to pick a fight. Ji-hee's back was to him, and she was still caught up in our moment.

Astor's wolfish smile was all teeth. "I see you've found some fun, Ji-hee." His voice dripped with innuendo making even the air around us feel dirty.

She stiffened in my arms. My plan was to ignore him and keep dancing, but Ji-hee turned, and I was forced to let her go. I stayed close at her side. He'd spoken Ji-hee's name, but his eyes that now glinted with a touch of something unhinged focused on mine.

I wasn't afraid of Astor. His petty jabs bothered me no more than the dirt on the bottom of my shoes, but I was afraid of the aftermath if I fought him. I couldn't let that part of me out. Jeff would flip. Plus, I'd be the one to get suspended, not Astor.

Ji-hee laughed, the delicate noise all wrong for the tension running unchecked between us. She touched her lips as if she could say more and erase the bad. "Harrison offered to dance with me." She smiled at Astor, doing her best to bring the energy down. "I do like this song."

Astor took a step closer to me, our chests almost touching. "Did he? How accommodating. Did he offer anything else?"

Ji-hee's voice went to ice. "Don't be a jerk. I can dance with who I want."

Astor's muscles became tight around his neck, but his eyes never left mine. I shot my right hand up, bringing his eyes away and at the same time my left hand pulled Ji-hee behind me. The effect was exactly what I wanted. He didn't notice how I moved her.

His focus was on the potential threat of my right hand. He moved to block, but instead of a strike, I let my right hand fall and drop harmless to my side. I smiled with innocent eyes and said, "It is a good song."

Regan appeared at my side. "Harrison." She sounded nervous. "Sorry I was gone so long." She glanced between Astor and me with a pucker between her brows. Calvin and Tiffany were close on her heels. Calvin gave Astor a friendly pat on the shoulder. "Cool dance, right?" he said.

Astor jerked his shoulder back and ignored Calvin.

Calvin raised both hands in exaggerated surrender. "Come on, guys," he said.

Astor waited. He knew he had me as close to fighting as he ever had. When I didn't make a move, he put his pointer finger against Ji-hee's forehead and tapped once. I started forward but Ji-hee smacked his hand away and put her other arm in front of me. "Don't touch me," she hissed at Astor.

Astor held up both hands. "You don't mind finding your own ride home then, right? I know you have that curfew, and I think the rest of us will stay longer."

"None of us are riding home with you, Astor," Tiffany said.

"Fine by me." Astor smirked in my direction like he'd won before turning on his heel and blending into the crowd.

Regan moved closer to Ji-hee. "Are you okay?"

Ji-hee laughed, but it came out with the nervous tension we all felt. "Yeah, that guy just isn't my type."

"Astor isn't anyone's type," Tiffany said.

Calvin blew air out slowly and gritted his teeth. "What a freaking jerk. Now how are we getting home?"

"We could call my dad," Tiffany said.

Calvin's face fell. "Your dad hates me, Tiff."

I knew Han-bae was listening. He'd been standing to my back left, just barely in my peripheral. I'd caught him watching us when Astor showed up. Only I had the feeling he'd watched somewhere in the shadows from the moment Ji-hee and I started dancing.

He stepped forward now. "I can drive us all home after the dance." His tone was friendly and bright. "I brought my Suburban."

"I'm in," Tiffany said, and Calvin nodded enthusiastically, no doubt relieved that Tiffany's Marine father wouldn't show up and wipe the floor with him for not securing his daughter's ride.

Regan eyed Han-bae. "You'll give us a ride home?"

Han-bae really turned on the charm for her with arms open and a natural smile. "Yeah, no problem."

Ji-hee stayed silent and was doing her best to appear neutral. I couldn't tell if she was still upset about Astor or if she didn't want to go with Han-bae. One thing I did know was that Han-bae wasn't our friend.

17

HARRISON

I hadn't thought I could hate Han-bae any more than I did at school but seeing him open the door for Ji-hee to his brand-new Suburban did it.

"Ji-hee, why don't you sit up front with me," he said.

Regan leaned close and whispered in my ear. "Just open my door and get in the back. If you make a scene over this it will scare her off."

I realized my hands were fisted at my side, and I leaned forward like I was ready to spring. I shook myself and climbed in after Regan. Tiffany and Calvin piled in next to us on the other side, laughing, but then climbed back to the farthest row of seats behind us. They were extra quiet, and I didn't need to turn around to know they were kissing. Normally it would bug me, but I was so focused on Han-bae right now nothing else seemed to matter. His shiny Suburban with lit running boards and leather interior, who did he think he was? Ji-hee wasn't going to fall for this.

But then Ji-hee laughed at something he said. He'd turned the music on, some Kpop band that I didn't recognize, and faded it to the back. None of us could hear a thing they said.

Regan leaned forward before I could. "Han-bae, can you turn the music down? It's so loud back here."

Han-bae bristled, and it was Ji-hee that reached out and silenced the music. She turned around and faced us with an apologetic look.

Regan smiled at her. "You might want to drop off these two first," she said, pointing behind her.

Ji-hee glanced into the darkened rear and made a face. No one liked PDA.

"Tiffany lives on Olive Street," I said loud enough for Han-bae to hear. "Turn left on First West and then it's your second left."

Han-bae didn't acknowledge what I'd said but leaned toward Ji-hee and spoke again. Under his breath this time so I still couldn't hear him.

"What did you say?" Ji-hee asked. "Sorry I can't hear you over the engine."

"Never mind, I'll tell you later, after we drop everyone else off."

That wasn't happening.

Regan placed a hand on my arm and gave it a warning squeeze.

But I couldn't help myself. "I'm walking Ji-hee to her door tonight," I said.

Han-bae glanced back at me in his rearview mirror with a sneer. "I'm dropping you off first," he said.

Ji-hee turned back to me with a smile. "I don't need anyone to walk me to my door." To Han-bae she said, "Harrison lives just a few houses down from my place so it's fine if you drop us off at the same time."

Han-bae chuckled. "I was joking. I'm taking Tiffany home fist." He turned left and then left again onto Olive while we all sat in awkward silence.

"It's the one with the truck in front and the light on," Regan said pointing up the street.

Han-bae slowed in front of Tiffany's house, and I turned back to Calvin. "Dude, time for Tiffany to go home. Her dad is watching out the window."

"What?" Calvin squeaked. "Really?"

Regan laughed. "He's not but it's time to unlock lips." She looked at me. "I'm sleeping over at Tiff's tonight, so I'll see you at school on Monday."

"Wait, you're sleeping over?" Tiffany said.

Regan threw her a glare. "Yes," she hissed. "Let's go."

Tiffany shrugged and both girls climbed out. I followed, walking Regan to the door, but Calvin stayed safe in the darkness of the backseat.

Tiffany went straight in, leaving me and Regan alone on the porch.

"Thanks for going with me tonight," I said. I looked back at the SUV, anxious. It was too dark to see Ji-hee through the window. I hoped Calvin was talking nonstop like only he could. That would keep Han-bae occupied.

Regan looked done, but she still leaned close and hugged me tight around the waist before speaking. "You need to relax with Han-bae if you want even a ghost of a chance with Ji-hee," she said. She's pretty closed off already so don't let your ego runaway."

I smiled down at her and nodded, but my stomach was in knots. All I could think at that moment was that I wanted to get back to Ji-hee and pull her from Han-bae's stupid shiny black Suburban.

Regan let go, and I waited for her to walk inside before sprinting back.

JI-HEE

Harrison climbed back inside just as Calvin finished the longest run-on sentence I'd ever heard. He was talking manic-fast, maybe because he was nervous. I noticed his eyes kept darting to Tiffany's front door.

"Can we go now?" Calvin said, before Harrison was even all the way inside.

Han-bae, who was clearly annoyed at Calvin, put the car in gear.

"Do you know where our neighborhood is?" Calvin asked.

Han-bae nodded absentmindedly. "I know where Ji-hee lives."

My mouth felt suddenly dry. "How do you know where I live?" I asked, trying to keep my voice and face casual.

Harrison shifted behind us. "How *do* you know?" he asked. "That's super creepy."

Han-bae had said he was lonely and gravitated to me because I was familiar, because I was Korean. But I was getting tired of this.

Han-bae laughed. "I just saw Ji-hee's address my first day when I was in the office. Mrs. Smars had her schedule and paperwork sitting out on her desk. I kind of have a photographic memory so it stuck. I've never actually been to her house."

"Sure," Harrison said, his voice dripping sarcasm.

It was all lies. Han-bae didn't have a photographic memory. In a few of our classes he couldn't remember what homework was written on the board. I tried to push all my suspicions down. I didn't think my paranoia was unfounded, but I couldn't show that I was on the defensive. Letting Han-bae think I believed all his garbage was the only way for him to eventually get sloppy and make a mistake. I just needed one big misstep, and I could trace him back to wherever he came from and find out what he was really after. I stifled a yawn. "I'm tired. Let's just go home."

Calvin made a noise in the back seat that reminded me of a dog snuffling. I almost felt bad for him that he was this scared of Tiffany's father.

When we pulled into our neighborhood Han-bae made a show of looking at the numbers on the houses before he found mine. By now I was sure he'd been to my house before. Probably watched me more than I'd previously realized.

"Well, thanks for a fun night, guys," I said before quickly opening my door.

Han-bae and Harrison spoke almost in unison. "Wait."

"I'm walking her to the door," Han-bae said darkly.

I reached for my purse where I had set it next to me in the seat, eager to hop out before they really started arguing. The seat was empty. "Where's my purse?" I asked, searching next to me. I quickly looked on the floor and at the spot between my seat and the door. I turned back to Harrison. "Do you see my purse back there?"

"The little blue one you had on your wrist all night?" Harrison asked.

I nodded. "I took it off and thought I set it on my seat, just right here."

"I didn't see you with it when you got in," Han-bae said. "Did you leave it at the school?"

My mind raced, retracing my steps. I'd gone to the bathroom and had it in there. I thought I had it when I left. But what about dancing with Harrison? I couldn't remember. I'd been so caught up in my dreamy state that I didn't feel anything other than how wonderful it was to be in his arms. Did I leave it in the bathroom? "Someone call my phone," I said. "It's in my purse."

Harrison touched his screen, and we all waited in silence, listening for a buzz. "It went straight to voicemail," Harrison said.

"I had plenty of battery." A cold feeling spread across my chest. I swallowed and my throat burned with an icy coating. "My grand-mother's ring. It was in my purse. I can't lose it," I said. "Can we go back to the school?" I asked.

"The school's closed by now," Calvin said. "We were some of the last to leave, remember?"

I swallowed and turned pleading eyes to Harrison.

"I can email one of the teachers that was there," Harrison said. "Was the ring expensive?"

I shook my head. "No. It's just important to me."

"Can you track your phone from a computer?" Calvin asked. "That's such a bummer to lose your phone."

I shook my head. My phone should have rung. It should have buzzed under one of these seats or someone from the dance should have answered and assured me that my purse was safe. It would only go straight to voicemail if someone took my phone out and powered it off. "The phone's not a big deal," I said. "I can buy a new one tomor-row. It's my grandmother's ring that I care about."

Harrison opened his phone and tapped the screen. "I'm emailing Ms. Smars, and we can all look when we go back on Monday."

Tears pricked at my eyes. I had to leave before I started crying. Without saying goodbye, I hopped out of the Suburban and started walking briskly away. I got close to the front door, but a hand clamped down on my wrist. I jerked to a stop, and Han-bae spun me to face him. His face contorted with pain. "I'm sorry, Ji-hee. I didn't know that—"

Before he could say more, Harrison appeared next to us. I blinked in confusion. Harrison's hand shot out, shoving Han-bae hard enough to make him stumble back and drop my wrist. "Get your hands off her," Harrison barked, stepping between us.

Han-bae regained his footing and his eyes burned with anger. "She doesn't belong to you. She's not even your date," he said. "Just leave us alone." He tried to reach past Harrison, maybe for my hand.

Harrison smacked it away. "You're not touching her," he said.

I turned and ran for the front door. The light was on, welcoming and safe. I pushed down on the handle and let out a breath of relief that it wasn't locked. Before I went in, I turned and looked behind me.

Both Harrison and Han-bae stood apart, tense and angry, but they were both watching me. I turned my back on them and went inside.

18

HARRISON

My parents came home a few days after homecoming. But it took another whole week after that for the glow of vacation to wear off. Finally Mom asked about the dance.

"How was homecoming, by the way?" She poked around in the fridge for something and pulled out the vegan mayonnaise Gretchen had purchased, then frowned.

"It was fine," I said, a little too hotly.

Mom looked over at me. "Do you want to tell me about it?"

I really didn't.

"Is it because your grandparents didn't want Ozzy to go? He had a last-minute practice, and Gretchen gave him the choice on whether or not he went."

I shook my head. Gretchen was a liar. "It was no big deal."

Mom moved from the fridge to rummage through the pantry. "Do you want to know what I think?" When I didn't say anything, she continued on. "I think Ozzy was nervous to go on a date. He's never been before, and skating was an easy excuse for him to not go. You should get another group together and invite him for winter formal.

Dad and I will be here and make sure he's more prepared." Mom closed the pantry door and turned to me. "What do you think?"

If I told her what really happened, she'd tell Jeff, and then they'd get mad at Garrett and Gretchen. Which for some reason I didn't want. It felt too much like tattle-telling. I also knew it would cause problems with paying for Ozzy's trainers. I wouldn't put it past the Evil G's to say they wouldn't help with the bill anymore. I swallowed my simmering anger right along with the hurt. I looked down at the floor before I spoke. "That's a good idea. I think Ozzy wants to date. He loves skating but he's definitely into girls now."

Mom beamed at me. "So, besides Ozzy, how were things? How was it with Regan?" She opened the vegan mayonnaise bottle and smelled it, wrinkling her nose before throwing it in the trash.

"It was okay, I guess."

Mom raised an eyebrow. "Sooo *not* okay."

"What do you mean? It wasn't bad." I'd never told Mom why Regan and I broke up, and I wasn't sure what she was getting at.

"Did you and Regan get back together?"

"No. Not even close," I said. "Did you want us to get back together?"

Her face remained blank, but she grabbed a sponge and started wiping the counter. "You can date who you want." Mom never meddled in my social life so her next statement took me entirely by surprise. "Regan just doesn't seem like the girl for you," she said.

I snorted. "She's definitely not."

"Will you be going out again?"

My mouth twitched. "I'm hoping to go out but not with Regan." I grabbed my coat from the chair and headed for the door.

"Wait," she called, and I turned back. "You like someone? Someone new?"

"Yeah, I do, but she doesn't like me back."

"Why not?"

"She was in our group for homecoming." I shrugged. "I think I came on too strong." I was too embarrassed to explain that me throwing a fit over Han-bae definitely made things weird. She was already hurting over losing her purse and that ring, then I picked a fight. Not cool.

"Do I know her, or her parents?"

"She lives with the Kims," I said.

Mom's eye's widened in surprise. "Chul and Sydney Kim? That young couple just down the street?"

I nodded and felt warmth creep to my face.

"I think I've seen her outside with Sydney. What's her name?"

"Ji-hee," I said, my face hot now. "But she's kind of avoided me since homecoming."

Mom smiled and busied herself with tossing more food from the fridge, giving me time to compose myself. "You don't come on too strong," she finally said. "You're just protective. You've always been that way. It's who you are, Harrison."

I grabbed an apple from the counter before heading out. Having Mom read me so well somehow made me feel better, like I still had a chance with Ji-hee. And she was right about the protective thing. It was a part of me, something I couldn't turn off.

I lost both my front teeth early over Marci Jordan. A third grader made her cry at recess, so naturally, I took a swing at him. He pummeled my face, but I never once regretted it. Marci was nice to everyone. Defending girls didn't feel like a choice to me, at least not a conscious one.

But with Ji-hee this part of me seemed to intensify. She was like a booster shot to my protective instincts. I could tell this bugged her, but I couldn't seem to help myself. I hoped doing it covertly was enough. Only Han-bae was so obvious about his attachment, making the protecting without getting noticed that much harder. He watched Ji-hee as closely as I did, always glowering in the background like a cloud over my days. She wasn't unkind to him. I would call it politely distant, like a contact name in your phone that you forget is there. It was the one thing that kept me hopeful. She wasn't dating Han-bae and kept him even farther away than she kept me.

She was friendly with me, only with walls. Solid, Harrison-proof walls. She never pushed me away, but she never let me in either. I still hung around a lot but it stung. It stung like a thousand scorching insects burrowing into my chest, leaving me with a heavy, bad feeling all over. At night it hurt to breathe, and sometimes I forced myself to get up in the full dark for runs just to ease the pain in my chest. I'd go until I could barely walk. Only then could I sleep. But I'd endure all of it and more, if it meant I could get Ji-hee in the end. I wasn't giving up.

Everyone says that guys hate the friend zone. And that's true, we do hate it. But what most of us will never admit is that we'll take that over being invisible every time. Invisible is annihilation of love. If you can stay friends with a girl, you might be at the very bottom of her romantic prospects, but you're not zero.

JI-HEE

I dreamed of Harrison almost every night now. It sounded so melodramatic, but it didn't change that he was always there filling my nights like a cringy romance book. Last night I dreamed that he kissed me, and I woke up with a pounding heart.

I knew this was all just my subconscious rebelling against the betrayal of my own heart. If I would just tell Harrison how I felt about him, or at the very least, not smack him down every time he hinted at a date, the dreams would go away. But I couldn't tell him. I wasn't allowed to feel that way about anyone.

Diana passed me the ball, and I missed it, letting a girl from the other team make a steal. "Ji-hee pay attention," Harmony yelled from somewhere behind me.

Ms. Liv blew her whistle, and we all walked to the bleachers to sit. Diana wiped her sweaty brow with her too long tee shirt. "Are you here with us, or still in la la land?" she asked.

"Sorry." I flashed her a cheerful smile that said I was fully engaged. "I'm here now."

Harmony dribbled the ball in and out of her feet. "You know who else is here, but isn't?" She jerked her head over toward Harrison. "He's totally not into the game today."

I glanced at where he leaned against the wall. When he wasn't actively playing, Harrison had taken to going off alone and staring at the floor like it held life's most important secrets. He seemed almost depressed, but I didn't know what to do about it. I rubbed my ring finger on my right hand. I felt the loss of Grandmother's ring daily, another reminder of everything good that had been taken from me. I wasn't adding Harrison to that list.

Neither Harmony nor Diana knew why I ignored Harrison, and I wasn't going to explain how in my world being engaged in high school wasn't impossible, that having your parents sign a marriage contract to boost stocks was considered normal. They'd never understand it. I was engaged to a boy I'd never met, and I didn't even know his first name. I basically knew he was the only son of the elusive Bitgaram family and that he lived in a boarding school somewhere in Switzerland. If I actually managed to stay here long enough to graduate, I fully expected to get a call from Gun, or worse, Mother telling me it was time to fly home because I'd get married in a week.

Han-bae walked past us and climbed the bleachers to sit above me. This was his normal move at the end of class, and it drove me crazy. I hated having him at my back, but Diana followed him with her eyes and got that look she always fell into when he was around.

Harmony tucked the ball under her arm and sat on my other side. She spoke low, in a near whisper so only Diana and I could hear. "Why don't you just go out with Harrison?" she asked. "He's into you."

"Hundred percent," Diana agreed.

Harrison was perfect in both my dream world and out. But that was the problem. He was too perfect, too attentive, too protective, too everything. If I gave in and went on even one date, then we would be like this snowball starting small but gaining strength as we tumbled down the mountain. We wouldn't even be a snowball by the end. Harrison and I would be an avalanche. Which, who wouldn't want to be buried by love? It sounded wonderful.

Only Mother would ruin it.

"I can't be interested in Harrison," I whispered back.

"Why not?" Diana asked.

I shook my head. "It's just complicated."

"You could find someone else." Harmony shrugged. "I mean if you're taken then Harrison might stop his miserable grieving and move on."

I knew Harmony had a thing for Harrison. She tried to hide it, but I could tell. When she said he could *move on* what she really meant was that if I was dating someone else, he could move on to her. I couldn't begrudge her hope either. She wasn't being a bad friend. She wasn't flirting with him, and I'd never laid any kind of claim on Harrison. But if I started dating someone else, she'd jump on it.

Harmony licked her lips as she stared at him. "Right now, it's like watching someone bleed out," she said. "It's hard not to want to help him."

Diana nodded. "Put that guy out of his misery."

"He'll be okay," I said. "He's got a lot going for him."

Harmony snorted. "Not to mention he's gorgeous."

"Are you sure you won't regret letting him go?" Diana asked.

Harmony elbowed me and nudged Diana with her foot. "He's coming," she hissed.

I kept my eyes glued to the floor.

"Ji-hee?"

I raised my head but hadn't properly steadied myself for a Harrison-so-close moment. His dark eyes burned into mine, and his mouth twitched before he took another step closer. The tip of his shoe almost touched mine, and I craned my neck up to see him. His hair was tousled in the front, and the jersey tank top he wore for basketball clung to his chest.

So unfair.

I jumped up before he could say anything and sprinted out the door. They were all going to think I was crazy or maybe Harmony would say I was sick to my stomach or something. Diana couldn't lie under any circumstances, and if she started talking, she'd tell him every detail she knew about me. She'd mention that I hadn't been sleeping well. The girl couldn't not spill her guts. I hoped Harmony gave an excuse before that happened.

My face was hot from embarrassment and shame. Not just because I'd run out of the gym like a rabid dog, but that I'd almost stood up and asked Harrison if he wanted to get dinner with me. I'd let a fraction of my brain play out an after-school scenario with Harrison. And that was the number one rule. No Harrison fantasies.

Maybe I broke the rule because I could feel Harmony circling. I hated the idea of her ever being with him. But most likely it was that I was getting weaker. I wanted to be with Harrison somewhere other than in my dreams.

19

JI-HEE

Sydney somehow talked me into joining her and Chul for a night of bowling. I didn't actually know how to bowl, yet here I was, third-wheeling in the back of their car. Chul parked in an old roped off lot, not well lit, and mostly empty for a Friday night. My new phone buzzed in my back pocket. I pulled it out to see a text from Han-bae. I didn't read it.

"Are you coming?" Chul poked his head through the car door and looked back at me. Sydney was already out and waiting.

"Yeah, sorry." I got out to follow them through an alley. I was expecting one of those multiplex fun centers that was a smorgasbord of games, laser tag, and bowling, but the building we walked to was stately old brick with patina-green awnings. A modest iron railing ran around the roofline with two smallish stone angels on each corner. The heavy door creaked its age when Chul opened it for us, and I followed them into an open space that smelled like aged wood and oil with just a hint of mint chocolate. The chocolate surprised me until I looked past the four outdated bowling lanes that filled one-half of the room. Instead of an adjoining greasy kitchen serving fries and beer, there was an old-fashioned soda bar with red upholstered stools under a glossy wooden counter. Two elderly people sat on one end and shared a giant ice cream float. But it wasn't the room practically frozen in time that made me catch my breath. It was Harrison standing behind the counter, polishing glasses.

Sydney turned back to me. "What do you think?"

I swallowed. "I like it."

"They serve the best ice cream custard here," she said. "You should go get yourself a treat." Sydney glanced over at Harrison and then smiled at me. "You know where to find us when you're done."

Before I had a chance to wonder if Sydney was playing matchmaker, she marched off to the bowling lanes. Chul was quick to catch up, and I noted with a twinge of longing how he always held his wife close, either her hand, or an arm around her waist.

I watched them for a long minute, too afraid to face Harrison. I doubted he'd even spotted me from where I was standing. When I finally got the guts to turn, Harrison stared right at me with a big open smile. I tried not to smile back.

He wore a gray button up oxford, and his messy dark hair begged to be played with. I walked forward slowly and felt myself blush. I wished he would look away or scoop ice cream. Something. Anything. But Harrison watched me openly, completely obvious. I don't know if it was that smile or those eyes, but I just kept walking.

HARRISON

I'd fought with myself all day to get Ji-hee out of my head, yet here she was, right back in my sights. And this time, she'd come to me.

JI-HEE

Harrison deserved to have a clear warning. I took two more steps and formed the words in my mind. The words that would be fair to him.

Hey, Harrison. I know you're into me, but I have major issues. I have a big shameful secret. Serve me up some ice cream and then pretend I'm not here. I took two more steps and tried to say the words, but they sealed themselves up in my mind. Like there was this other Ji-hee, a selfish version of myself that wanted Harrison despite any fallout. I tried again to make myself back out of this. Only Harrison stood there, perfect.

I moved to the shiny red barstool, but I didn't sit down. The wooden counter was scarred and scuffed, just like my heart, but Harrison pressed his wide hands down on the top almost as if he appreciated every scratch. He leaned forward and grinned at me. "Hi."

I let myself smile and it felt like a dam breaking inside my chest. "Hi, Harrison," I breathed. I tried to say more but my mouth felt full of glue.

He searched my eyes, and then, as if he could magically sense all my inner conflict, his deep voice took on a reassuring note. "Do you like ice cream?"

I nodded.

"All kinds or is there something you don't like?"

"I'm allergic to blueberries."

He reached forward over the bar. It wasn't hard, his arms were long, and he took my hand to gently pull me onto the stool. "I'm going to make something off menu, a custom dessert, perfect for you."

I laced my fingers tightly together in my lap and tried to calm my flutters. "I'd like that."

He turned around and started grabbing ingredients. I watched him work. His movements were easy and quick, like he was familiar with his job. My phone buzzed, and I pulled it out of my pocket. It was Gun.

You need to call me.

I texted him

Later

He texted right back

Right now!

I sighed. "Hey, Harrison?"

He turned slightly. "Yeah, I'm almost done."

"No, sorry. I need to make a call. I'm going to step outside for just a minute."

He glanced up from something he was stirring in a metal bowl with a nod.

I slipped off the stool and turned to scan for Chul and Sydney. They were still at their lane. Chul was standing behind his wife with his arms wrapped around her shoulders it that oh-so-cute way he always did. He murmured something close to her ear, and she laughed before pushing him off to grab a bowling ball. The roof could fall in, and they'd probably keep flirting. They wouldn't notice if I left.

I walked to the door, but before I could open it, I got another text from Gun.

Where are you? I can't reach Chul. Are you someplace safe?

I snorted as I walked out. It was full dark now, and the front of the bowling alley wasn't well lit. One broken lamp post across the street sputtered, and just faint light came from both windows. Other than a homeless man on a bench, the street was deserted.

I texted back.

What's the big emergency?

My phone buzzed and a call from Gun lit my screen. I answered it after three rings, trying to sound bored instead of mad. Silent disdain was better than letting him see my anger. Anger meant I still cared. "Hi, Gun."

"Ji-hee. Are you with Chul?" He spat out the words, quick and cutting, which bugged me even more.

"Kind of. Why?"

"We have a problem. Can you give him the phone, please."

I sighed. He used to hate Chul, and now if he couldn't reach him, it was the end of the world. "He's busy playing perfect husband with Sydney. I'll tell him you called when I see him."

Gun's voice sounded strained. "Tell me exactly where you are. Where is Chul? Can he see you?"

Something wasn't right. "Look, Gun, I've been taking care of myself for years now. Either tell me what's really going on or I'm hanging—"

"You're not safe. Go find Chul, NOW."

I hung up the phone. Gun might be my older brother, but he'd lost any say in my life and Chul . . . was too busy with Sydney if I had trouble. "It would help if you didn't send me to live with my former crush," I muttered the words as I whipped around angrily to march back inside.

Only that didn't happen. Harrison's voice was the first thing my brain grabbed onto as I smacked into a solid wall of muscle. "Whoa," he said.

I was acutely aware that Harrison's warm hands held me close. He smelled just like he did at the dance. I inhaled. Soap layered with a more mesmerizing scent, something my brain wanted to drink in. I pushed away before I could lose my head.

Harrison held on for half a second too long, then reluctantly let go and took a step back. His gaze became dark pools in the dim light as he looked down at me. "Are you okay? I didn't mean to eavesdrop but it's dark, and not every neighborhood is safe. You can make your phone call in the back office."

I was glad it was too dark for Harrison to see my flaming face. "How much did you hear?"

Harrison grimaced. "That you live with your crush."

I bristled. "Former, as in no longer, dead, over, and it was barely a thing to begin with. We went on one date, and it was a pity date at that. Chul felt sorry for me."

Harrison folded his arms and the beginnings of a smile tugged at his lips. "Yeah, Ji-hee, you're a smart girl but dead-wrong on this one. No guy would find you anything close to pitiful."

I snorted. "Not the case at my old high school. The boys there—"

"Are clearly idiots." He laughed and it caught me off guard with his deep rumble.

I sighed. "It doesn't matter. I'm here now, and both Chul and Sydney are actually cool about everything."

Harrison took a step closer. "So you don't like Chul anymore?"

"I really don't. I was a freshman."

Harrison nodded. "Who was that on the phone, if you don't mind me asking?"

"My stupid brother."

"He sounded worried for you." Harrison's eyes studied mine. "I can help if you need anything."

My phone started to buzz in my pocket. I pulled it out and powered it off.

Harrison pointed. "Your brother again?"

Before I could answer, a dark Suburban turned onto the street and slowed as it came to the curb. The window lowered and Han-bae leaned out. The little hairs on the back of my neck raised up in alarm. How did he know I was here?

Han-bae eyed Harrison and then raised his chin. "Ji-hee, I found your purse."

I could see the outline of another man in the passenger seat. He was too hidden in shadow to make out more than his large size. Han-bae twisted and reached behind him. When he turned back, it was with my favorite blue clutch from homecoming. He dangled it out the window by the strap with one finger.

My heart lurched. He had my purse all along. During the ride home when I turned back to talk with Harrison and Regan, he must have slipped it into his lap and powered my phone off. I'm sure he wanted to snoop through my stuff, look at emails, texts, and pictures. I squeezed my hands into little fists and focused on keeping my features serene. Grandmother's ring better still be in there.

Gun's words echoed through my thoughts, *You're not safe.* But I couldn't run. I needed Grandmother's ring almost as much as I needed air. I eyed the angle of his arm out the window. I could probably grab my purse and retreat if he wasn't expecting it.

I smiled and let my voice take on a friendly, almost gushing tone. "Oh, wow. Where did you find it?" I started forward with my hand extended, but Harrison moved fast.

In one motion he grabbed my hand with his right one and snatched the purse in his left, all while keeping his body between me and Han-bae. I never even got within a meter of the car "Thanks." Harrison spoke with firmness as he spun us both around, and then he was moving me back inside.

It all happened so quickly. I barely had time for more than one brief view of Han-bae's face over my shoulder. He was livid.

HARRISON

I knew Ji-hee was wary. I'd felt her muscles tense next to me, but if I knew anything about this girl, it was that she was good at hiding her feelings. Maybe her plan was to play dumb to the danger and get the purse before retreating. Only that doesn't always work. What would have happened to her if I wasn't there? Nothing good. I was pretty sure she didn't notice the two, possibly three men sitting in the back, and I couldn't make out much with the beefy guy in the passenger seat. But from what I could see, none of them went to Bishop High or were anywhere near our age. These were grown men with a hired thug vibe.

I still held her hand and pulled her behind me as my heart hammered in my chest. I let go only when we were inside the back office. There was a small window in the door, but I pointed to a cracked leather armchair next to a messy desk. The chair was far enough in the corner that even if someone came to the door and peeked in, it was hard to see. "Have a seat. I'll be right back." I handed her the purse as she sat. She immediately unzipped it, searching inside. I had already started toward the door, but my curiosity over this ring had me rooted to the spot.

She pulled out a simple band and slipped the ring on her finger with a sigh. "I'm never taking this off again."

She held up her hand and gazed at the thin strip of gold as if it were worth more than any diamond or treasure. I smiled to myself and slipped out to the bar area.

The ice cream concoction I'd scooped for her was in the freezer and I grabbed that with two spoons. It gave me just enough time to scan the doors in case Han-bae had followed us in. He hadn't.

The owner, David, was at the front counter taking payment from a family about to leave. Chul and Sydney were still bowling. Everything looked normal, but I couldn't relax. The way Han-bae had looked at Ji-hee, the car full of quiet muscle, all my instincts told me to stay on guard. I went back in the office and placed the bowl of ice cream on the desk next to Ji-hee. "I hope you like this."

Ji-hee smiled. "Thanks, but . . ." She searched my face for clues. "Why are we back here? I hope you're not worried about me."

The unsettling feeling I had over the guys in the Suburban would be hard to explain, and there was also the phone call from her brother. I couldn't hear his words, but the tone was frantic. I was hyper aware that Ji-hee didn't like me fighting her battles, but this was something I couldn't ignore. "I thought it would be fun to take my break with you," I said. "Do you mind eating in here with me?"

Ji-hee picked up one spoon. "No, you just seemed jumpy, so I wondered. But I'm glad you're not worried."

"Not at all." I grabbed the folding chair from behind the desk and moved it close, straddled it backward as she took her first bite.

"Wow, this is good." She took another bite and made a giggling noise. "No, seriously, this is sooo good. What is it?"

I loved her ice cream laugh. I didn't even know there was such a thing. But there was and Ji-hee had one. I leaned closer and grabbed the other spoon. "If I tell you the secret recipe, will you give me a bite?"

She stared at my lips before nodding.

"One scoop of our vanilla bean custard." I put a spoonful into my mouth and spoke around it. "One scoop of bourbon caramel custard and I topped it with marshmallow cream, pistachio fudge sauce, and crushed shortbread cookies."

"It's perfect." She licked some sauce off her spoon, and I tried to look away, feeling caught in some kind of atmospheric Ji-hee trap, like everything she did felt magnetized and made me want more. She wasn't aware of it, either, making her all the more attractive. I shook myself before I did something stupid like kiss her. I really wanted to kiss her. "I have a question for you," I said.

Ji-hee spoke around a full mouth. "What?"

"Did you invite Han-bae here tonight?"

She looked down and shifted. "No."

"Then how did he know where you were?"

Ji-hee frowned. "Um, I'm not sure."

Even through the closed door I heard David's voice raise sharply. He sounded like he was arguing with someone. I stood up and approached the door, then leaned cautiously and peered from the side of the window. Han-bae was standing next to David. My eyes continued to scan until I found two big men that didn't belong. They were searching the lanes of the bowling alley and a third walked back toward the restrooms.

I turned to Ji-hee. "Will you stay here and wait for me?" She stilled with the spoon in her mouth, and her eyes went big. I kept my voice soft. "It's okay, Ji-hee. Han-bae seems upset, but I can calm him down. Just don't come out." I waited for her to nod and then slipped silently out the door. No one saw me. It had a lock on the doorknob which I pressed before closing it tight behind me.

I walked quickly to David. He wasn't a large man and Han-bae was poking him in the shoulder as he grilled him.

"Where is she?" Han-bae barked the words like he was some kind of authority. "She's my sister, and I need to talk with her."

Han-bae was such a liar. I rolled my shoulders reminding myself to keep it cool. Getting into it with him would only terrify Ji-hee more, and I'd already screwed that up once. I tapped Han-bae on the shoulder. "Hey. Are you looking for Ji-hee? She just left." I pointed to the rear of the bowling alley with the green exit sign.

Chul and Sydney must have heard the commotion and were making their way to us. Neither one looked happy. They both stopped next to Han-bae.

"Did you just say you were her brother?" Sydney asked. Her voice hissed with acid.

I noted how carefully Chul watched Han-bae interact with Sydney.

Han-bae took a step back and gave us all a disarming smile, then he switched from perfect English to broken. "Not brother. Just trying to return purse. Where she go?"

Sydney cocked her head and narrowed her eyes. Then started rattling off words in Korean I didn't understand. She raised her voice when she pointed at each of the three men searching the bowling alley. One of them had stopped at the office door.

20

JI-HEE

Someone rattled the door, and I was almost certain it wasn't Harrison. I could see shadows along the glass, so I pulled my feet up into the chair and tried to squeeze myself into a tighter space. My chair sat positioned on the same wall as the door, but far back into the corner so no one could see clearly through the window.

A fist banged again, jarring the door. "Open up," the voice bellowed.

Definitely not Harrison.

This was stupid. I wasn't going to hide in the corner. If Han-bae was somewhere out there causing all of this then maybe he needed to hear that I was getting sick of him following my every move. I just wanted to find out what he was hiding. I jumped up, ready to unlock the door but froze when I saw a large man through the glass. His back was to me. Before I could decide what to do, something heavy rammed against him, and his whole body slammed into the door. His greasy hair slid along the glass. I heard a painful grunt from the man, then Harrison's voice, low and threatening. "Employees only."

"Get off me," the man growled back. I thought of the shady figure seated in the passenger seat next to Han-bae. He wouldn't have brought someone violent with him. Would he?

There was another crash, this time with breaking glass. The man outside was gone. I whipped open the door. Harrison lay on his side, shattered glass around him and a small trickle of blood above his eyebrow. His glare was directed to my right. As I slowly turned to look, a large hand clamped down on my shoulder.

I gasped in surprise as dark eyes and bushy eyebrows set in a meaty face loomed over me. The guy had hanging jowls, a healthy midsection, and arms as big around as my waist. He leaned down close to me with a twisted smile. "You're the pretty we're lookin' for."

I shuddered as his breath wafted over me with the potent smell of old cigarettes and decay.

Meathead dug his fingers into my shoulder. "I've got her," he shouted.

I reared back and tried to wiggle from his grip, but his hands shot to my waist, painfully squeezing and hauling me up like he was going to throw me over his shoulder. Cold fear gripped my gut. I frantically twisted, trying to pull away. My nails scratched and clawed at his fleshy arms, but it was like a mouse poking at a walrus.

I didn't see it, but I felt the impact of Harrison hitting Meathead before he let go. I fell and landed with a painful thud on my side. I rolled to my front and hopped up in one motion, all before Meathead stumbled past me. He smashed into the barstools with a horrible crunching sound. Harrison charged after him, a storm of fury. He turned and barked at me as he passed. "Get back in the office."

His yell jarred my already stunned brain. I would not hide in the office. I was going to fight too. I took a step forward, determined, but then Sydney was at my side.

She moved with swift determination as she grabbed my hand. "Don't be stupid. There are three of them."

I looked past her shoulder to see Chul landing blows on yet another man. This guy was a lot smaller than Meathead, but Chul was still working hard using kicks and punches to his advantage. I watched, hypnotized, until Sydney hauled me back into the office and locked the door.

"Help me," she said, grabbing onto one end of the heavy metal desk and trying to lift. I scurried to the other side, and we managed to drag the beast of a desk to the door. It groaned as we pushed. We both panted from the effort and adrenaline. I was shaking but my mind felt slow and sluggish. My black tee-shirt had been torn at the hem when Meathead dropped me, and I fingered the frayed edge like it could somehow bring me comfort.

"The owner called the police." Sydney nodded toward the door. "But my guess is this will be over soon. Chul and Harrison will chase them off before the police get here."

"Who are they?" I asked.

"There was a Korean guy," Sydney said. "He was looking for you."

I knew Han-bae was behind this, but it didn't make any sense. A small fear began to nibble away at my last remaining calm. I shook my head. It couldn't be that. If he was connected to the Bitgarams, then maybe he was just a random person they sent to spy on me.

Nothing more.

But the Bitgarams weren't random, they were deliberate, and now Han-bae had done more than spy. I was hiding, and the one boy I liked was getting hurt for my sake.

I pulled out my phone and powered it back on. There were eight missed calls, all from Gun. I touched the screen and my brother answered on the first ring.

"Ji-hee!" His voice came out strained and panicked. "Are you okay?"

"I'm okay," I said quickly. "I'm with Chul." I wasn't really sure everything was okay, but I hadn't been fair earlier. Gun deserved to know I was safe.

"Listen to me, Ji-hee, you need—"

I interrupted him. "Did the Bitgarams send someone here to the States? Someone to spy on me?"

"Not someone," Gun said. "Jung, your fiancé is there in California. I just found out. You need to find Chul and lie low."

My hands started to shake. "How long has he been in California?" I asked, trying to keep my voice steady.

"He left his school in Switzerland around the same time you left London. They knew I'd registered you at a public school. I thought the whole fake Marklem Academy thing would throw everyone off, but they followed you."

Tears pricked at my eyes. I couldn't believe how stupid I'd been. Han-bae was Jung. He'd used a fake last name, but it was Jung Bitgaram. Why hadn't I seen it before? He was one of the Elite. He had no history or social media presence, and he was my age. The one person that met those requirements was the stupid guy my mother had signed my life over to. I'd been so set on watching Han-bae and waiting for him to make a mistake, that I missed the obvious. And never would I have thought his *mistake* could be violent. Sydney could have been hurt. Harrison was hurt, and I really hoped Chul could hold his own with that guy out there.

I cleared my throat and swallowed my tears. Crying over this wasn't going to help. "Jung is here," I said. "He's been attending the same public high school as me under the name Han-bae."

The line went quiet and then Gun said, "That's Jung's middle name, Bitgaram Han-bae Jung."

Sickening pain wove around me, like a noose drawn tight until I could only hold very still.

"Just don't leave Chul's house," Gun said. "If Jung is anything like his mother, then he's dangerous."

My hands were shaking harder now, and I felt cold all over. I couldn't tell my brother that it was too late. Han-bae had lied to get close to me and now what? Was he trying to take me back to Korea? But why? We were already engaged, not that I had any intention of honoring that. And it's not like he came to check me out. Mother had sent videos of me and tons of pictures.

I, on the other hand, had never seen *his* picture. Mother said he was private. Now I knew. Not private, maybe psychotic was more his thing.

"Promise me, Ji-hee. Stay with Sydney and Chul. Don't go to school and don't leave their house."

I could feel the walls closing in on me here. My life in California was going to be cut short, but whatever time I had left I wanted to spend it with Harrison. This realization surprised me, and yet, it didn't. All these years I'd yearned for normal and now that I had it, I wouldn't let it go without a fight. I was going to school. I wouldn't hide. I'd done enough of that in London.

Another loud thud landed against the wall.

"Gun, why would Jung be here? Why would he come to California? We're already engaged."

"After you left for California Mother and Myang got in a fight. Myang didn't want you to leave London and was angry at Mother for allowing it. I thought that would be the end of it but, Jung followed you there."

My breath caught in my throat. I didn't hear any more of what my brother said. They were Elite. There was no reason the Bitgarams were hanging on this tight, unless Han-bae or Jung or whoever the heck he was dug his heels in. Han-bae could have any girl he wanted so why choose me?

HARRISON

The police showed up before Chul finished zip tying the guy I'd pinned onto his fat belly. I had both arms drawn behind him and my knee in his back while Chul pulled the plastic tight around his beefy wrists. Then we both jumped back as the guy flopped around and rolled over yelling.

My boss, David, who hadn't stopped frowning for even a minute, glanced in our direction and scowled deeper. Like all of this was somehow my fault. It wasn't. But I was pretty sure my days as soda fountain manager were over. David was going to fire me for smashing a whole wall of dishes. He talked with the two officers who were handcuffing the two other men. Three had been detained to take the blame, but no one seemed concerned with Han-bae. The police said they'd like to question him, but he'd disappeared, evaporated into nothing when the fighting started.

This told me two things. One, that Han-bae was smart, and two, he was a coward. It was the smart part that worried me. I was more than sure he'd waited somewhere and watched to see who would win the fight. If it had been his guys he would have swooped in and stolen Ji-hee. Since it was us, he was regrouping somewhere. And that left a cold feeling in my gut. This was LA. Han-bae could always hire more guys, stronger and smarter. Maybe next time there would be six instead of three.

I walked to the office door with Chul. The guy didn't even look winded. My shirt was torn and the cut above my eye still oozed blood. Chul knocked on the door and spoke gently. "Syd, it's safe now." When there was no response, he knocked again. "Babe, you okay?"

We heard a muffled, "Hang on." The grinding sound of the ancient metal desk sliding against the tile screeched through the door and then it whipped open. Sydney rushed straight past me into Chul's arms. Ji-hee followed close behind but seemed embarrassed and wiped at her eyes.

Chul gripped his wife with a smile as she showered him with kisses. "I was worried," she mumbled over his lips.

It was hard not to stare.

I took a step toward Ji-hee but one of the officers moved in front of me. His quick scan where his eyes surveyed less of our surroundings, and more of us, made me feel like I'd done something wrong. "I understand you fought with one of the robbery suspects," he said.

Robbery suspects? What was he talking about? "Uh this wasn't a robbery. A guy named Han-bae—"

Chul spoke, swift to interrupt. "Han-bae was just confused. He doesn't know English very well and was trying to return my friend's purse. He left right after my wife spoke to him, and then these three men started threatening us. I don't think Han-bae had anything to do with these other guys."

I balked. How could Chul tell such a blatant lie? He knew Han-bae was behind all of this. But when I opened my mouth to speak Ji-hee took my hand and gave it a warning squeeze.

I started to explain. "One of the men tried grabbing Ji-hee and—"

"Ji-hee was in the office with my wife," Chul said.

The officer held up a hand to stop Chul and looked right at me. "And that's when you proceeded to fight this man?" He motioned toward the big guy now moaning on the floor as two paramedics tried to inspect his wounds. "I watched the video footage. Where'd you learn to fight?"

"I took TaeKwonDo when I was a kid," I offered, more as a joke than anything. Jeff had been the one to teach me how to fight.

Nobody laughed.

The officer nodded and wrote it down. "I've already got the owner's statement. Good thing you boys were here. No money or goods were taken."

I started to speak. There was no way this was a failed robbery. Is that what Chul had told them? But Ji-hee touched my face. "You should go get some ice on your head." It was just a slight brush near the cut above my eye, but it made me tingle all over, and I got the impression she was trying to warn me to wave off again. "After we get your eye fixed will you drive me home?" She asked. "Chul said it was okay."

"Uh, yeah, yes," I stammered. "Of course."

"You should listen to your girlfriend," the officer said. "Go get your head checked out with the EMT."

I looked at Ji-hee to see what she would say, but she just gave me a gentle smile, her face filled with concern. My chest went tight.

The fact that he didn't seem to be asking where Han-bae had gone or wondering why guys that were robbing a place would leave a register but come after a girl in the back room should have made me think more. And I would think more on it later. But at that point one word eclipsed every other thought in my brain. *Girlfriend.* Ji-hee hadn't corrected the officer when he said we were together, and that gave me something more powerful than fear. It gave me hope.

21

JI-HEE

We both stood outside the bowling alley and mutely stared at the rain. With the fighting and the police, neither of us had noticed that a heavy downpour started. But now that I was outside, I wondered how I'd missed it. Sheets thundered into puddles that flooded the uneven asphalt.

"Wow. It's really coming down," he said. "Are you okay to run for it or do you want me to pull the car up?" He cleared his throat. "I guess it's not really a car, more like my mom's minivan. It's just over there." He pointed but his tone sounded apologetic, like a warning not to expect too much.

"I'm down to run." I smiled to myself. I'd seen minivans but had never been in one. It seemed more novel than any luxury car, and I'd been in plenty of those.

He shrugged off his jacket and held it over me before we stepped out from the awning and ran to the forest green minivan with rusted out wheel wells. He opened the door for me, and I hopped in without hesitation. The seats were worn fabric, almost threadbare. But it was comfortable, *and* I was alone with Harrison.

He started the engine, and it rumbled before he put it in gear and began driving.

I tried to think of something to say, anything to distract from the questions that hung in the air between us, questions I knew he wanted answers to. "I guess you're wondering what's up with Han-bae," I said.

"More like wondering why you and Chul don't want to report him to the police. We both know that wasn't a robbery. All three of those guys worked for Han-bae, and they were there looking for you."

I winced inwardly. Straight to the point. I squeezed my hands together in my lap. Explaining my world, my life, to Harrison felt about as easy as jumping off a bridge. "Chul doesn't want to report anything with Han-bae because my family wants to handle it themselves. It involves both of our families."

Harrison was quiet as I spoke but gripped the wheel a little tighter. "So did you already know Han-bae before you moved here?" he asked.

"No. I pieced it all together tonight. I think Han-bae was trying to hide his identity from me. We'd never met, but I knew of his family, the Bitgarams. He was going by the last name of Yun here."

"Why would he do that?"

"I don't know, but my brother will find out." It was true. I really didn't know. At least not all of it. I had more questions than answers, but I wanted Harrison to have this much truth, at least.

Harrison shifted. "Is this the same brother from earlier on the phone?"

I nodded. Glad he didn't remind me that I called him my stupid brother. It felt foolish now. "Yes, I only have the one brother. His name is Gun."

Harrison watched the road ahead and didn't speak for a whole minute. He finally said, "And do you trust that he can do this better than the police?"

"Yes. In my world things are settled among families. The police are rarely used."

"So, what? Are you like from a mafia family or something?"

I laughed. "No. Han-bae's family and mine are just wealthy."

"How wealthy?" he asked.

"My family has some money, but we'll never be as rich as Han-bae's." I turned to study him carefully. It was the first time I'd openly admitted my wealth, and I didn't want to upset him. Harrison seemed touchy about money. He reminded me of Grandfather who viewed all our luxury with distrust, like it was what ruined his daughter. And maybe Grandfather was right. Maybe my family would be loving, and I'd be a normal Korean student studying for the *Suneung* college entrance exam if mother had married into a middle-class family instead of Father. Maybe I would have grown up happy.

But right now, I was glad I didn't. If I had, I never would have met Harrison.

I watched his face for acceptance. I needed him to be okay with my wealth and all the crazy that followed it. "Does it bother you?" I asked.

"Han-bae's interest in you bothers me. It bothers me a lot, and I hope your brother and Chul take care of it," he said.

"They will," I answered, quickly. I waited but he didn't say more. He hadn't answered my question, not really. Before I could think of how to reword it and try again, Harrison parked in my driveway and started to get out. I was sure he planned to open my door, but the rain was still coming down.

"Wait." I stopped him with a hand on his arm. "You don't need to walk me." I turned and jumped out fast before he could protest. The rain pelted my face as I ran for the door, but Harrison appeared right next to me before I got halfway there. He held his coat high over my head as we moved together to the porch. Harrison dropped his arms and took a small step back but stayed close enough that the faint smell of pine floated over me.

He reached out and pulled a lock of wet hair from my face. "Your house is dark," he said.

I tried to control my breathing. "Chul and Sydney aren't back yet, but I have a key."

Harrison scanned the dark street. "I don't want to leave you alone. It's not safe."

I scoffed. "Their house is a vault. I'd be safe from aliens, zombies, and for sure Han-bae."

Harrison laughed. "Okay then." He stuck both hands in his pockets and looked down at his shoes. "But, hey, since we didn't get to finish that ice cream, do you want to come over, and I can make you some more? We don't have all the fancy stuff, but I think we have chocolate syrup and vanilla." He raised his eyes tentatively and looked at me.

"I can't," I said. I wasn't sure why I was saying no at this point, other than now that I was finally alone with him, I was nervous.

His face fell. "Okay, yeah, it is getting late. Maybe I'll see you tomorrow." He turned on his heel.

I watched him go, striding across the lawn toward his van. Each of his steps took him farther away, and each one felt like someone was smacking my chest with a bat. "Harrison," I called out, my voice a little louder than I wanted.

He stopped mid-stride and turned to me.

I wasn't sure what made me finally dive in, but when I saw his face, half hopeful, I got this feeling. It's the kind you read about but think doesn't actually exist. It was like my soul went—*Oh, there you are.* And right then, I think I kind of knew that there would be no turning back for me.

I knew it just by looking at his stupid, beautiful face and I ran.

Thick fear made each step heavy and painful. The crushing thought that this wouldn't work, that I never get anything good pounded through my brain, but I still didn't stop. I skidded to a halt, breathless and soaking wet as I craned my neck to squint up at Harrison through the rain. "I changed my mind," I said, breathless.

He took my hand, and it all melted away.

22

JI-HEE

Harrison's house was dark when he opened the front door. I followed him, shivering in my soaked jeans and belatedly wondered if I should have changed at my house before coming over. "Where's your family?" I asked, as we both dripped all over his foyer.

He flipped on lights. "They're out for my brother's skating competition," he said. "Here, follow me." He pulled me by the hand to a bathroom, then draped a sunny yellow towel over my head. "I'm going to change, and I'll grab you some warm clothes too. Be right back."

The room was bright and clean with a daisy shower curtain and a little kids shark toothbrush holder that held three toothbrushes. So different from how I grew up, but Harrison's house was exactly like him, warm and solid.

He was back soon holding a neatly folded hoodie and what looked like sweatpants. "Here, these are my little brother's. They'll still be big on you, but they should work."

"Thanks," I said, closing the door, more than a little embarrassed about borrowing someone else's clothing, but mine were so wet you could ring them out. I dried myself and changed before looking in the mirror. My hair was in knots, so I finger combed it the best that I could. Luckily, I hadn't worn mascara or that would be a mess. When I came out, sleeves pushed up and pants rolled at the waist, Harrison momentarily stopped digging through the freezer in the small kitchen adjacent to their family room. He turned to watch me and whistled as I walked out.

I did a little twirl and spread my arms out wide. "From Christian Dior—the baggy collection," I said.

Harrison folded his arms and smiled. "Everyone is going to want this look now that you've modeled it."

"Yeah, no," I said, laughing and walked into the family room. A beige sectional sofa took up most of the space with a small child's table and chair in place of a coffee table. Across from the sofa a tv hung on one wall and framed family pictures covered another. I took a step toward the pictures.

Harrison went back to searching his freezer. "I look dorky in those, so don't laugh," he called back to me.

"No judgment," I said, now burning with curiosity to see Harrison scrawny with braces. But I was disappointed because all of the pictures were recent with Harrison looking nothing shy of perfect. Only, I wondered for a moment if he was adopted. Everything about him from his size to coloring was completely the opposite of the rest of his family. His parents were both blonde with blue eyes. A striking contrast to Harrison's almost black hair and deep brown eyes. And where his little brother, Ozzy, was like a carbon copy of their father, lean with the same smile and an almost graceful neck, Harrison towered over both of them. But the warmth in their expressions and the father's protective arm around Harrison's shoulder all screamed loving family. For Lee family portraits, my parents had mastered frigid stares. They expect us to look perfect, not loving.

I could feel Harrison's eyes on me, and I hoped my fascination didn't bother him. "Your family is wonderful," I said softly. "How old is your little sister? She's darling."

"Becca is five going on twenty-five. Don't let that innocent face fool you. She's as bossy as she is cute," Harrison said coming into the family room. "Bad news, someone ate all the ice cream."

I did a mock frown which made him laugh. "Do that face again," he said.

I shook my head and quickly sat.

"That was the cutest frown ever. Do it again."

"No way," I said as he sank down into the sofa next to me.

Harrison took my hand. I'd lost track of how many times now, but his touch still sent electric currents racing from my fingers to my heart. The closeness made it harder to talk. The smell of his skin and warmth of his body, the way his jaw moved when he spoke—it all sent my brain into a tailspin.

I swallowed. "Does your head hurt?" I touched my own head above my eyebrow mirroring where he had his bandage.

"No."

"I'm sorry you got hurt, though. What will you tell your parents?"

"The truth." He snorted. "What are you telling yours?"

I shook my head. "My parents are different. I don't tell them stuff."

He watched my face carefully, and I tried not to squirm. "No, I'm starting to get that they're not like mine." He brushed his thumb over the top of my hand in a slow circle. "But Chul and Sydney are cool."

I laughed, all nerves. "Sometimes. But you saw how they are, all kissy, kissy. It's kind of embarrassing."

Harrison brought my hand up to his mouth and brushed his lips across on the top. I had to stifle a gasp. He grinned wickedly. "Yeah, I hate kissy, kissy."

I pulled my hand back and lightly smacked his arm, but heat rose to my face.

Harrison jumped up. "How about drinks instead of ice cream."

"I don't drink alcohol," I said.

Harrison paused on the way to the kitchen and scratched at his jaw. "Yeah, I was thinking like Coke or Gatorade, but we do have something stronger if you're feeling dangerous."

I cocked an eyebrow. "What's that?"

"California tap water, slightly warm, unfiltered, pure and concentrated. It will mess you up."

I laughed. "I'll take a Coke." I sat down and leaned back into the couch. It was old and kind of lumpy, yet still soft enough to sink deep into. Harrison came back with the sodas and sat down next to me as he popped open my drink. It was cold from the fridge and burned slightly as I sipped.

"A little sugar might make you feel better after the night you had."

I sipped at my drink again. "Stupid Han-bae," I muttered.

"So, you agree he's stupid?" Harrison raised both eyebrows, a clear question. "I've wondered if you noticed how much he follows you."

"I know more than I've let on."

"Just be careful. After tonight Han-bae will be more desperate."

I learned careful before I learned how to crawl, but I knew that wouldn't comfort Harrison. "My brother is very protective. He won't let anything happen. But I hope he doesn't try and get a bodyguard. Our family has employed one before, mostly when traveling. I don't want that." I looked down at the carpet. "They get in the way and hover."

He shook his head, even looked a little upset.

"What?"

"I could tell that you had money. I just kept hoping I was wrong, and it was Chul's money or something. I wanted you to be like a poor relative that he had taken under his wing."

I sat up straighter. "Poor?"

Harrison nodded. "I was hoping for like dirt poor. Don't worry, I'll get over my disappointment."

"You're disappointed?" I laughed. I couldn't help it. This has to be my favorite thing about him so far. I tried to keep it in, but another laugh slipped out.

Harrison cracked a grin. "Stop."

I covered my mouth, but the laughing got worse.

Harrison's own smile grew. "You know you're laughing at a poor peasant. That's what I am next to you."

I spoke around my hand clamped over my mouth. "You're not."

Harrison smiled but his voice held hurt. "Why is this so funny to you?"

I stopped and wiped at my eyes. "It's less funny and more just ironic. I'm so used to people sizing me up and judging me. You're the first person to ever think it was a bad thing that I have money. Most of the people I know think I don't have enough."

"You've been hanging out with the wrong crowd then. That settles it. If you don't want a bodyguard, I'm the next best thing. I won't hover, but I'll stay close if you let me." He looked down at our clasped hands, then he lowered his voice. "I don't think I've ever felt the way I did when I saw that guy try to pick you up." Harrison's eyes bore into mine almost pleading and I felt slightly hypnotized by the shadows that gripped him.

I wanted to lean closer and tell him everything was okay. But that would be the real lie. Without any warning, sadness spread across my chest. It filled my lungs with each breath and pushed against my ribcage.

Living here, seeing Chul and Sydney every day as a couple, and then getting close to Harrison, just being around normal people again, was a crushing reminder of how much I'd been denied. I wanted family and love, and it was right here. All I had to do was reach out and take it.

In probably one of the most impetuous moments of my life I turned to Harrison. "Do you want to go out?"

"What?" He blinked. "Oh." He cleared his throat and turned red, like he'd understood me but then overthought it. "Where else do you want to go?"

I shook my head and leaned closer. "No, do you want to date me? Be my boyfriend?" It must have been the intensity of my voice or the hard stare I leveled him, but Harrison frowned with concern like I'd just stepped onto a high wire without a pole.

I raised my chin slightly and held him with my gaze. "You don't want to?"

He gripped my hand tighter. "I want to. I just want to make sure you do. You've had a hard night. Will you feel this way tomorrow?"

"I know what I want. I want us to see each other all the time, save each other's seats, eat together at lunch, hang out on the weekends. I think that's how it works. We might even kiss." I tried to sound confident but felt a blush creep up my neck. My last sentence came out a mere whisper. "I've never kissed anyone."

Harrison moved fast. One minute we were miles apart, the next, his hands held me, one hand warm at the base of my skull, fingers laced in my hair, and the other softly against my face. His lips were already on mine and the fire that sparked was like the first strike of a match, crisp and new, with a perfect flare. Harrison made it all effortless. His hands and mouth turned coaxing, and I softened against him, moving even closer. That was all it took. In an instant our little match exploded and raged until I couldn't tell where I ended and he began. I could only hold him and wonder at how so suddenly, we fused and bound together.

That's what it felt like to kiss Harrison, like if we stopped—and I never wanted to stop—part of me would remain and become part of him. Falling for Harrison was changing me. I knew that now. I would have to bend and reform in ways that I didn't yet understand.

And I wanted it.

23

HARRISON

I drove the few blocks to Chul and Sydney's house in Mom's old Honda Odyssey. Ji-hee had already seen it but that had been at night. In the light of day there was no hiding that it had so many smashed fries in the seats, no amount of vacuuming would ever get it clean. It bothered me, but Jeff needed the car today.

I rang the bell and waited. The camera on the security system glowed green. Three cameras above me and one to the right moved into focus.

Chul's voice came over the speaker. "Hey, Harrison. Ji-hee will be right out."

"Okay," I said. I kicked my shoe against the cement of the porch. Chul had never invited me inside their home, and I was curious to see how they lived. Maybe now that Ji-hee and I were together she'd invite me inside.

The door opened and Ji-hee walked out. I expected her to beam at me and gush. I wanted her to. Her eyes flitted from mine, and then she ducked her face before walking past me. "Thanks for giving me a ride." Her voice was too high.

We'd texted last night after I dropped her off. After our kiss. Then

I was up at five thinking about her. I texted her at seven to see if she wanted a ride to school, and she'd said yes.

I stopped her by grabbing her backpack and swinging her around easily. When she faced me, I took a step closer. She smelled like flowers or cherries or both. I couldn't decide. "What's wrong?" I asked.

Her eyes went round, and she blinked into the sun. "Nothing," she said.

"Are you upset?"

"No."

She was.

She rubbed the tip of her nose like it itched so I leaned down and kissed it. She opened her mouth in surprise, and I met her lips.

The kiss was meant to be a soft caress, but Ji-hee sighed into it and that sound was like a switch in my head. All the self-control I thought I had went out the window.

I broke the kiss and stepped back, feeling hot all over. I cleared my throat. "Are you worried about seeing Han-bae at school?" I asked.

She looked down and twisted her grandmother's gold ring on her finger. "No, not really. I'm just unsure."

"About what?" I asked. I wished she would look at me.

"About us."

It was like a kick in the gut. No, a kick to the head. "Are you regretting our kiss?"

She ducked her head and a small smile curved at her lips. "Of course not. I'm not regretting that we are a couple." She sucked in a shuddering breath and quickly said. "But I'm not sure what the rules are. Or how to act."

I didn't think. My arms wrapped around her, drawing her close. Closer.

I held her until it felt like I could breathe again. I didn't know the rules either. The rule with Regan had been don't make her mad, which is about as far from love as you can get. The rule with my family was don't be different, also lacking. But any rule for Ji-hee had to be as pure and perfect as she was. "What rules do you want? I'll follow any rule you give me." I would too. The parts of me that Ji-hee tugged on felt invincible, like nothing she could ever ask of me would be too much.

"I don't want to give you rules," she said. "I think we both know the basics. But . . . I don't want to make mistakes. I want you to think I'm normal."

I laughed. "I've never thought you weren't."

She shook her head. "But I'm not like you. I'm cracked and broken, full of secrets. You're like the lead in a movie. You live in a suburb. You're super-hot. You drive a minivan."

I winced. Maybe in Korea a minivan wasn't a negative status symbol.

She didn't stop. "You have this wonderful family that loves you. You go to a school where everyone's biggest concern is who to sit by at lunch. Your best friend lives down the street. Your house has pictures with everyone smiling on the wall." She wrapped her arms protectively around herself. A motion I realized was well practiced. "I'm not like that," she breathed. "It scares me that I won't be normal enough for you."

I didn't have the words to comfort her. Ji-hee didn't just come from a different country. I was acutely aware she was from a different world with her wealth and whatever ghosts had chased her here. Calling her normal was like calling an erupting volcano an everyday thing. Normal wasn't the word you'd use. Majestic, awe-inspiring, freaking cool. Ji-hee was all of those things. "You're far above normal," I said. "I don't want you to be anything but you." I leaned down and kissed her again.

We entered calculus class late while holding hands. Calvin let out a whoop and grinned at us, but I was too busy scanning the room for Han-bae to celebrate. Ji-hee did the same. Her posture relaxed as we both realized he wasn't there.

"That's enough out of you, Calvin," Ms. Smars said. She gave me a hard look and said, "Find your seats."

"He's not here," I whispered as we wove through the seats. I passed Regan on my right, and she gave me a discreet thumbs up from her lap. We sat on the back row across from each other. I leaned over. "What do you think that means?"

"It means he won't be coming back," she said with confidence. I wondered what she wasn't telling me about him.

Class was over too soon. Ji-hee had dutifully listened to Ms. Smars give the lesson and then finished her assignment.

I'd tried not to stare at her legs.

Today she wore a white skirt that landed just at her knees, some seriously expensive looking tennis shoes, and a pale blue tee shirt. No one wore skirts to Bishop High. But Ji-hee did and I freaking loved it.

JI-HEE

It was weird eating lunch with Harrison. Maybe because I'd spent so many days convincing myself that I didn't want to, that the very last thing I would ever want in the whole wide world would be to have Harrison sit down next to me. It was a tough lie to sell myself. And now that the lies were over, and we were sitting together, eating together, walking in the halls together, it was even more amazing than any of the little fantasies I'd tried to fight off.

When I lived in Korea, we had a gardener that would let me help plant in the spring. He'd dig holes and have me pull new plants from little plastic containers and then place them down in the hole, filling it in with dirt and water. When the roots came out of the containers, they were always bound up tight in knots. I'd imagined those roots taking a sigh of relief and uncoiling themselves in the soil, no more plastic barrier, no living in a shed. That little plant could stretch and grow as tall as it could reach in the sun.

That's how I felt with Harrison. It felt like stretching and unwinding after being in a dark shed.

Harmony and Diana still sat with me at lunch. Harmony wasn't jealous, or if she was, she hid it well, and for that I gave her loyalty points. Diana was just her usual awkward self and even asked Harrison if he was worried about his reputation.

"Why? Why would I worry about my reputation?" he asked.

"Well," Diana shrugged. "We're like the outcasts of Bishop High."

"Come on Diana. We're not that bad," Harmony squirmed in her seat, clearly embarrassed by Diana's self-deprecation.

"We are though," Diana argued. "I mean. You guys are the only friends I have in this school. Most of these kids have known each other since kindergarten and I was homeschooled until last year."

"That doesn't mean anything," Harrison said. "You guys are all new. You just need to get to know the rest of the school. You'll make more friends."

"That and you need to stop sewing your own clothes," Harmony pointed out. "Seriously, you should let me take you shopping so we can buy you some real jeans."

I took a bite and tried not to roll my eyes.

"What?" Harmony asked. "Spit it out Ji-hee."

"It's just that all of her clothes are better quality than anything that you'd find in the mall. I mean, look at her shirt. It's skillfully tailored. You don't find stitches like that in off-the-rack retail."

"I guess," Harmony said. "It's just seriously retro. Like grandma retro."

I smiled at Diana. "You have your own signature style. All the great icons did. Keep your clothes, maybe just add some jewelry."

Diana took a sip of her milk and nodded. "My mom won't let me shop at stores, anyway so even if I wanted to wear jeans and tee shirts I couldn't."

"Maybe I can bring you some shoes," Harmony added. "You can keep them in your locker and change before you go home."

I nodded at this. "Losing sandals with the athletic socks look will take you next level with fashion."

Harrison leaned close and whispered. "Your friends are nice. Nicer actually, than a lot of my friends."

I smiled and fed him one of my french fries. "Thanks," I said.

"Can you come to my house after school?" he asked.

I shook my head. "Sydney and Chul want to talk with me about something important."

"Did they say what it was?"

I dropped my voice. "I'm pretty sure it's to tell me Han-bae has hightailed it back to Korea and I'm free to enjoy the rest of the school year."

"Will you text me after? You can still come over."

"Sydney wants to have some girl time tonight but—" I met his eyes and made sure to smile brightly "Pick me up in the morning?"

Harrison nodded. "Okay, yeah."

I leaned over and brushed my fingertips along his arm. I would never get tired of being this close to Harrison. "Do you want to eat at my house tomorrow? Sydney can't cook to save her life, but if I ask, Chul will make Korean food. Want to try it?"

He grinned. "Yes."

I loved that his smile was some mix of deep caring and mischievous boy. But it made my heart ache a little because I'd just lied to him.

It was true that I couldn't go to his house today, but it wasn't because of Sydney or Chul. I needed to be alone when I talked with Han-bae. My phone call had to be a knock-down, sweep-the-place-clean kind of conversation. I needed to obliterate any hope Han-bae ever had, and when I was done, he would know there was no chance, less than zero, of us being together. We weren't friends, and I would never agree to marry him.

24

JI-HEE

I unlocked the front door and hurried inside Chul and Sydney's house. The love birds wouldn't be home for another hour, plenty of time to call Han-bae.

"Hello, Ji-hee."

I whipped my head around. Gun sat serenely on the living room sofa like he belonged there. "I missed you, little sister." His voice sounded rough, like he'd been crying, but Gun never cried.

I stood there, too startled to say anything. I hadn't seen my brother in three years. He was different than I remembered him, more angular, and his eyes had a heaviness to them now.

Before I could turn away from those eyes, ignore him, and pretend I hadn't seen his pain, little cracks formed around my hardened heart. I didn't want to forgive him this easily. I swallowed hard. "Hi," I said. My voice came out flat. Only I couldn't bring myself to say more.

Gun stood up. He was taller too. "Nice to see you," he said.

"What are you doing here?" I asked.

"My little sister is getting harassed. You think I wouldn't show up?"

I sighed. "I've told you, I can take care of myself."

Gun walked to the foyer and gave me a gentle hug. "I want you to come home now." I pushed away and Gun's arms dropped to his side. He stood there with slumped shoulders looking even more dejected than I did. Which wasn't fair. "Mother knows Marklem Academy is fake," he said.

My stomach dropped to the floor. "You told her?" A question and accusation all at once.

"I did. When I realized Jung Bitgaram followed you to California."

"You idiot," I snapped.

"Mother needed to know how serious it's gotten. I thought a pretend school in California would hide you long enough to give Mother time." Gun took a deep breath. "But none of this worked."

I threw my hands up in the air. "What could Mother possibly need time for?"

"Time to unwind her mistakes." Gun grimaced. "To come to grips with the idea that she can't let the Bitgarams have you no matter what it costs us."

Something about the way my brother stood, the look in his eyes, the way he spoke, alerted me to danger. Like someone had just placed a live wire on the ground between us and now it was writhing around. I felt the hairs on my arms prickle with alarm.

Gun blew out a breath. "Mother wants—"

"Honestly I don't care what she wants," I said. Fear or no, I wouldn't back down on this. I wouldn't leave Harrison.

"She's still our mother."

I folded my arms. "I'm not going back to Korea."

"You'll be safer there."

"Like I was safe in London? What's your plan once I'm back home? Hide me in my room? Mother won't want me to show my face once this scandal erupts. I'm sure when she tells the Bitgarams that the marriage is off they'll spread rumors about how I was an unsuitable match for Han-bae. The fall out of this will be way worse than Daeshim and those stupid pictures." I laughed. "Or maybe this time you'll send me somewhere *safer* than London. Why not a maximum-security prison? I'm sure Mother can bribe the right judge to lock me up and throw away the key."

Gun scrubbed a hand down his face and sighed. "Enough of the dramatics. Mother's not hiding you or locking you up."

"You sent me to reform school for drug addicts when I was basically a kid. I'm hardly being dramatic, brother."

"No, not me. *I* didn't send you anywhere. I was a kid too," he snapped. "You've acted like this was my decision, but I begged Mother not to send you away. I screamed and yelled and threatened. In the end I was just a dumb high schooler with no idea who or what we were dealing with." Gun was breathing hard. "I didn't do anything, Ji-hee. I was only powerless to stop it."

I glared. "Don't give me that. Don't act like you suffered on my behalf. You were the one to pack my bags in the car. You sat with me on the ride to the airport and told me London would be okay. You lied to me Gun."

"I didn't lie," he said. "I hoped it would be."

"You hoped?" I gritted my teeth together. "Do you know they did a full strip search the moment I got there? They took my clothes and my phone. We weren't even allowed to wear shoes in that school."

"I didn't know it would be that bad. There was almost nothing online, just that it was an all-girls school."

"Then why send me there? Why Gun? Why did Mother choose such an awful place?"

Gun crossed his arms over his chest. "It was Myang Bitgaram who suggested the school."

I stilled. "What?"

Gun rubbed his eyes. "Myang planned it so well, but none of us were paranoid enough to see what was really happening. She wouldn't tell Mother how she knew, but she said she'd heard you were in trouble. Then she presented the school as someplace to keep you safe. Shortly after that Myang offered even more protection with a marriage contract to her son. She told Mother they would invest in JAYNE talent after you were married."

"I thought it was Mother who talked Myang into the contract, not the other way around. Myang didn't know me. Why would she risk her only son marrying someone she didn't know? We have nothing to offer a family like theirs."

"Oh, Myang Bitgaram knew all about your life. By the time you were a freshman at Daeshim, she knew who your friends were, and that you'd gone on a date with Chul. She'd been following you very closely."

Acid churned in my gut. Gun couldn't mean what I thought he was saying.

"She met you *before* she approached Mother. She went to your elementary school. It's taken me forever to dig through everything, but Myang Bitgaram was listed as a guest speaker in Mrs. Cho's class for your third term. You would have been ten years old."

My mind raced trying to remember. I'd never seen so much as a picture of Myang. No one had. Everyone in the Elite seemed to know of them, but they were more like legends. The Bitgarams didn't show up at any of the events. They didn't do social media. They didn't donate or build museums. So, few people had actually met them.

"I think Myang went to your school for one reason, to find a wife for her son. I'm sure she was after someone Elite but not of the highest tier of wealth, someone financially vulnerable so she could control and manipulate the situation with money. She wanted a girl that she could groom to be exactly what she wanted for her son."

"What are you talking about? I can't be controlled. I'm me, Gun."

"That's just it, though. For three years she did control you. She was the one that paid the photographer to take those pictures of you. She tried to make our family think you were being blackmailed but it was all just to make Mother vulnerable enough to send you away."

I stuttered. "I thought . . . Didn't Min order the pictures and then she paid that photographer to blame you?"

Gun shook his head. "It was never Min. All of that was Myang. I have proof now."

I swayed a little on my feet.

"But that's not all of it," Gun said. "She bought the reform school in London the year before you arrived there."

My mouth hung open. "She owned that freaking school." My voice rose. "The school that treated me like trash."

"The day after you left, Mother tried to arrange a visit, but the school wouldn't let us see you."

"Schools can't do that," I said. "Why didn't you call our lawyers?"

"Mother did, only to have Myang sweep in and convince her to drop the whole thing. She said that the school might have some unconventional methods but what mattered was your safety."

"And Mother bought that?" But of course, she did. Mother always put money ahead of us.

Gun raked his hands through his hair. "I tried everything. I even flew to the school myself and tried to get in. Nothing I did worked, and Mother is too scared to go against Myang."

I swallowed, feeling queasy.

Gun let out a heavy breath. "If Chul hadn't helped me I wouldn't have been able to get you out. When I realized that Myang owned the school, I told mother enough was enough and to break off the engagement." He shook his head. "She said the contract is unbreakable."

"No engagement is unbreakable," I said.

Gun shrugged. "Mother still wouldn't end it, so I made up Marklem Academy. I had to bribe a bunch of the staff in London and pull a full-on con just to get you out. Then I got Grandfather involved. I knew you wouldn't get on a plane if I called you."

It made some sort of mad sense now. The guard getting me up in the middle of the night, Grandfather acting so strange. Gun had schemed to get me out because Myang would never have let me go. "Myang is absolutely crazy to do all this, and over a stupid marriage contract. She could have any girl she wanted for her son. It didn't have to be me."

Gun nodded. "Totally crazy. But Myang is worse than mother. She probably planned this from the day she met you. Do you remember her? Think back. Did a woman ever come to Mrs. Cho's class when you were little?"

I remembered. I sat down. Right there on the floor, right in the middle of the foyer I sat down before I fell down.

My teacher Mrs. Cho seemed nervous and then, by the end, agitated. After, we were told she quit, but all the girls knew she'd been fired. We were Elite, and our school was to train us into the adults that would run empires. No mistakes were allowed. Somehow, Mrs. Cho had made a mistake.

"Alright girls," Mrs. Cho beamed at us. "We have a special visitor all the way from Switzerland. Mrs. B is going to be speaking to you about the importance of tradition in modern families."

Seo-yeon elbowed me and nodded at the woman standing at the head of our classroom. "I want to be just like her when I grow up," she whispered.

I stared at the woman's long shiny hair swept gracefully around one shoulder. She had a strange name, but she could have been any of our mothers with that blue Hermes Birkin balanced on one arm. Only this woman also wore a ruby and diamond encrusted tiara.

Mrs. Cho kept glancing at it oddly, but Mrs. B ignored her. She acted like it was the most natural thing in the world to wear a tiara to school. Mrs. B stepped ahead of Mrs. Cho, as if she were the one in charge that day. She smiled with a perfectly made-up mouth, but her hands looked bony and sharp. All of her looked sharp. "I'm sure you're wondering why I'm wearing this crown today," she said.

Most of the girls stared with glittering eyes. Seo-yeon giggled next to me and rocked side to side in her seat. I stayed perfectly still.

"I'm wearing this today because I'm looking for a very special girl." Mrs. B began pacing the room. "I'm looking for a girl that I will make into a princess."

There was a unified gasp, and then the girls in the room started whispering, some raising their hands. Seo-yeon grabbed my arm and shouted. "Oh, me." Which earned a sharp look from Mrs. Cho.

Mrs. B stopped pacing and studied our reactions. I didn't like her eyes. They were like hard black rocks. They made her look like a doll instead of a mother. But she kept coming back to me, staring with beady doll eyes. I knew why. I wasn't a princess. Maybe I would be asked to leave.

Seo-yeon shot to her feet. "I'm a princess. Choose me. Choose me."

Mother told me that princesses never wanted to play in the dirt, but I did. I liked the soft dirt in the garden and the bugs. I loved the wet sand at the beach, even though Mother made me sit under the umbrella shade with her on a silk blanket so I couldn't feel the little grains between my toes. Mrs. B would choose Seo-yeon instead of me. I was glad. I didn't want to give up on dirt.

Mrs. B made a delicate sound that might have been a laugh, but it sounded mean. "I will interview each of you to find the real princess."

"Excuse me," Mrs. Cho interrupted. Her face had clouded, and she clasped both hands tightly together like she did when someone failed a term test. "You are supposed to be a guest speaker. I wasn't told about any interviews."

Mrs. B swung sharply toward our teacher, and Mrs. Cho seemed to shrink lower. "What I mean is." Mrs. Cho spoke softly. "We don't really have time for more than an hour. I know the girls would love to hear about keeping tradition."

Mrs. B nodded to her assistant in the back of the room who left quickly. "What I'm doing was tradition during the Joseon dynasty. You should know that."

Soon Mrs. Cho was called away to the office and Mrs. B conducted interviews in the back of the room for the rest of the day. She interviewed me last. I was glad, but even more glad when she left. I was tired when she finally announced that only one of us was a princess. "You will get your crown when you are older," she said on her way out.

It wasn't me. Everyone knew it was Seo-yeon. She bragged for weeks until I was sick to death of princess talk. But Mrs. B never came back with her tiara, and we eventually forgot about the whole affair.

"Ji-hee, what's wrong? Get up. Please." Gun reached down and lifted me from the floor by my arms. "Are you okay? You're so pale."

I stood but wobbled on unsteady legs. "It was her. It was Myang." I grabbed my brother's hand urgently. "She came to my school."

"That's what I'm trying to tell you," Gun said softly. "It's always been her."

Tears welled in my eyes, and I moved in a daze as Gun led me to the sofa with heavy lines creasing his forehead. I could see it now; his eyes were red and swollen. He *had* been crying. "It's okay," he said. "I'll protect you from her."

"I need a moment to think," I said.

Gun nodded and sat down next to me.

Mother became friends with Myang when I was in eighth grade. I knew because at first, she talked about her nonstop. Whenever Myang was in Korea she invited mother to her residence for private lunches. Mother would come home exhilarated, talking about the money the Bitgarams had. *"More than the Kangs, even,"* she'd whispered.

But none of us paid attention. Gun and I were just glad she wasn't nagging about how we needed to network at school more. Father was always too deep in his drinking to notice anything amiss. Not once did we stop to wonder why the richest of the Elite would choose to befriend one of the lowest.

And that's what my family was. The fact that we only had one family jet, that Gun and I never had our own didn't seem shameful to me. It did to Mother.

If Myang had watched me, if somehow, she'd chosen me that day she came to my school, Mother would never have seen it. The little things she should have picked up on, those red flags. She would have missed them all, if it meant she could be friends with all that money.

Myang's game plan had been to mold me into some kind of Stepford Wife. She'd sent my mother into a spiral of fear that my reputation would be ruined and then isolated me in a school she controlled. It was the kind of fear and manipulation tactics that were used in war. But we were Elite. Everything with us was war.

I didn't blame Mother anymore. It would be like blaming a dog for wanting a bone. And if it was Myang we were up against, then Gun couldn't have done more than he did.

"I'm not going back," I said. My voice was dull from the shock of it all, but hearing my own words began to stir something in me.

"You have to," Gun said.

I sat up straighter a slow anger beginning to boil. It started low and spread outward until each of my bones seemed to vibrate with seething.

"Do you know where Myang is?"

"She's in Korea. She flew there after you left London and Han-bae came here."

"Han-bae isn't here," I said. "He wasn't at school today. I think he went back to Switzerland."

Gun shook his head. "Chul has been tracking his location, and he hasn't left the country."

I felt a stab of worry. "Where is he right now?"

25

HARRISON

The doorbell rang a minute before Mom poked her head in. "A friend is here to see you," she said.

Maybe it was Ji-hee. I rolled off the bed and tucked my phone into my back pocket as I walked down the hall, glad something finally stopped me from doom scrolling. When I rounded the corner Han-bae sat at the kitchen table. I jerked to a stop but kept my face blank, trying to assess any treat he could be to my family. Mom stood at the stove stirring something that smelled like split pea soup. That's where I wanted to keep her. I calmly entered the kitchen and nodded at Han-bae with an all-business look. "Let's go for a walk."

Han-bae stood up and followed me. It made me twitchy to have him at my back so I turned slightly until I could see him in my peripheral and opened the door for him to leave first. I thought about closing and locking it in his face, but I wanted to know why he was here, so I followed him out. His I'm-a-stupid-rich-kid Suburban was parked and still running in front of my house.

"Let's talk in my truck," he said.

I bristled. "You could have just texted me that you wanted to talk outside."

"Your mother invited me in."

I cocked an eyebrow at him. "Because you rang the doorbell."

He sighed. "I wasn't sure you'd talk with me unless I actually showed up at your house, and I really need to talk with you," he said.

And I really needed to rub his face on the cement, but I pushed my anger down. If I wanted to protect Ji-hee then I had to know what was up with this guy beyond he was a jerk with money. I folded my arms. "Okay, let's talk."

He walked around his Suburban and got in as I causally approached. Inwardly I was cautious as I opened the passenger door and let my eyes flick to the back. No thugs. I climbed in and turned to Han-be but he didn't say anything. I waited.

"You don't know everything about Ji-hee," he finally said.

"Clearly, you don't know anything," I shot back.

"I know that she's my fiancé."

That stopped me. Everything stopped, maybe even my heart. "Explain that," I said quietly.

Han-bae sighed and wiped his hand down his face. "My mother and Ji-hee's mother signed a marriage agreement. Then, about a year ago two of our lawyers showed up at my school with a bunch of documents for me to sign. They said it was for a marriage with a girl named Lee, Ji-hee. I don't actually know what it was that I signed. The lawyer didn't give me a chance to read any of it, but I know it involved business agreements. I saw the words, JAYNE talent agency, and that's the business owned by Ji-hee's family. My guess is that after we get married, my family will invest and get part of the stock." He sighed. "Not that we need any more stock but that's how it's done in our world."

"If you didn't know what the papers said then why did you sign it?" I asked.

Han-bae laughed. "Saying no to my parents gets me more than lost phone privileges."

I shook my head. Was this guy lying? He had to be. Ji-hee couldn't be engaged. She was my age.

"Look, I know to you it sounds shocking but sometimes children are treated like commodities. Ji-hee's family has a relatively small portfolio. They only own one company, and my mother saw a way to exploit that to get what she wanted."

"What did your mother want?" I asked.

Han-bae looked me square in the eye. "She wanted Ji-hee. My parents are dead set on controlling every aspect of my future, down to who and when I marry. This is normal in a world with billions at stake, but my mother is extreme."

"So what? You're saying Ji-hee's taken and I should back off. That you're in charge and she has no choice?"

"No. I came here to try and protect Ji-hee."

I laughed. "Protect her? You didn't protect her from those guys you hired?"

Han-bae held up a hand. "Not me. I didn't hire those idiots. My mother did. I was just trying to run interference before they got to her. If you hadn't butted in, I could have gotten her to come with me and controlled the situation."

I raised my voice. "That's not what it looked like."

Han-bae stayed quiet and nodded. "I get it. You don't like me, and I really don't like you, but knock the chip off your shoulder long enough to listen. I'll tell you what's going on, and maybe we can help each other."

I narrowed my eyes at Han-bae. "Why should I trust you?"

"Because we're worried about the same person. I'm never going to force Ji-hee to do anything, but my mother will. She'll start by hurting those closest to Ji-hee, like her brother. If that doesn't give her control, then she'll hurt Ji-hee. And if Ji-hee doesn't bend she'll destroy her."

My mouth felt dry. "I'm listening."

Han-bae leaned back in his seat. "As far as I can tell my mother started this plan sometime near the end of my freshman year. She sent me a picture of Ji-hee and told me that my future wife attended a school in London. I wasn't happy about it, but I knew better than to argue with my parents. I believed that since my mother choose her, they were like friends or something. I had this false story in my head that my mother was training her to be a spy, and that my future wife would dictate to me the way my mother does. I'm sure it sounds paranoid, but I moved to my boarding school in Switzerland when I was ten years old. That was the best day of my life. Having freedom from my mother was, and still is, the main drive in my life."

I shook my head. "Enough with the sob story. I don't feel sorry for you."

Han-bae rolled his eyes, but the guy was weak. He sat up straighter. "I knew I couldn't entirely get out of the life that was planned for me, but I hoped whomever I married would at least be an ally. I wanted to know what kind of girl Ji-hee was and how deep she was in my mother's pocket. So, I dug around until I found the name of her school and paid some guy to get her file." Han-bae looked at me. "Did Ji-hee tell you about the place she was at in London?"

I shook my head.

"It was a type of reform school but for the very worst of kids. My mother purchased it so she would have full control while keeping Ji-hee there. Her file said that she wasn't allowed outside communication with her family. She was on the strictest tract, the one reserved for violent kids. And that's when I knew. Ji-hee wasn't friends with my mother. My mother was trying to break her."

"If she was supposed to marry into your family then why would your mother want to hurt her? How does that help anyone?"

Han-bae looked at a loss for words but then simply said, "Because my mother's crazy."

"Nuts," I agreed.

"My mother has always believed in force, that control is the only way to parent. She thought this would make Ji-hee compliant. She wanted a daughter-in-law with a clean slate. Someone who didn't love anyone, including her family. Someone with no close relationships."

I took a deep breath. Hearing this made me sick. I wanted to punch the dashboard and part of me still felt like it was a good idea to punch Han-bae's face, but I focused on control.

"I know her," Han-bae continued. "She would have thought that when Ji-hee graduated she could swoop in with attention, love, and most importantly money. She thought Ji-hee would become dependent on her."

"That'd never would work on Ji-hee," I said.

"No, it wouldn't, and I hoped that when we both graduated, we could run away together."

I tried to keep my rage in check, but weird rich family aside, the idea of Han-bae and Ji-hee running off together was wrong on so many levels. The first being that she didn't like Han-bae.

"But then Ji-hee went and messed it all up," he said. "She left the school early."

"Hold up," I said. "What do you mean by *messed it up*? How is any of this her fault? You said it was an awful school. Why wouldn't she leave."

Han-bae shook his head. "She was safe there. My mother was going to leave her be until she graduated. And I don't know what her brother was thinking. She took a public flight here. My mother found out where she was within hours of her landing. The only reason she hasn't flown out here personally is because I begged to come first. I was hoping I could convince Ji-hee to come back to Switzerland with me. I'm pretty sure my mother will allow her attend school there. I'd protect her, and when the time is right, we can both live abroad."

I held up my hand. "Stop, just stop. Ji-hee's not going anywhere with you."

"If you cared about her then you'd tell her to go."

I laughed. "That's not how it works."

Han-bae frowned. "You can't keep her safe."

"I'm not telling my girl to run off with a guy that thinks he can help her but can't. You said yourself that you knew better than to go against your parents. You'll do whatever your mommy tells you to do."

Han-bae's face went dark. "You don't know what Ji-hee's up against. The only way Ji-hee wins is if she comes with me."

I'd heard enough. I got out of the car.

.   .   .

I waited until after dinner before sitting on my bed and typing out the text to Ji-hee.

How can you be engaged?

I stared at the words. They looked so surreal on the screen. That word *engaged*. It was a word for your late twenties, early thirties. No one got engaged at seventeen. I deleted them. They sounded like an accusation, and how could she answer that question? What could she say that wouldn't humiliate herself and infuriate me?

I wished Han-bae was lying, but I didn't think he was, at least, not completely. Maybe Ji-hee never agreed to it. She probably hadn't been given a choice. Then what right did I have grilling her on it? If I asked point blank, I didn't see a scenario that worked for us. Everything felt like a dead end.

Getting Ji-hee to go out with me, to actually be my girlfriend, felt like winning some cosmic version of the lottery. But it had only been one day, and now, someone just told me my ticket wasn't valid.

I called her.

She picked up on the first ring. "Harrison." Her voice came out a little shaky. "Are you at your house?"

"Yeah. Why?"

"Did Han-bae stop by? Chul said his truck was there."

I pinched the bridge of my nose hard before answering. "Yeah, he was here."

"Did he . . . what did he say?"

That question hung like dead weight between us until I answered in the easiest way that I could for Ji-hee. If there was going to be any kind of crash landing, I wanted it soft for her. I swallowed hard. "He was here, and we talked. I set him straight and told him you weren't a couple and to bug off."

"Did he say anything else?" she asked.

"Nothing important," I said.

I could hear Ji-hee talking to someone off the line. "He did go there," she said.

"Ji-hee?"

"Yeah." Her voice quivered like she was about to cry.

"It's okay."

She sniffed on the phone.

"Can I come over?" I asked.

"I'm not . . . I'm not sure it's a good time right now," she said. "My brother is here."

My throat burned dry and hot as I spoke. "That's okay," I said. "Can I pick you up in the morning?"

"Um, no." She didn't say more but made a little desperate sound in the back of her throat.

"Are you sure?" I asked.

"I'll need to miss school tomorrow." Her voice came out strained. "I just have a few things to work out with my brother."

I nodded even though she couldn't see me. But what could I say to that?

"Bye," she said.

I hung up and the emptiness surrounded me.

26

JI-HEE

Last night Harrison sounded mad or maybe sad. I wasn't sure there was a difference in my mind. Both were wrong. I never wanted him to be anything but happy with me. But when he asked to come over, I wondered if he wanted me to say no. Like he was just asking because that's what he was supposed to ask me, and that thought made me more determined to fix things with Han-bae and by fix, I meant erase. We had never been an item. I didn't agree to an engagement, and I wanted out. What more was there for him to understand?

I could smell charred bread when I got out of the shower and knew Sydney had tried cooking again. Last week it'd been eggs and the first day I'd been here she tried to fry tofu. That ended with a slick oily mess in the sink. Sydney had this magic power. She managed to burn every food item she touched. There was lingering smoke in the hallway, but when I entered the kitchen, I let out a sigh of relief. Chul was flipping pancakes on the griddle. Sydney sat at the bar and dreamily took a bite dripping with syrup.

She turned when she heard me approach. "Oh, you're up. It's still so early. I thought you'd sleep longer." She patted the soft stool next to her. "Come, sit and eat. Chul made us my favorite. Sorry about the smell. I burned a whole loaf of bread trying to make french toast."

"It wasn't a whole loaf," Chul said, defending his wife.

"Everything but the heels," Sydney said.

"Hmm . . ." He looked down and concentrated hard on the griddle. "Maybe we should start looking at hiring a helper. Just someone to cook a little when we're both busy."

Sydney grinned. "Nice try, but no. Besides, I love your pancakes, and you make them every time I mess up in the kitchen."

Chul sighed and flipped another pancake. "It's just that we have a lot pancakes."

It was true. Chul didn't cook very many Korean dishes because Sydney was so picky. She'd eat black bean noodles, but none of my favorite soups or kimchi. Most of our meals were take-out or pancakes. I sat down just as Gun walked in from the garage door. "Are you packed, little sister?" he asked.

Sydney slid a plate with a stack of pancakes in front of me. "No, I told you last night," I said. "I'm not leaving California."

Gun groaned and walked over to sit down next to me. "I'm going to explain it one more time. Listen carefully," Gun said.

I crossed both arms and leaned back in my chair. "You can explain it a hundred times, but I won't agree to go back with you."

"We can keep you safe in Korea. It's home. It's where you belong," he said.

Gun was wrong. It wasn't my home. I sighed. "If I go back with you, I'll have to deal with Mother *and* Myang, not to mention all the gossip mongers. At least here, there's only Han-bae lurking in the shadows."

"But that's just the thing. He's actually lurking. You're not safe here."

"I have a boyfriend here. I have nothing in Korea."

"Is that what this is?" Gun smacked the table. "If you're thinking you can't leave over some dumb boy, think again. You're too young for anything serious."

Sydney made a noise that sounded like she was trying not to laugh and covered her mouth with her hand.

I took a bite of my pancake and chewed softly instead of grinding my teeth. Who was Gun to tell me I was too young? I'd basically been on my own since freshman year. I swallowed and politely wiped my mouth with a napkin before speaking. "Brother," I said sweetly. "I will be looking over my shoulder in any country I live in. The Bitgarams can find me anywhere. Staying here and trying to reason with Han-bae is our best option right now. And as far as the dumb boy goes, he's not dumb and hardly a boy. His name is Harrison. You should meet him before you call him names."

"I'm not meeting him and Mother said I couldn't come back without you."

"The answer is still no." I looked at Sydney. "I can get my own place if you want."

Sydney was quick to jump in. "No way. We love having you. Stay as long as you'd like."

Chul flipped another pancake. "If you're in the States, you should absolutely be with us. You wouldn't be safe on your own. But what will you do about the engagement? Your mother still hasn't agreed to break it."

"As long as I'm not in Korea, Myang's contract doesn't hold. They can't force me to marry someone if I'm not there, and if my mother wants me home, she'll have to drag me."

Chul winced and I knew what he was thinking. My mother could easily hire any number of security personnel that would carry me kicking and screaming onto her own private jet. He was right, but that was the only way I would go. I wouldn't leave Harrison willingly, and I would never, ever marry Han-bae.

I loved my mother in a distant sort of way. She'd birthed me and allowed me to be raised well by nannies. But that didn't mean she could ruin my life. She'd already done that once. I turned to my brother. "I won't follow her anymore, and you shouldn't either. Let Mother do what she will. It can't be worse than losing who we are."

Gun leveled me with a hard stare. "You've forgotten how cruel she can be."

"I haven't forgotten. I can just see more clearly that she doesn't own us. In seven months, I'll be a legal adult."

"She can disown you," he said. "She can leave you penniless."

"Then I'm penniless." I shrugged. "But I still own my life." My brother stared at me with all the fear and pain he'd felt from the last three years. He didn't hide anything, and I took it from him with open arms. Gun tried so hard. He'd worked to shield me from the worst of it, but both of us had so many bullet holes I couldn't count them anymore. "I'll call Mother in a few days. After she cools down. You go home," I said.

He shuddered like a cold breeze circled around him. For a moment I thought he'd argue. But he took a deep breath and then said, "Okay, I don't know how long this life here will last, but I'm willing to let you have your way with two conditions." He held up a finger. "First is you agree to stay here. I don't want you staying in a hotel alone, or worse trying to rent a place."

Sydney clapped her hands and smiled.

"What's the second?" I asked.

"Chul and I need to go have a talk with Han-bae."

I started to say I'd go with them, but Gun held up his hand.

"Alone," he said. "We need to talk with him alone."

I wouldn't argue with Gun anymore. Not when he'd agreed to let me keep the only thing I wanted. Harrison.

HARRISON

"What do you mean she's not coming?" Calvin said. He pointed over my shoulder. "I see Ji-hee right there."

I turned around and there she was. The morning sun glowed from the front hall windows behind Ji-hee as she walked toward me, moving and breathing with all the allure of a modern-day goddess.

Her hair flowed down, just below her shoulders, in soft layers that bounced against her deep red shirt. She wore dark blue jeans that were baggy at the bottom but hugged the curves at her waist, hips, and thighs.

I liked so much about Ji-hee that had nothing to do with her looks, but I really liked her in those jeans. I tried to imagine what she would look like if she was ugly, but I couldn't. She was just Ji-hee, and that made her pretty. So pretty.

"Close your mouth," Calvin said. "You're acting like you've never seen a girl before."

Ji-hee stopped at my locker and touched my hand. It was like a hundred questions wrapped up in that one touch. *Are we good? Are you mad at me? Can we hold hands?*

Ji-hee didn't know what Han-bae had told me, but she was worried. I could see it in the set of her jaw. She didn't need to worry because none of it mattered. I didn't care if Ji-hee had a thousand dark shadows hanging over her life. I still wanted to be with her.

I took her hand in mine, lacing our fingers together. "You're here," I said. "I thought you couldn't make it today." I pulled her closer and the light scent of flowers touched my nose. She tilted her face up to mine and her lips parted just a fraction. I was going to kiss her. Here in the hall in front of all the idiots at school. It would be embarrassing and everyone would talk, but I was going to grab her and kiss her.

"I'm outta here," Calvin said.

Ji-hee took a big step back, but I still held her hand in mine. "My brother left earlier than we thought for the airport. I already said goodbye to him."

It took my brain a second to reboot from wanting to kiss her to talking. I met her eyes. "Are you okay?"

She spoke softly. "My brother and Chul went and talked with Han-bae this morning."

I let out the breath I'd been holding and again closed the space she'd put between us. "Did they threaten to end him if he didn't leave you alone?" I was hopeful.

Ji-hee lowered her eyes. "You don't need to worry about him anymore."

A stupid-rich, lying, scheming maniac tried to kidnap my girlfriend. How could I not worry? "What happened when they talked?" I asked. "I thought he'd already left."

"I don't know what they discussed," Ji-hee said. "My brother only told me that Han-bae was leaving for good now."

The bell rang before I could process more. She pulled her hand from mine when we walked together into first period. I let her, even though it felt cold, and followed her to the back of the room where she sat. I took the seat directly across from hers then hooked a foot around the leg of her desk and dragged it closer, right next to mine. She weighed almost nothing, so it was easy to do.

"What are you doing?" She whispered and looked around to see if anyone had noticed. Ms. Smars was still at her desk. No one else would care.

"I want you closer," I said. It was clear that Ji-hee, while confident, wasn't comfortable with what it really meant to go out. I was.

"Well get in trouble." Ji-hee's eyes flitted around the room.

I grinned at her. "Only if I kiss you." Her eyes widened and I leaned closer. "Sitting together is okay."

"Yeah, but this is practically in your lap," she said.

"Actually, that does sound fun." I pretended to reach both hands toward her waist, and she squeaked. "I'm kidding," I said and tried not to laugh.

I'd been focusing so hard on Ji-hee that I didn't see him until it was too late.

Han-bae sat down in front of my desk and turned around. He ignored me but spoke boldly to Ji-hee. "You didn't think I would go home, did you?"

27

JI-HEE

I tried to forget the day I learned that I was engaged, the phone call, the tears after. But sometimes memories just show up, wander in and make themselves comfortable without us knowing. It's like finding a spider in the corner of your room. No one is ever happy to see a spider, but it's not completely unexpected either. Sometimes bugs get in the house.

Only seeing Han-bae walk in, all cocky and smiling felt more like a monster under the bed. I was surprised, very surprised. But I wasn't afraid. Han-bae didn't know this, but as a little girl, if I had ever actually found a monster under my bed, I couldn't have screamed for my parents. No one would come. Sure, I could have yelled for Gun, but then what if the monster got him too? No, if I had a monster problem, I'd get a bat.

"Han-bae," I nodded at him and kept my voice polite.

He turned in his seat, fearless in his suit and tie. He looked exactly like the kind of man my mother had described in her phone call that day, *smart and driven, a man that would go places.* I wondered at how I could have missed this before. But there was something there now that I knew who he was, something I didn't like. Han-bae looked possessive. "I can't say that I'm happy to see you here," I said with coolness in my voice. "My brother said you agreed to leave and go back to Switzerland. There's nothing here for you."

Han-bae lost his smile. "You're here," he said softly.

Harrison went very still next to me.

"I'm not leaving without you," Han-bae said.

I narrowed my eyes and switched from English to Korean. "I thought my brother made it clear that you shouldn't show your face at my school."

Han-bae replied back in Korean. "I told him I would leave, and I will, when you agree to come with me."

I laughed. "I can't believe you think I would go anywhere with you. You lied about who you are."

"I didn't lie to you. I thought you might recognize me. I'd hoped your mother had sent you a photo of me."

"I wasn't allowed to get mail at that school in London. The messed-up school your mother sent me to."

Han-bae faltered. "I didn't know how they treated you until later. I'm going to fix that. But I hoped me being here would give you time to get to know me." His stupid eyes turned soft. "I already knew a lot about you, but you didn't know anything about me."

"I don't want to get to know you, and there's no fixing anything. You can't give me years of my life back," I hissed.

"You're right. I can't change the past, but we're engaged. Let me give you a future. One that you deserve."

"We are not engaged. I'm canceling the contract, and I don't want anything to do with you, ever."

Han-bae reared back as if I'd slapped him. He took a deep breath. "Look, I didn't know my mother was doing those things to you. I knew she'd chosen you for me, but I didn't know the extent of it. I hoped—" His hand reached out toward mine.

Harrison moved fast. A loud crack sounded, and then Han-bae's hand was pinned down flat against my desk. Harrison spoke low and quiet as a few heads turned with curious eyes. "I don't know what you're saying, but Ji-hee doesn't want you to touch her."

Han-bae strained against Harrison's hand and glared at him. "Let go of me," he growled in English.

More students turned in our direction, and Ms. Smars began looking up from her phone with an annoyed expression. I'd been stupid to talk to him here.

Han-bae jerked hard, moving his whole body and my desk, but Harrison kept his arm and hand firmly pinned. He smiled at Han-bae calmly.

"Harrison." Ms. Smars' voice rose with command as she stood. "I can see you. Let Han-bae go."

Harrison didn't move. "Leave my girlfriend alone," he said, still in that same quiet voice.

"Harrison, I'm serious," Ms. Smars said.

Harrison removed his hand and Han-bae turned back around, seeming unruffled but a vein throbbed in his jaw.

Ms. Smars had both hands on her hips as she glared at Harrison. "That's enough boys." Both Han-bae and Harrison remained quiet, but the classroom began to buzz, sensing the almost fight. Regan glanced over and shot me this sympathetic look. She raised her hand.

A deep sigh came from the front of the room. "Yes, Regan. What do you need?" Ms. Smars asked.

"Can I use the bathroom?" she asked.

Ms. Smars sighed again. "Yes."

"Can Ji-hee come with me?"

Ms. Smars eyed her. She wasn't one of those teachers that never had any idea what was going on with the students. She knew that Harrison and Regan used to go out. Now Regan wanted to leave class with the new girl that Harrison clearly liked. She'd say no.

Ms. Smars waved her hand. "Just both of you hurry up," she said.

But then again, Ms. Smars was also one of those teachers that didn't seem to care. I stood up and Harrison stood with me.

"They don't need you, Harrison," Ms. Smars snapped.

"I'm okay," I whispered and motioned for him to sit back down. He made a grumbling noise but sat. Han-bae stared straight ahead and didn't even glance at me as I walked out.

The hallway was quiet with most of the doors shut, and I took a deep breath, feeling less claustrophobic somehow.

"Better?" Regan asked.

I still didn't trust Regan. She was nicer, way nicer than she'd been those first few days, but I also knew that if Harrison gave even the slightest inclination that he wanted her back, she'd stomp me flat like a bug under her shoe. "I'm fine." I folded my arms and leaned against the wall. "What's up?"

Regan put one hand on her hip. She looked like my old nanny right before giving Gun a lecture. "Harrison can't get kicked out of school. He needs to graduate. Maybe keep him and Han-bae apart."

I pursed my lips, hoping she was done.

"I don't know," she continued to babble. "I have a weird gut feeling about that guy. I guess I just don't really trust him. You know what I mean?"

Regan had zero clue as to the gravity of what she was saying. Keeping Han-bae away from one of the few people I cared about in the world was top priority, and she'd just taken me away from the fight. Who knew what would happen now that I'd left. "I've got it under control," I said.

She inspected her nail. "I guess you do." She acted like she wanted to say more, but I was distracted by the buzzing of my phone. I gave her a dismissive look and pulled it from my jeans pocket.

"Is it Harrison?" she asked.

I ignored her and looked at my phone. I had one text from Mother. She never texted. Ever.

I almost didn't open it, but then Regan said, "Fine. If you don't want to talk, I'm going back to class." As she turned to leave my finger hovered and then touched the screen to open the text. One very short sentence appeared.

Grandfather passed away.

HARRISON

Regan came back in the room and gave me a pointed look, then nodded to the hallway. I raised my hand.

"Yes, Harrison."

"Can I go to the bathroom?"

Ms. Smars scrunched her lips to one side. She looked like she was about to throw a book at me. "Do you think I'm stupid?" she asked.

"No," I said. I tried to look sorry. "You're not. Can I go check on my girlfriend? She's upset."

Ms. Smars' face didn't exactly soften, but it went from I can't stand high schoolers to— let's at least be fair. "Five minutes," she said. "Don't make me come get—"

I was out of my seat and through the door before she could change her mind. I thought I'd have to go find Ji-hee, but she was slumped down on the floor right outside class, her head bent forward. "Ji-hee?" I squatted next to her. Both her hands rested in her lap, and her hair hung over her face. It looked like tears dripped onto her hands. "What's wrong?" She didn't move. "Are you okay?" A surge of panic washed over me. Maybe she was hurt.

She rolled her head up, and her eyes locked with mine. "I have to go to Korea. Today. Right now," she whispered.

"Why?"

"My grandfather." Her chin quivered. "He died."

My mouth hung open. I scrambled to try and think of something to say. The words weren't enough, but I said them anyway. "I'm sorry."

"It's okay." Her voice sounded far away. "He was old and happy, and everyone loved him."

"That's . . . that's good," I said lamely. "I mean, I'm glad he was happy." I was bad at this.

Ji-hee reached out and took my hand. Her eyes shined from the tears. "I want you to listen," she said.

I sat down next to her and focused. I gave every cell to Ji-hee. Whatever she needed I was here.

JI-HEE

The strangest things, these little details around me came into sharp focus. I held onto them to keep the tide of pain and panic back. I noticed how Harrison's dark hair held more curl today and fell down over his right eye, the touch of his knee resting next to mine, the sound of the light above us as it hummed.

"I'm listening," he said softly.

I tried to focus and talk. I needed to get these words out. We didn't have much time, and he needed an explanation. I wanted to tell him that I'd go there and then come right back. But none of it was certain. When I opened my mouth, it all poured out in a desperate jumble. "I have secrets. Maybe when you learn them, you'll hate me forever. Maybe I'll leave, and my mother will sabotage me, or maybe Han-bae will say something, and you'll see me differently. Maybe I have nothing good to offer you. But until my life implodes, I want to be with you."

The muscles in his shoulders pulled against his shirt as he gripped my hand. "I know Han-bae's family and yours formed a marriage contract."

I didn't speak. I tried to but words wouldn't come.

His jaw was set in that determined way that had become familiar. "I don't care about any of it." He had this look that said he'd go to war for me, that if both of our backs were at the fire, he wouldn't run. "If you don't want to be with him, you don't have to." He leaned down and brushed his lips along mine. "Say that we belong together," he whispered. "Just us."

"I'm all yours," I said.

28

HARRISON

I parked Mom's minivan in temporary parking at the airport and hoped that when the school's automated system called to say I'd missed class, she'd think it was a mistake. She might because I'd never, in my entire high school career, skipped school. I missed one day when I got my wisdom teeth out, but that was it.

"Do you mind coming in with me, just to security?" Ji-hee asked.

"I was planning on it," I said.

She sighed. "Is it dumb that I wish you could go there with me?"

A thousand percent it wasn't dumb. It was exactly what I wanted to hear. Knowing that Ji-hee was flying away with the very real chance of Han-bae following her there—probably on a stupid private jet—made my hands sweat against the steering wheel. "Do you want me to go?" I asked. "I will." I had my passport at home and almost three thousand dollars sitting in my own savings account. It was for college. Every drop of sweat was for college, but it was mine. I could drive home, get my stuff, and then be sitting next to Ji-hee on a flight to Seoul. My parents might figure it out by dinner time when I didn't show up.

Ji-hee's eyes widened, but then she shook her head. "No," she said, almost resigned. "But I'm glad you would if I asked."

I sat for a minute, quiet. It would be crazy if I went. I'd be grounded until forever. But it'd be worth it. I just wasn't sure it would help her. I felt like I was sitting at a chess board and didn't know the rules. I'd do anything for Ji-hee, but I had this deep feeling that I had to be smart, that each step I took would have a ripple effect, and only if I was careful would the end be with us together.

She sat next to me with a dull expression, clearly exhausted, and this was just the start for her.

"Let's go," I said and got out to open her door. She had no luggage. When we left school, I'd driven her back to Chul's house, and she'd come out with a purse just a few minutes later saying all she needed was her passport and wallet. I guess she'd buy whatever she needed when she got there. How would it be to have enough money to do that?

We walked from the parking garage through the crowds of hurrying travelers and straight to a ticket counter. I listened a few feet back as Ji-hee bought a seat in first class that left in forty-eight minutes, barely enough time to get through TSA and then to her gate if she ran.

Ji-hee turned away from the counter and took two quick steps to me. She wrapped her thin arms around my waist like I was a life preserver and tilted her face up to mine. "We don't have a lot of time."

I nodded looking down into her eyes but didn't speak. I wanted her to tell me everything on her mind. Something was there besides the grief from losing her grandfather. She'd been quiet for most of the drive to the airport, and now she trembled slightly in my arms. I waited.

"I'm scared to go home," she finally said.

I nodded. "Is it more than Han-bae?"

She laughed but there was no humor in it. "Han-bae is still a worry but mostly it's my mother. She's kind of a maniac, and I haven't seen her in three years."

"I figured she might have a screw loose since she agreed to marry you off, practically as a child bride," I said.

This time her laugh was real as she nodded. "I'll be okay, though. I always am."

I tucked a loose lock of hair behind her ear. "Call me when you land."

"I think it will be close to four in the morning your time."

I touched her nose. I loved her nose, her skin, all of her. "You can call me any hour, and I'll answer. I want you to call."

"You make things so nice," she breathed.

"Do I?" I pulled her closer. Even her breathing drove me crazy. "Tell me how I make it nice."

"You make me feel wanted," she said. "That's kind of intoxicating for me. It makes me want more. What if I become this black hole of need?" Her eyes flicked to my mouth before coming back to my eyes.

My hands found her waist, and I lifted her up until our lips met. Our kiss was fierce. She had it all wrong. I was the one that needed her, not the other way around. I'd always be the guy with the messed-up-hero complex, wanting to save someone. Knowing she needed me felt right, like my own personal polarity lined up perfectly when she was near. "You can want more. I'll always give you more," I whispered.

She gripped me harder. "Then promise you'll miss me."

I pulled away and grinned down at her. "I won't be able to breathe right while you're gone," I teased.

We were out of time, but she kissed me again, and it was different. She let some of her worry and pain seep into the kiss. I didn't understand it completely until I was driving home. My mind played over our conversation, our kisses. When I lined the emotions all up and put the Ji-hee puzzle pieces together, I wished I could have gone back and said more.

Ji-hee asked me to miss her. That's what she really longed for. Sure, she was scared of her crazy mom, of Han-bae, and she was sad to lose her grandfather. But Ji-hee's real fear was being forgotten. Her time at that London school must have been full-on abandonment. Even though she was the one flying halfway around the world, she was afraid I'd leave her. I never would.

JI-HEE

I could still smell Harrison. I'd asked him to give me his jacket in case the plane was cold. First class never was, and they give you a blanket, but he'd given it to me without a thought. I snuggled down into the soft denim that smelled like perfection and closed my eyes. I tried to bank this feeling; to store all the Harrison up and make it last this whole horrible trip. Flying back to Seoul and returning to my old world was the same as entering a desert where the sun only scorched and each grain of sand was made of sadness. If I could take my personal Harrison power bank with me, I might survive it. My phone pinged, and I opened my text to see a message from my brother.

Mother told you. I'm so sorry, Ji-hee. I haven't landed yet, but I have Wi-Fi if you want to chat.

I quickly sent an email to Gun with my itinerary and then texted back.

I'm heading home. On my flight and about to take off. I just sent you my flight info. My heart and head hurt for Grand-father. It's too much to know that I'll never see him again. I didn't even call him.

Gun replied right away.

You know he didn't like to talk on the phone.

I texted back.

Yes, he was a simple paper letter kind of grandpa, and I didn't send one of those either. I should have.

His return message took a moment to come through.

Just got your email. I land four hours ahead of you. I'll pick you up. I hope you are doing okay. I think we all feel like we didn't get enough time with him.

I replied.

I'm sad but all of us are. Everyone loved Grandfather. He was the good parts of our childhood and now that's gone.

Gun texted me back.

Maybe not gone. We're still here and like you said, he's the best parts of us. I'm glad we're friends again.

I was done being mad at my brother, but it felt weird saying we were friends again. Like when you step off a roller coaster and the ground under you just doesn't feel like you can trust it. Only I knew I could trust Gun. I think in London part of me still knew it, but under the cloud of grief it was hard to remember. I texted him back.

Me too. You busted me out of that place. Thanks for sticking with me.

His next text appeared.

Of course.

I sighed. Glad to be right with Gun, especially now, before the funeral. Nothing else was right in our family but we were. I'd replied to Mother's text at school. Right away I'd said I would fly home. I even tried to call her, but she didn't answer, didn't respond. I bit my lip and texted Gun the question I really wanted answered.

Mother only sent me a short text. **Did you get a chance to call her? What are the funeral plans?**

When his reply finally came through, I barely had time to read it before we started rolling onto the runway.

The funeral is in three days. I spoke with Mother's assistant. He will arrange the food rites and memorial. She collapsed after her frenzy of wanting everything to be perfect. The doctor came a few hours ago and prescribed sedatives. I actually feel sorry for her. She's driving herself mad with guilt, saying it's her fault that he passed on.

I tried to reply, but we were already in the air, and I lost signal. It was no surprise to hear that Mother wasn't taking it well. I wished she could find peace. Grandfather was seventy-seven and had lived a happy life. I closed my eyes, wrapped in Harrison's jacket and drifted to sleep, acutely aware that I now lived in a dimmer world, a world without Grandfather.

29

HARRISON

I timed it so school had been out for ten minutes when I pulled into my driveway. I hoped my parents wouldn't know that I skipped, but as I powered my phone back on, the thirteen unanswered calls and twenty-eight texts said otherwise. I pressed the garage door opener and saw that Jeff's car was already inside. He was never home this early. Not good.

"Where were you?" Jeff asked as soon as I walked through the door and into the kitchen. He and Mom sat at the table. Mom's eyes were red, and she gripped her phone tightly in both hands.

"Uh." I looked between them, my mind scrambling for what to say.

Ozzy walked in from the front hallway. He was supposed to be at the rink. He gave me a barely perceptible shake of the head which meant one of two things: One—Mom and Dad are freaking out, remain calm, no sudden movements. Or two—Mom and Dad are way past freaking out. So even if you have a really good reason, you're so dead. I knew it was the second one. I swallowed and took a breath. "Mom, everything is okay I—"

Mom's hands started to shake. Her face turned bright red. "How is the fact that my son ran out of school without being excused, okay?

You just disappeared from the middle of first period and went missing for hours. You even powered your phone off." Tears brimmed in her already bloodshot eyes. "We were about to go to the police."

Right then I heard the front door open and the unmistakable voices of the Evil G's just around the corner. "I don't know why they asked us to take Becca to gymnastics," Garrett said. "But you can reschedule your nail appointment."

Ozzy gave a small groan and walked back to his bedroom. I was on my own.

Garrett entered first followed by Gretchen sweeping into the room in her dramatic fashion. "Jeffery, I'm so glad you're here," she said. "You work too much." She walked to him and bent down to give him a delicate pat on the shoulder. "Now where is my darling grand-daughter?" She looked at Mom. "Do you mind if we take her dress shopping after gymnastics? The dress she wore last Sunday was short at the knees. It should always be tea length at her age, you know."

She and Garrett ignored me completely. I might as well have been invisible.

Mom tried to surreptitiously wipe at her eyes, but Gretchen never missed clues.

"Oh, dear," she said in her fake singsong voice. "You're practically crying. What's upsetting you? Tell us."

Before Mom could explain Becca bounded from her bedroom. "Nana," she yelled, running into the kitchen. She stopped short when she saw me and changed course throwing herself at my legs.

I wrapped my arms around her and squatted down. "Hey," I said, giving her a hug.

"Why did you run away?" She blurted, and stuck out her bottom lip.

Gretchen and Garrett's heads swung my direction in unison. They both stared, Gretchen looking unabashedly almost hopeful.

The three of us sat in the office with the door closed, but I was pretty sure Ozzy listened outside. Both of my parents tried to rush the Evil

G's off for Becca's class, but I was surprised when Garret seemed to want to hang back. I wasn't sure why. He kept looking at me and then at the floor.

After they finally left, Mom sat across from me next to Jeff on the love seat. I sat in the only other chair in the room, the hot seat, which she'd planted right in front of them. She folded her arms and looked at me through half closed eyes, something she did when she was trying not to lose her temper.

Jeff leaned forward, his elbows resting on his knees. "Harrison, what's this all about? Is this because of the vacation?"

"What vacation?" I asked. "Are you guys leaving again?"

Jeff shook his head and touched my knee. "No. Ozzy told us what happened with Australia?"

"What do you mean?" I asked. I hadn't told a soul, other than Calvin, about being uninvited.

Mom blew her bangs out of her eyes and yelled, "Ozzy. Get in here."

Ozzy immediately opened the door. Proof he'd been outside listening all along. "I'm here, Mom. You don't need to yell." He crossed the room and dropped onto the floor next to my chair in one graceful motion. "I ratted you out, brother," he said.

"Everyone was panicked," Mom said, defending the statement. "Someone had to tell us what was going on."

"Will someone now tell *me*," I said.

Jeff leaned forward. "When the school called and we realized you were missing, we called your brother to find out if he knew where you were. He didn't, but he did know something that both of you should have shared a long time ago," Jeff said.

"Before we went to Australia," Mom snapped. "You both should have told us. We wouldn't have gone without you, had we known." Mom's voice sounded raw, like she'd swallowed something too hot, and I realized she was trying not to cry.

Ozzy scooted closer before speaking. "Do you remember the Fourth of July BBQ where the steaks caught on fire?"

I nodded feeling sick.

"I heard what the Evil G's said to you."

"I told you not to call them that," Mom said.

Ozzy ignored her. "I was in the kitchen when the grill caught on fire, and the door was open. I heard what they told you about not going with us to Australia. They basically said that you weren't part of the family." Ozzy glanced down. "I was miserable when we left without you."

"We all thought he had the flu because he barely got out of bed," Dad said.

"I should have said something," Ozzy said. "I should have yelled at them, but I was scared. They were paying my bills, and the new coach meant me qualifying for the next Olympics. But I don't care anymore. I'm sick of seeing the way they treat you. The rest of us have to walk on eggshells just so Gretchen—"

"Nana, she's still your Nana," Mom said.

"Mom," Ozzy raised his voice, and she flinched. "Sorry." He immediately looked down. "Sorry, I won't yell, but she's not. She's not my Nana or my anything if she refuses to be Harrison's."

Jeff nodded. "I appreciate you sticking up for her." Jeff softly squeezed Mom's knee. "But Ozzy is right, if my parents aren't accepting Harrison then we have to draw a line in the sand."

Mom's eyes filled with tears. "I thought they were getting better at accepting Harrison. But I think they just got better at hiding their rejection."

"It's okay, Mom, I'm fine," I said.

Ozzy looked at me with raw open hurt and shook his head.

This was why he'd been acting so weird, so upset. We grew up sharing bunkbeds and stealing cookies together. I used to lace and tie his ice skates before he knew how. This was my family. My real family. Jeff wasn't my stepdad. He was my dad, and I was part of them. I should have fought for them.

"It's not okay. You should have told us," Mom said again. "Why, didn't you?"

I lowered my head. "I didn't want to make it harder on you guys."

"Is this why you ran away?" she asked.

"I didn't run away. I drove my girlfriend to the airport. Her grandpa died."

Mom's eyes got bigger. "So why turn your phone off? Why not ask?"

"You would have said no," I said.

"Regardless," Dad said. "Ask next time or you're grounded."

"I'm not an idiot, though. I wouldn't have run away," I said.

"That's right. You're not," Mom said, back in her reassuring mode. "You were being mistreated, and we should have seen it. We saw some of it, just little things, but we should have known they were mistreating you."

"I think there was a lot we should have noticed and didn't," Dad said. "I made a lot of excuses for both of my parents, but in hindsight it only made them bolder. You're my son, Harrison. You'll always be part of me and part of the family. No one, not even my own parents will ever change that."

"But what about paying for Ozzy's lessons. I don't want you guys to fight with them and screw that up," I said.

"I'll quit skating," Ozzy said.

"No one's quitting anything," Dad said. "We can pay for it, if they don't." Dad reached out and pulled me closer by the back of the neck. Before I knew it, he had me in a giant bear hug. Ozzy stood and hugged both of us.

The part of my chest that had been tight since the stupid BBQ eased. It was like I'd had these awful stitches that burned and pulled right across my heart, and I'd just gotten used to the pain. Now someone had come by and clipped them out. It felt like I could breathe again.

"Can I ask a question," Ozzy mumbled into Dad's shoulder, the shoulder that was being smashed against my nose.

Dad broke away. "What is it?" he asked.

Ozzy leaned back. "Why did you invite them over here to take Becca if you know they did all this?"

Dad's eyes went hard. "After they bring Becca home your mom and I are going to have a long chat with them."

30

JI-HEE

How strange it was that flying away from Harrison reminded me of leaving home that first time. In London I'd moved through waves of guilt and grief, so homesick and lost. My only thoughts had been about going back to Korea. Now I was just as sad, maybe worse, but instead of wanting home, I desperately wanted to go back to Harrison.

I checked my phone again. By now he would have heard the message I left. I glanced out my airplane window. A blur of buildings rose up below, like a picture not yet in focus. In a few more minutes our wheels would touch down, and I would be back in Seoul. I knew this more from the knots of tension forming at the base of my skull than I did from the approaching runway.

I wiped at my eyes and tried to think of what Grandfather would want me to do over the next few days. He would tell me to hold my head up high and not worry about the barrage of questions that would be unavoidable over the next few days. The gossips would still question where I had been, maybe ask why I never came home for a holiday. And it wouldn't just be the gossips. Everyone who was anyone would be at the funeral.

Grandfather hadn't been the wealthy owner of a conglomerate, but his son-in-law was. My father was born into the Elite and this guaranteed that the rest of them would unfailingly come to us for two things: marriages and funerals. I wasn't sure if death and unions were what really defined the upper crust of society, but those events were where we showed our solidarity.

The exception to this rule was if you were part of the Bitgaram family. Most people didn't even know what they looked like. Even my engagement had always been some kind of super-secret, never announced with any of the proper ceremonies. At the time I didn't think much of it because the Bitgarams were different. Only now, I knew better. They hid their identities behind a mountain of money because they didn't want the rest of society to know that they were actually monsters. But not even a Mt. Everest of cash could erase what they had done to me. It was a relief to know that none of the Bitgarams would be at Grandfather's funeral.

When I finally made it out of the airport Gun was waiting for me in a yellow Lamborghini. His face was drawn, and he looked even more lost than when he'd come to me in California. I made myself smile and waved as I approached. He got out and opened my door. I stopped and waited for my brother to look at me, but he didn't. "Gun." I said his name. His shoulders slumped and he only stared at the pavement.

"Gun, it's okay." I placed a hand on his arm, but he still didn't look up at me. His body started to tremble and then he just dropped. Gun squatted down, right there on the very public curb, and made a noise that was half sorrow, half breaking.

I drove us home.

The next two days were slow and long. Grief, Mother, Father, more grief, all of us hurting, and the devastating weight of knowing that we couldn't hold onto Grandfather for comfort.

The only bright spot was that Father stopped drinking and remained sober for two days during the Wongi ceremony and the wake.

Both evenings, when everyone else had gone to bed, I called Harrison. He listened to me tell him small details of my day, then asked questions and let me say more. I told him things, the bad things about London, the parts of Mother I hated, and even the small parts I loved. But mostly, I told him why Grandfather was so special.

When the third day arrived, the day of the actual funeral, Gun and I were ready. Parlor number seventeen was the nicest one in the funeral home. Grandfather's picture was surrounded by a wall of white chrysanthemums with sticks of incense below. Most of the mourners had come and spoken in hushed tones, making their bows and some offering prayers. The condolence money box in the outer hall filled so fast that one of our staff had to come and empty it hours ago, only to have it fill up again.

Mother slumped with Father against the parlor wall. In the last hour Father had started drinking again, and now he slept deeply on the floor. Gun and I stood resolutely with our hands clasped in front of us, when a thin woman dressed in a simple black dress and a beautifully made-up face entered. Two men, clearly her security, flanked her on each side as she swept into the room. She looked familiar enough that I was sure we knew her. It was embarrassing how many faces I'd forgotten in three years. But they'd been long years, and maybe I wanted to forget them. I rubbed my eyes tiredly, trying to rack my brain for a name to connect with this woman.

My simple answers to the many questions had gotten easier, almost like reading from a script.

I was in London. Studying. Very busy. I loved it. Sorry I never reached out. No, I'd gone on a social media fast a few years ago. Yes, I was an unusual girl. Of course I'd stay in touch.

I was ready as this woman walked closer. I knew Gun would contribute enough to end any interrogation quickly, without making it seem suspicious. We were a team again.

I faltered when the woman smiled wide. Suddenly she felt wrong in our place of mourning. No one smiled like that. Not in the parlor. The slightly drunk mourners in the dining hall would laugh at shared memories while eating yukgaejang. But smiling in here, at the family? Who was this woman? I glanced down at the condolence envelope in her hand. The backside was facing out where you would typically write your name in the bottom left hand corner. There in bold black letters that stood out against the pale paper was one horrible name. Bitgaram. I froze and took half a step back. I reached to touch Grandmother's ring on my right hand.

Gun moved closer, frowning next to me and then suddenly Mother made a noise from her spot behind us and stood with a gasp. "Myang," she said. "We didn't expect you."

Myang smiled even wider which seemed like an affront to physics. Her face stretched thinner as her lips widened showing all of her teeth. "Of course I would come. My daughter-in-law is mourning."

Mother rushed to my side and slipped an arm around my own, grasping me at the elbow in a firm grip. Her breathing had changed to little, short pants.

A sour taste touched my tongue as fear rose up from my stomach. "I'm not your daughter-in-law," I said softly.

Father gave a grumbly snort in his sleep behind us, and Myang covered her mouth with a delicate hand. "He must be exhausted. You all are, I see. But you, Ji-hee, you are as stalwart as ever, standing up front for your mother. That's why I selected you. Always so steady, even when things are hard." She lowered her hand and gestured to the man at her left. He pulled a set of folded papers from his suit jacket and placed it in her open palm. Myang unfolded them and tilted her head to one side. "Ji-hee, my dear. This is a certificate of marriage registration issued by the district office proving that you *are* my daughter-in-law. Not in the future, currently." She pointed to the document which had been sealed by the state office with their insignia. I held my hand out and she handed it to me.

Right there at the top it listed the names of the spouses, Bitgaram Han-bae Jung and Lee Ji-hee. At the bottom my name was printed *and signed*. Mother had signed for me. I could tell it was her signature, and she had gotten Father to sign his name as well. The date was from just a year ago.

Mother hadn't betrothed me. She hadn't agreed to a contract. Mother had signed for my marriage and let them register it. In the eyes of the Republic of South Korea, Han-bae and I were married.

I raised my eyes and met Myang's aggressive gaze. "I'm filing for a divorce. This marriage won't stand."

Myang tsked. "There is a penalty for you to take such drastic action. Check the prenup, Ji-hee. Dissolving this marriage means your family hands over *all* stock for JAYNE talent agency."

Mother's hand slipped limply from my arm, and she stumbled back with a wail. "You can't have it," she cried, as she sunk to her knees.

Myang ignored her and spoke directly to me. "I don't know if your brother has told you, but he's made some heavy investments of his own." Myang nodded. "He's been growing the business and it's doing very well, but JAYNE stock is personally securing these investments. The same stock that I will take, if you file for divorce. Your family will be bankrupt within a month."

Gun snatched the papers from my hand and began leafing through them. I knew he had no idea that mother had signed away our fortune, or that I was actually married.

Married.

She'd lied to us. In her greed, Mother thought that marrying into the Bitgaram family secured everything. Myang promised investments for JAYNE. Her money would take it from the largest talent agency in Korea to maybe the largest in the world. Mother would no longer be the bottom tier of the Elite. All that money hanging within her grasp and she would have signed over her own life if it had been on the table.

"Ji-hee," Gun's voice went tight with panic. "I didn't—" He flipped the next page and kept reading. "This can't—"

I held up my hand to stop him. "I know." I said firmly. None of us could fall apart right now.

But Mother's wailing only grew louder. "It's not your money," she screamed.

Mother's personal assistant walked in from the dining hall. He must have heard her wails.

"Mr. Cho," I snapped. "Take mother and Father to the car now."

Mr. Cho pulled out his phone and quickly texted before approaching Mother. He squatted next to her and whispered something calming that I couldn't quite make out. Two more of our staff appeared in the parlor and moved to help.

"My parents are tired and need to go home," I said.

Mr. Cho eyed Myang and seemed to understand that more was happening than just a grieving family. He helped Mother to stand while the other two practically carried Father out the doorway.

I turned to Myang. "I'm going to have our lawyer look these over and get back to you." Gun seemed to have gathered at least half his wits because he folded the papers and tucked them into his suit pocket.

"Oh, my sweet, Ji-hee. I'm not here to offer condolences, though. I'm here to collect what is mine."

I bristled, understanding what she meant. Gun did too because he stepped closer, putting himself between me and Myang. The man to her left met the action by taking his own step forward and then reached out to place a very solid looking hand on my brother's shoulder. We all froze, each party waiting for the other to make a move.

It only took that single second to know with absolute certainty that, yes, this ship was going down, and if I didn't give up my spot on the lifeboat, Gun would go down with it. The men that Myang brought with her came for violence, I could see it in their faces. I turned to Myang. "Let my brother go, and I'll come with you. I'll leave with you right now."

31

HARRISON

I laid on my bed and checked my messages again. Then my voicemail. I even checked my email. Nothing. Ji-hee never texted or called after the funeral. Maybe she was so tired that she'd just crashed and was still asleep. But it should be morning there now. Like it was past 10:00 a.m. I texted her again.

How are you holding up?

I pressed send and a few minutes later my phone rang. Her name lit up my screen, and I answered it. "Hey," I said, trying to keep the excited, happy, thrilled-that-you-called tone out of my voice. I was all of those things, but she was sad. Her grandfather had just died. Ji-hee needed sensitivity right now, not a sappy boyfriend.

But the voice that answered me was like a pin sliding into my bubble of joy with a loud and startling pop. "My sister can't call you."

"Oh, hey, Is this Gun?" I asked.

"Yes," the voice said. Gun sounded mad and almost dead, like if a zombie could talk it would sound like this guy. But I wasn't going to judge. They'd just lost their grandfather.

"Well sorry to bother you during this time of mourning. I just wanted to say hi to Ji-hee. Is she resting?"

"No, she's not. She can't talk to you anymore so stop texting her phone."

The phone went dead. The guy had hung up on me. I got that this wasn't his best moment, but he didn't have to be a jerk. I rolled over on my back and stared at the ceiling. I should just let this go. Ji-hee would call me tomorrow or better yet, she'd fly home tomorrow. But something in my gut didn't sit right. I opened my phone and looked at her last text. She'd said the funeral was winding down. That they would leave soon, and she'd call. I looked at the time stamp. It would have been early evening her time. Unless she'd gotten a lot more attendees she should have called before going to bed.

Maybe she was just exhausted.

Maybe she was talking to her family, and her brother was mad that I kept texting.

Maybe Han-bae . . .

I sat up and swung my feet to the floor. My parents were out there with the Evil G's again. This was like the third night they'd all sat in the office with the door closed and talked for hours. Last night Mom and Dad came out drooping and tired, while Gretchen came out with puffy eyes. Garrett had stepped out of the office and looked right at me. It wasn't with anger or sadness; it was more like he was seeing me for the first time. I had just let him, holding his stare. He'd broken away first before taking Gretchen who'd started to do this weird crying hiccup and escorted her to the door. I still hated them, but I wasn't hurt anymore. My parents were standing up for me.

I ninja walked past the office, then quietly opened the front door. I made it halfway across my lawn before I thought about what to say to Chul. I didn't care that it was dinner time or that he might not appreciate me dropping by without texting. That bad feeling in my gut was worse. The more I thought on it, the more I knew something wasn't right.

I rang the bell and waited with my arms folded. I expected a voice over the intercom and a full scan from all their cameras, but Sydney opened the door.

"Come in, Harrison," she said, like she'd been expecting me. Her face was drawn and she didn't smile. Sydney smiled at everyone.

As we rounded the corner to the living room, Chul was a blur of pacing with a phone pressed to his ear.

"But how could that have happened? I thought half of the stocks had already been transferred to your name." He was quiet a moment and then shook his head. "None of that is legal so why did she go?" He stopped talking and seemed to frown deeper as he listened. Then he said just two words. "Poor Ji-hee."

I froze. Everything I feared crashed into me. I didn't know what was happening but whatever it was concerned Ji-hee.

"Have you heard from her at all?" Chul asked. He was quiet again and his pacing picked up. "Are you going to go over there? I sent you the address. They hid it well but . . ." Chul snorted. "Not that well."

Sydney touched my arm. "Are you okay, Harrison? Do you want to sit down?"

I could barely move. I mumbled a no thank you and continued to listen to Chul.

"Alright, man. Keep me in the loop," he said. "We'll fight this. Later." Chul hung up and walked to me. "I'm sure you're wondering why you haven't heard from Ji-hee. Have a seat and I'll fill you in."

I still couldn't move, so I just stood there and stupidly stared at Chul.

He sighed. "I get it. I've been where you are. It's a punch in the gut, but you can't freeze up. Turn on your brain because you're going to need it."

I shook myself and sat down. "I'm here," I said. "Tell me everything."

By the time I walked back home I'd burned through all the emotions at least a dozen times and landed back at how I was going to kill Han-bae.

Chul and Gun didn't have a plan. Not really. It was lawyers and annulments, and it would take forever because Ji-hee and Han-bae were freaking married, or at least a document said they were. The only thing that saved my brain from blowing up like a nuclear bomb was the fact that it had all been illegal. They weren't actually married. Ji-hee had never agreed or signed anything. Her weird mom had. Which was why Chul and Gun thought they could fight this in court. But in the meantime, no one could contact Ji-hee. She had left with Han-bae's mother because she was trying to save her brother. Ji-hee was basically a prisoner in the Bitgaram home.

Their plan wasn't a plan.

As I walked home all of this looped through my brain like a scratch on a record. I played the scene out in my head. Ji-hee had tried to buy time. I'm sure she thought if she went with them her brother could get their lawyers on it, but naturally he had tried to stop her leaving and that ended in Gun getting beat so bad that Chul said his arm was in a cast. So instead of buying time, Ji-hee had to watch her brother get the snot kicked out of him while some guy carried her off screaming.

If I'd been there . . . but I hadn't been.

Only that wasn't the worst part. No one could contact Ji-hee. She hadn't had her phone on her when they hauled her off, and not even the police could help. Apparently the Bitgarams were so rich they were untouchable. It didn't seem real to me. It seemed like the script of a movie or a crazy nightmare.

I opened my front door and made a beeline for my bedroom. I was grabbing my passport and then I'd beg Calvin to drive me to the airport. I didn't make it past the kitchen.

"Sit down, son." Dad's deep voice startled me as I rounded the corner. Both of my parents sat at the kitchen table and looked calm, almost pleased. Garrett and Gretchen sat across from them looking defeated. I would have enjoyed their pain, except there just wasn't room in my brain for anything other than how to save Ji-hee.

"I can't," I said. My hands were shaking. I stuffed them in my pockets and hunched my shoulders to keep steady. But this only made me look like a defiant teenager, the exact opposite of what I wanted to portray right now.

Dad's mouth formed a hard line.

I spoke quickly. "You remember that girl, Ji-hee?"

"Yes, your girlfriend, right?" Mom said.

"What about her?" Dad asked. His patience was usually longer than the Great Wall of China, but I could tell his parents had used it all up in the last few days.

"She's in trouble," I said. "She flew home to South Korea and now her family is falling apart."

"Are her parents getting divorced?" Mom asked.

I shook my head. If I told Mom the truth, she'd freak out and not let me go. And I had to go. "No, but she needs me. Can I fly out there for a few days?"

Dad folded both of his arms and started to say something. I knew it would be about responsibility and the cost.

"I'll take him," Garrett said.

The room went quiet, and we all stared at him.

"I've been to Korea on business a few times. I know how to navigate and where to stay." He looked at my dad. "I want to help my grandson."

Calling me his grandson was a checkmate move. Dad couldn't say no now. He'd just railed on Garrett for three solid days. Given his parents a taste of their own medicine, and from what Ozzy had overheard, threatened to cut them off from ever seeing any of them if they couldn't accept me. Now Garrett was doing his first big gesture. Dad had to say yes.

"I'll only be gone a few days," I said.

Dad hadn't looked away from Garrett. They were locked in this stare down that made us all uncomfortable. Finally he spoke. "What about school?"

"I have all A's. I always have A's, and I'll keep it that way."

"What about her mom and dad? Do they care if you visit?" Mom asked.

"They're not even with her. She's alone."

"Oh, that poor girl," Mom said. She looked pointedly at Gretchen and added. "We would never abandon *our* child."

Dad had always been big on how to care for women. Treat them with respect, and if they ask for help, be there. "This is my girlfriend," I said. "She needs me right now."

When I made it that simple, he couldn't argue. Dad breathed out hard and stared at the floor.

"Please, Dad," I begged.

"He'll be fine, Sweetie," Mom said. "We can let him go."

I wanted to high-five Mom. I knew this probably seemed like a big romantic gesture, and she was a sucker for that stuff. It made me feel slightly slimy for deceiving them, but the sick-to-my-gut feeling over Ji-hee eclipsed all that.

"You still have your passport?" Dad asked.

I nodded but my legs were already running down the hall. "I love you guys," I yelled.

Ten minutes later I was packed and sitting on the porch waiting for Garrett to come and drive us both to the airport.

32

JI-HEE

The door locked from the outside, but it's not like I could go anywhere. I had no phone, no money, no car. I sat on the floor of an attic bedroom with heavy velvet curtains drawn over windows that had been nailed shut. The room was opulent with a crystal chandelier hanging above where a bed should be. Only there was no bed, no chair, no anything. The room was completely bare of comforts. But I wouldn't give them the satisfaction of asking for so much as a pillow.

At least there was an ensuite bathroom. This morning I'd showered, but with no change of clothes, I had to put my funeral dress back on.

I wasn't sure of the time when Myang entered. One of her men followed her in carrying a large upholstered chair which he deposited in the middle of the room. I sat opposite the door with my back to the wall and knees drawn up to my chest. I didn't move or get up. If she wanted to talk, she could do it from there.

"It's so dark in here. Open the curtains, Chan-woo," she said to the man.

Chan-woo. I was sure this guy was the one that broke Gun's arm last night. I'd be sure to remember his name for some payback later.

I'd find out the other guy's name too. I'd find out everything, because the one thing I did have was time. I was stuck here with nothing to do and nowhere to go.

Chan-woo walked to both sets of curtains and slid them apart to let in what I guessed to be the noon-day sun. I hadn't eaten since yesterday's breakfast, and my stomach ached with hunger.

As if they read my mind, two staff came to the door and wheeled in a cart full of food. It smelled heavenly with a steaming pot of ginseng chicken stew, along with rice and all the sides. My mouth watered. I was going to eat my weight in chicken. I waited and let the maid bring me a tray where I still sat on the floor. I murmured my thank you and started to eat. Some people might have refused food and sulked, but I'd had time to think about my situation. I was already beaten, and not eating wasn't going to help.

During the long night I didn't sleep. Instead, I got all my crying out. I'm not ashamed to cry. Only I wouldn't in front of them. Never.

I didn't cry when they repeatedly kicked Gun in the face or when they shoved me in the car and sped off. I waited until they walked me up three flights of stairs, deposited me in this room, locked the door and left. I waited for the light peeking around the draperies to go from dim to black, and for the dark house to grow quiet and desolate. I waited for my shock to turn to despair, and then I waited even longer. Finally, I crept into the bathroom and climbed inside the deep clawfoot tub. And only then did I let myself sob into a towel. Grief burned me up from the inside out as I cried for Gun's bloody face and broken arm, for my mother's ultimate betrayal. I cried for my father who was so addicted that he couldn't protect his family. But mostly my crying was selfish. I cried the most for losing my freedom, for losing Harrison. If it had just been Mother, even Father, I'd burn the Bitgaram's marriage certificate and laugh when they took our company.

But it was Gun.

The brother who'd tried to protect me so many times. He didn't know how to live without the money. I had to wave my white flag for Gun.

At least that had been my plan while crying alone in a bathtub. Only now, seeing the tightness in Myang's face awoke the tiniest glimmer of hope. Myang sat in her pillow-soft chair, made-up in her tailored dress and diamond wrapped wrists with shimmering lips and leather heels. She looked stunningly perfect, but there was something else, something most people would miss. She looked unsure.

Myang carried herself with a natural haughtiness. It was the ultimate mask. Most people couldn't see the real her. But I'd developed the skill of seeing past a mask. I could read people that didn't want to be read. The irony of it was that I never could before London. Something about being ripped from your life and everyone you love can force you to develop survival skills that a normal person doesn't even think about. The subtle shift in the moods of the guards, in what made them laugh versus what made them annoyed could mean the difference between simply losing a meal or being locked in solitary. Saying the right thing, the exact right thing, all depended on reading the person. So, thanks to Myang, I had this semi-psychotic skill of manipulation. I'd been relieved to bury it once I arrived in California, but I'd happily get it out and dust it off for her.

I watched carefully, her breathing, the way her eyes moved just a little too fast, and how it was hard for her to look at my face for longer than three seconds. Somehow, she had lost control of the situation, and I needed to find out how. I pressed my thumb and finger against Grandmother's ring. If my grandparents were here, they would tell me to fight. They would say don't let them take you or the company.

So I started my battle with the most obvious. "Where's my husband?" I asked, using the term *husband* purposely. She wouldn't expect me to see him this way after last night. It might lower her guard.

Myang's lip twitched, and her eyes slid past me. That was the problem, then. Han-bae wasn't playing her game. Too bad she wouldn't break *his* arm to get what she wanted. But Myang had probably been trying to control Han-bae his whole life. He was sure to have one or two get-out-of-jail tricks that he saved for his mother's most extreme behavior. I needed him as an ally.

"I would like to speak to my husband," I said.

"Jung is in Switzerland. He couldn't come." Myang's brow creased just a little too much when she said this.

"If we're married, I want to be near him. Are we going to Switzerland?" I knew she had a home there. She'd spent more time in Switzerland over the last ten years than she had in Korea. Why would that change now? Unless her son was refusing to see her. The marriage wouldn't really work in her favor if she only had a bride but no groom to control.

Myang pursed her lips. "I thought you said you wanted a divorce."

I spread my hands out dramatically. "Well, I did last night. But can you imagine how I felt with you busting in with those papers? I mean, I never even had a wedding, and you were saying I was already married. I want a big wedding, you know."

Myang eyed me, not quite buying it.

"If I'm going to stay married, I want two. One wedding on an island with friends and another here with family." The words almost burned coming out of my mouth, but I worked to sell the dumb, moody teenager persona.

Myang sighed. "Of course we will do a wedding."

I kept up my harassment. "Well, we can't now because Jung isn't here. He told me in California that he wouldn't leave without me. He should keep his promise." I sighed. "I want to call him."

That got Myang's attention. Her eyes went from flat and bored at my tirade, to alert. She motioned to Chan-woo and he brought over a phone. I was pretty sure it wasn't hers because Han-bae wouldn't answer a call from his mother. She dialed and put the call on speaker. Then Chan-woo carried the phone to me When he got close enough, I had this insane second where I thought about grabbing his wrist and biting him hard. Like tear-through-tendons-hard. Let him see what it feels like to bleed. Instead, I took the phone and took it off speaker just as Han-bae answered.

"This is Jung," he said.

"Jung." I made my voice a little breathless on purpose. "This is Ji-hee."

"Put it on speaker," Myang said.

I ignored her. "I'm here with your mother. Where are you? Aren't you coming?" I kind of felt like throwing up in my mouth saying this. Honestly, playing this pouty girl, pleading for the guy to come save me, wasn't even close to my plan. If I could get Han-bae to come, and that was a big if, I'd probably try to break his nose before asking for any help. But just to keep the ruse going I added, "I miss you."

"Put it on speaker," Myang snapped. "Do it right now." I knew Han-bae could hear her.

"Listen to me," he said. "When you put it on speaker, I'm going to act like I'm dumping you. I'm not. I'll be there to help soon. I just need to wait for the right time."

Myang stood up and stormed toward me.

"Play along and I'll—"

"Your mother wants me to put it on speaker so we can all hear," I said as I pulled the phone away and tapped the speaker button. Myang got to me and ripped the phone from my hands like she had talons.

"Do you hear that, Jung?" Myang said more calmly than she looked. "Your wife is here, and she misses you."

"I don't miss her," he said. "I told you, Mother. I'm finishing school. Ji-hee can do what she wants. I'm not interested."

The phone went dead, and it was clear to all of us, except Myang, that her son had hung up on her. She just stared at the blank screen and blinked stupidly. Finally, she screeched and threw the phone at the window above my head, shattering one of the panes. Shards of glass rained down over me, and I instinctively squeezed my eyes shut and hunched my shoulders.

I waited a long moment before I opened my eyes and looked up, she'd already left the room. I was alone with the door closed again. I stood and shook my hair down toward the floor, letting tiny pieces of glass fall. I straightened and went to the cart the maids had left to serve myself another bowl of soup. One without glass shards.

Myang didn't know it, but her weakness was on the table now, and I was very hungry.

33

HARRISON

We didn't talk on the plane or in the taxi to the hotel, not even when Garrett ordered room service and climbed into one of the king beds without eating his meal. And I didn't care.

I think Garrett knew I didn't want to talk so he didn't try. It felt like he was waiting for the right moment, and that was so much like my dad. It bugged me to see that many of the cool parts of Jeff were also there in Garrett, they'd just been hidden before. I didn't want to know that, but spending this much time together, I couldn't not see it. Garrett kept right on acting like an older, richer Jeff. He even had the same soft snore as my dad. I wanted it to stop so I could just go on hating him, but after the long flight I finally had to admit that Garrett wasn't one-hundred percent horrible. Maybe just ninety-five.

It was close to 9:00 p.m., which meant it was like 5:00 a.m. to my body. I was wicked tired, but I snarfed down the burger and fries that Garrett ordered for me, and then because he was dead asleep, I ate his shrimp noodle dish that tasted weird but super good. After that I drank two energy drinks to stay awake and opened the map on my phone. The address Chul had given me that was supposed to be

Myang Bitgaram's residence was an hour and twenty from the hotel if I took a taxi.

I was nervous. Now that I was here, my plan didn't seem that much better than Gun and Chul's. It wasn't really a plan, just show up and storm the castle. I wished I could at least speak Korean. I grabbed my wallet and phone before turning to leave.

Garrett sat straight up in bed. "Where are you going?" he asked. He didn't even seem groggy. Fully alert, like our bunker had just been bombed and he was ready to fight.

"Uh, I'm heading out," I said.

"I know that. Where?"

I didn't answer so he did for me. "To go find your girl that's in trouble?"

I let out a heavy sigh. "Yeah."

"Okay." He reached over to the nightstand and grabbed his wallet, took out a wad of cash and then a credit card. He held it out to me. "Take this so you have money. You have my number in your phone. Call if you need help."

"Uh, I have my own money so—"

Garrett stood up and walked to me then grabbed my hand and put the money in it with the card on top. "Now you have more," he said. "Do you want me to go with you?"

"No," I said, quickly. But I kind of did want him to go, and I really hated that.

"I will," he said. "I know your story has more to it than what you've told your parents. I don't know what it is, but I suspect from the way you've been acting that it could be dangerous. I'll go with you." He was already turning to grab his pants, but I stopped him.

"You're right," I said. "About all of that, but I need to go alone. I appreciate the offer, though."

"Your parents want you to be safe," Garrett said. He let that hang there for a second and I didn't miss that he'd called them my parents and not my mom and Jeff. He was acknowledging me as part of the family.

It was the worst kind of awkward, but it also felt like he needed to say it. We both knew that earlier when he offered to take me to Korea and called me his grandson that it had all been for show, to suck up to my parents. But maybe a small part of this was to say sorry. I let out a breath before saying, "We're good."

Garrett didn't smile, but he looked me in the eye when he answered with a nod. "Yes, we are good."

The house was completely surrounded by a wall with security cameras, and to make it even more interesting, a solid metal gate with a guardhouse stood at the entrance. I raked my hands through my hair with a groan. This was dumb. The wall was massive, at least twelve feet high, and I didn't even have a rope. I thought about doing the obvious and just walking up to the gate and ringing the buzzer or bell or whatever they have in Korea. Instead, I stuffed my hands in my pockets and started to walk around the perimeter one more time.

Lights from a car across the street flashed. I froze. Maybe it was like a Korean neighborhood watch, and someone was about to report me for obviously casing a house. The lights flashed again, and the window rolled down. It was too dark to see, but Han-bae's voice was unmistakable.

"Get over here, you idiot," he said.

I had very few choices. One, I could go drag him out of the car and beat him to a bloody pulp. That one would land me in jail and definitely wasn't the right thing to do. But I really, really liked that choice. Second, I could go talk to Han-bae and at the very least gather intel on what the situation was. Chul had said that Han-bae wasn't at the funeral parlor when his mother was there, but that didn't mean he wasn't in on the whole thing.

I jogged over to his car.

"Hurry," he said, when I got closer.

I walked around before opening the door and slid into the passenger seat of a beautiful Maserati.

The car went dark once I closed the door, but I could see his outline. He was tense yet didn't seem shocked to see me. "I'm glad you're here," he said.

"Really?" I almost laughed out loud. "Don't you have my girl-friend locked up in your mansion there?"

I could feel Han-bae's glare. "This is all my mother. I tried to warn both of you that she'd do something like this. So, if you can't leave your ego in the backseat, get out of my car. Ji-hee has bigger problems right now, and I need help getting her out."

He was right. On basically all of that. I swallowed hard. "I'll help," I said. I meant it. I'd put my differences with Han-bae aside because this was Ji-hee. "What are we doing out here?"

Han-bae raised a pair of night vision binoculars to his face. "I'm waiting to see if Chan-woo leaves for the bar. He usually goes out for an hour or two around this time. If we make a move, it should be when he's gone."

"What do you mean by make a move? And who's Chan-woo?"

"Chan-woo is the head of my mother's security detail. He's the meanest muscle my mother's ever hired. He loves carnage. Got kicked out of the Marines for killing a guy. When we go in to get Ji-hee, we don't want to run into him."

"Is he the guy that bloodied her brother, Gun?"

Han-bae put the goggles down and looked over at me. "I didn't know about Gun. Did he get hurt?"

"Completely smashed by someone at the funeral parlor."

Han-bae shook his head. "Probably Chan-woo. He never leaves my mother's side when she's out."

There was a noise in the yard and Han-bae brought up his binoc-ulars. "Someone's leaving." The gate in front of the house slid silently open, and a BMW pulled out before it slid closed again.

"Is that the guy?" I asked. It was so dark, and we were at an angle almost around the corner from the front gate. I couldn't see anything.

Han-bae nodded as he watched. "I think it is. Hard to tell, but yes. Yes, I think that's Chan-woo." He dropped the binoculars. "Okay, let's go.".

"Wait," I said. "What's the plan?"

Han-bae already had his door open, so we were all lit up. He turned back and glared. "Just get out."

I got out and closed my door quietly. "It just seems stupid to not take a minute and make a plan. How are we going to get in there?"

Han-bae walked to his trunk and popped it open. He had a rope ladder inside. "We go over the wall with this."

"There are cameras everywhere," I said.

"Not everywhere. I've snuck out enough times as a kid that I know a blind spot. Plus, it's a smaller crew at night. As long as Chan-woo isn't there, we can get in and out."

I wanted time to think. I wanted blueprints or at least a description of where we were going. I wanted to know if they had guns. I didn't like any of it, but I grabbed the ladder and followed Han-bae. He was wearing all black and pulled a dark mask from his back pocket. I was in jeans and a white tee shirt that basically glowed in the dark. This was the stupidest thing I'd ever done, and I was absolutely going to do it.

34

JI-HEE

I spent the rest of my day breaking out the remaining glass in the window by tapping small pieces with the bottom of my high heel wrapped in a towel to keep it quiet. After I had the full pane removed, I studied the yard. From my view it looked like the entire estate was in an L shaped formation surrounded by a wall that was too high to scale unless someone conveniently left a handy ladder sitting around. That left leaving through the gate as my only choice to get out.

No one brought me food at dinner time, so I ate cold rice and congealed soup. I drank water from the bathroom sink and did sit ups and push-ups to burn off nervous energy. It would have been awesome if there was at least a book in here or some paper and pens, anything to keep me from thinking about how stupid I was to try and break out of here on my own. Part of me wanted to just sit tight and wait for Han-bae, but the other part of me hated that idea more than the idea that we were married. And we weren't really married. Mother signed and registered the document. Not me. That meant none of it was legal and none of it was real. I could try and get it annulled, but I also knew Myang's lawyers would eat mine up like little snacks and still be hungry for more. And if by some miracle my lawyers gained any footing, Myang could always bribe a judge. Despite these cold truths I couldn't just sit here.

When it was full dark, I went to the now open window. A warm summer breeze tickled my face as I leaned out. I'd taken eight years of gymnastics before I went to London. I could tumble, land, and fall. Getting up onto the roof from here and then down off again was cake. Only it really wasn't. I'd be lucky if I only broke my leg and not my neck. But sometimes, even when you have zero chance of winning, you go for it anyway.

I took a steadying breath and put one knee up onto the windowsill, then the next until I was kneeling with both of my hands holding onto the top of the window frame. The window was tall, so if someone gave me a shove from behind, I'd have flown down three flights to my death. Very carefully, I lifted one leg over the windowsill, twisting until I could swing my other leg out. Now I was facing inwards, toward the house and kneeling on the very thin outside window ledge. The cement was rough against my tender skin, and I wished for about the hundredth time that I didn't have a dress on. The wind, which felt gentle while standing inside, seemed to push against my precarious balance. Very slowly, I reached up and took ahold of the rain gutter with both hands. When I had a firm grip, I rose to my feet. While standing the gutter was at my shoulder level. Maybe the next part wouldn't be as hard as I originally thought. I pulled and shimmied and pushed until my stomach was up and over the gutter. After that, I heaved my body onto the rooftop. I lay there, panting for a moment and tried to congratulate myself on the completion of the first task. Only it was the easiest one, and time was no longer on my side. If someone came to check on me, they'd figure out in about three seconds that I'd climbed out of the window onto the roof.

The moon was full, which was good. I could see. But also, not good because everyone could see me. There were cameras mounted at three-meter intervals, but they were aimed down toward the lawn. I stood slowly and waited until I felt confident in my footing. The shingles were sharp against my bare feet, but there was no way I could have walked up here in my heels. I took my first step and realized it was easier than walking on a balance beam. It was like walking on a slanted board, only every few inches was a sharp edge. Once I got a feel for how to step, I moved fast. I rounded the L and then came to the farthest edge of the house. The roof ended, and right below it was a second gabled roofline that pitched lower. That one dropped to another, even lower roof that spread out into an oversized garage. It was wide enough that it probably held a dozen or more cars.

Getting down from here would be easy. It was two drops, less than a few meters each. I could do it without breaking my legs or killing myself, but once I was at the garage level, I'd be stuck because one side of the garage had the gate where two guards stood, and the other was flanked by a guard house with windows all around. They'd practically rolled out a welcome mat that said: *Come jump down off the roof right here so we can easily catch you.* If I tried to get down anywhere from the garage level, all the guards would have a front row seat to my botched escape.

As I got closer, I could see inside the guard house. Two men watched monitors, and there were two more sitting at a table playing cards. The minute I hit the ground they'd be out the door with flashlights to drag me back by my hair.

I squatted down and watched them, then crept closer and grabbed onto the edge of the roofline before dropping down onto the lower tier. I moved silently along that roof and then came to the edge and dangled down again. I landed on the garage roof with a gentle thud, but none of it felt gentle to my bare feet. I crept forward feeling wet between my toes. I didn't have time to check for cuts, but I hoped they weren't deep. I was honestly too scared to feel much pain. I got closer to the edge of the garage and lay on my stomach, army crawling forward. I thought about laying right there all night. No one could see me, and maybe when they changed shifts or when a car approached there'd be a moment, a tiny blind spot, where no one was looking. I could wait and make my move then. I wiggled my hips and tried to get comfortable. Impossible with too many scrapes to count and a foot that now throbbed with my heartbeat.

One of the guards at the monitor jumped up and ran to the door, banging it open.

I raised my head a little higher. It looked like Chan-woo. Maybe there was a camera up here I'd missed. I was about to hop up and start running when I heard him yell.

"Han-bae, you brat. Get back here." Then he pointed. "And who is that?" Chan-woo raced out of the guard house and across their lawn.

I looked in the direction he ran. A bright light switched on, illuminating the entire scene.

A man in all black and a face mask froze, crouching in the bushes. I wouldn't have known it was Han-bae without all of Chan-woo's yelling. But only a few feet behind him crouched another man. Someone I would recognize from any distance. Someone impossible. Harrison.

The guards all started yelling and chasing as both Han-bae and Harrison turned and hightailed it in the other direction. They sprinted until they rounded a corner.

Guards shouted but I couldn't see them anymore. That's when I realized, they'd all left. Even the ones at the gate.

I was up and running before my brain could think more. I did the same shimmy to get down as before and then gripped the edge of the roofline. I didn't stop but dropped with a roll to the ground. Then I was half running, half limping to the gate.

There was a small security booth and inside would be a button. If it was similar to ours, you could open the gate just by pushing it. I made it inside and hit the big orange disk at the bottom of the keypad and waited, nothing happened. I looked around. There had to be another switch, but then the gate gave a distinct hum and began to silently swing inward. I was out and sprinting for the road before it finished opening.

35

HARRISON

Han-bae was ahead of me and almost over the wall by the time I grabbed the bottom rung of the ladder. I dropped to the ground on the other side seconds after he did. He hadn't waited and was already to the car. I was close behind, less than five feet away when something barreled into me. I went down face first and rolled, then brought my arms up in a defensive move. A sharp kick landed, and my ribcage exploded with pain. Instead of curling in, I took the hit and swept out with my leg, knocking whoever it was down with me. We were both back up in an instant, and then I was eye to eye with a guy I was absolutely sure wanted to wipe the ground with my face.

He barked at me in Korean. "여기 누가 있어"

Dad always told me to try and talk first. *Don't fight if you don't have to. Do your best to talk them down.* But I didn't think pulling out Google Translate right now was going to be helpful. I tried replying in English. "I'm Han-bae's friend. He asked me to help him."

"Okay," The man replied in passable English. "Looks like he's not your friend, though." The guy nodded behind me, but I didn't dare turn to look. "He left you."

I could hear Han-bae's car engine ripping down the street. I swallowed and my stomach flip-flopped.

The man sneered at me. "I'm good at cleaning up what Han-bae leaves behind."

Since this guy wasn't into talking I'd go with my dad's final advice. *If you have to fight, end it fast. Strike hard and finish it.*

I moved first, taking one quick step forward and striking out with my right fist. The guy dodged and his grin got bigger, like a cat that just found not only a mouse to play with, but a big fat one rolled in cream.

Before I could move, he lunged and took a shot to my head. I tried to block and duck but he got most of the hit in. He followed fast with a second and third strike in succession. So, I did the only thing I could, and ran at him, slamming against his body, propelling us back into the brick wall. I had him pinned, but my arms and back strained with the effort.

"Is your name, Chan-woo?" I asked around clenched teeth.

The guy grunted. "Han-bae told you about me?" he asked.

"Just a little," I replied. But then Chan-woo shifted his right shoulder forward, barely any effort for him. Fear washed cold over me as I realized he could easily get out of my hold. I raised my head to eye level before saying, "Ji-hee's brother says hi." Then I bashed my head into his nose. I followed fast with two hard hits to his jaw. Chan-woo responded by slamming an elbow into my face, knocking my head back with an explosive crash. Next came a strike to my ribs, so hard I thought I'd vomit on the spot.

A car screeched past us and skidded to a halt.

I stumbled backward as blood gushed into my eyes. Ji-hee's voice rang in my ears, but I couldn't see. I tried wiping the blood. Two hands grabbed the back of my head and brought my face down hard into a knee. The crack sounded like my skull split in two, but I knew it was only my nose breaking.

Ji-hee screamed louder. I couldn't understand what she was saying. She yelled at Chan-woo in Korean. Spitting out words like bullets.

I hadn't known I was lying on my back so I must have been out for a second. I rolled over, spit blood, and wiped my eyes in time to see Chan-woo slap Ji-hee.

In hindsight it was the worst and the best thing that could have happened. The worst because I couldn't handle seeing her take a hit, and the best, because up until that moment I was going to lose the fight. Chan-woo had been whipping me, and I was done. He was just as strong, only with decades of skill to back him up.

But Chan-woo shouldn't have touched Ji-hee.

I don't remember moving. I don't remember a lot of it, just that his back was to me and that gave me a sudden advantage. I jumped him from behind and got his neck in a hold. He brought us both down, but then by some miracle I was on top, punching him. He blocked, but I struck again and again, putting everything I had into each hit. I kept going, even after his arms fell away. I didn't stop until Ji-hee grabbed onto me, put her body in front of Chan-woo's.

"Stop," she said. "Stop. He's out."

When I dropped my fists, Chan-woo moaned and his head rolled to one side.

Ji-hee jumped up and pulled on my arm. "Harrison, get up," she shouted.

I think I stood because then we were walking. I looked over my shoulder, seeing only through a bloody haze. Chan-woo started to get up again, but we were to the car. Ji-hee opened a door and pushed until I crawled in. Then she was next to me and the car was moving.

I woke laying on something hard. I think it was a kitchen table. Two men were close and talking while one worked on my face. I could feel the tugging of stitches. Nothing hurt, I was numb, except my nose. My nose felt like it'd been run over by a truck.

I had a lot of drugs on board. I could tell by the weird floaty feeling. I tried to move, and then Ji-hee came into view.

"It's okay. Stay still. They're helping you." She squeezed my hand, which really didn't feel good, but then she pressed a kiss into my palm and that did feel nice. I tried to smile but my face wouldn't work right. She said something else. I couldn't understand her. I tried to roll, I don't know why. It just seemed important to get off the table, but something dragged at my arm, stopping me. The men shouted, all words that had no meaning. I tried to touch whatever was pulling at my arm. My fingers found plastic, tubes, and tape. I tried to talk, to tell Ji-hee that I needed to get up, but my mouth wouldn't work. The men kept shouting.

Then my arm burned or maybe it was cold. The floating stopped. I began to sink.

Down.

Down.

Down.

JI-HEE

Harrison was asleep when his grandfather showed up. Garrett Mills had called a little after two in the morning, but I was still awake with Harrison's phone in my pocket. I had a feeling someone would miss him, and I didn't want any police looking for a lost American boy. When I explained to Garrett what happened, he didn't seem overly shocked like I thought he would. I offered to send a car to bring him to our home in the morning, and his only request was that it be early. He arrived sharply at 7:00 a.m.

Father was gone again. This time to a new summer house in France, probably to drink all his lovely wine in peace. Mother was a no-show, and Gun was still sleeping. That left me to receive Garrett.

I could have turned it all over to Mr. Cho, Mother's assistant, but he had his hands full with arranging extra security and with Mother herself, who was clearly wrapped in self-pity. According to the staff, she hadn't left her room since the funeral parlor. Not even to see Gun when he came home from the hospital in a cast and certainly not when Han-bae brought Harrison and myself to the house late last night. Mother thought she'd lost her fortune, and maybe we had, but it was good she was keeping to her rooms. I wasn't ready to see her. When she finally emerged, she wouldn't apologize. She would expect absolute forgiveness. Only this time around, the forgiveness would come with some boundaries. Mother no longer had any say whatsoever in my life.

So maybe me meeting Harrison's grandfather was the right thing. If I was going to be in charge of my own life I might as well start here. I knew almost nothing about Garrett Mills other than what he had told me last night on the phone. No one in Harrison's family knew this trip was walking into danger. Harrison hid it from them. Garrett decided to come with him in case he needed a guide in a foreign country. This left me almost breathlessly angry. How could Harrison just come here and expect to *not* get hurt?

Last night when Han-bae and I half dragged Harrison inside my house I had this weird thought. I remembered this time I saw a little boy eating an ice cream cone, it was so hot out that the ice cream started to melt and it fell off into the dirt. Instead of crying like a normal kid, this little boy had knelt there in the grime and tried to eat it, only I think he got more dirt than ice cream. I just kept thinking about that kid while the doctors worked on Harrison's bloodied face. His boneheaded idea to fly all the way here and try to white-knight the whole situation was the mother of bad ideas. It hurt to see him moaning in pain, and it was all I could do to not yell at the doctors to give him more drugs.

I'd had Garrett shown into the Morning Room. Mother recently redecorated that part of the house in forest green and gold. Gun said our designer convinced her the jewel tones would renew her spiritual energy. I didn't think there was enough color in the whole world to renew Mother but maybe it would help sooth Garrett who sat on the farthest sofa next to the window. He stood as I entered. A trim man for sixties, with silver hair and a tan face. He wore off-the-rack slacks, and a well-tailored sport jacket.

"Mr. Mills," I said, approaching. I would have extended my hand, but both were covered in Band-Aids and gauze from my own escapade getting off the roof. "Harrison is still sleeping but if you would like to go to his room I can show you the way."

"That will be fine," Garrett said.

He silently followed me through the hallway that led to the East wing. My heart beat too fast and my mind spun with the gravity of letting Garrett see Harrison so injured, but I couldn't stop him. When we arrived at Harrison's door, I bit my lip and tried to think of something to soften what he was about to see. I'd explained all of Harrison's injuries over the phone, but his face still looked like hamburger.

Before I could speak, Garrett turned to me. "Ji-hee, I have a simple question for you."

"Of course," I said.

"Harrison came out here to protect you." He gestured to the house around us. "But you're a wealthy girl. Very wealthy. You probably have your own bodyguards or whatever people like you have. Yet my grandson came and got hurt. He doesn't have influence or power in your country, but he came anyway."

I tried not to wince, or worse, start crying again. Garrett was right. It absolutely shouldn't have been Harrison that got hurt.

But his question wasn't an accusation. He looked me dead in the eyes and said, "Would you have done the same for him?"

That stopped me. I'd been so distraught at Harrison for putting himself in danger that I didn't take even a moment to consider what I would have done if the story was reversed.

And just like that, I realized that yes, I would have flown halfway around the world and scaled a wall to fight for Harrison. Even if I knew I would lose, I'd still do it. That dirt-eating kid wasn't wrong after all. If you find the right guy, you wade through grime just for a sliver of a chance to save him. And that's what Harrison had done for me. He'd eaten dirt to make sure I was okay.

I spoke firmly. "Yes, Mr. Mills. I would. I would do the same for Harrison. I love your grandson."

Garrett smiled at me and his eyes went from guarded to genuine. "That's all I needed to hear." He opened the door and went inside to sit with his very bruised and broken grandson.

36

HARRISON

Ji-hee's doctors said I had some broken ribs, a fractured nose, and a list of other things. I tried to ignore most of it.

Garrett didn't.

He asked a lot of questions, talked to my parents, and then told them not to come. He said they could trust him. I still didn't really trust Garrett. Only that had been yesterday. Things changed when Han-bae showed up.

It was still morning when Garrett burst into my room and ripped the blankets back. "Get out of bed. Hurry," he said.

I groaned. It still hurt to breath, but I sat up. "What's wrong?" I croaked.

"Some idiot is here. He's insisting that Ji-hee go to Switzerland with him."

I got out of bed faster than I thought I could and then followed Garrett down a maze of hallways until we came to a library, like not just a room with a few books, but a real library with rows of shelves that extended to the ceiling and a large table covered with antique maps. A fireplace stood at the opposite end of the room flanked by two sofas. Ji-hee sat straight with her legs crossed and arms folded. Han-bae was there, right next to her, way too close.

I marched to Ji-hee and took her hand, helping her to stand. Ji-hee looked at me, startled. "You're here," she said. "How can you be out of bed?"

"I was bored," I said.

She eyed me, but I led her to the opposite sofa and had her sit down next to me. Every movement was exceptionally painful, each breath felt like I was coming apart at the seams, but I managed to keep my face steady.

Han-bae sighed. "I'm glad you're feeling better, Harrison."

"Are you?" I asked, "You left me with Chan-woo."

Han-bae's ears turned red, and he looked past me. "I saw Ji-hee running away so had to go get her. I came back for you."

He hadn't and we both knew it. Ji-hee had been the one out of the car and he'd done nothing to prevent her from getting slapped, but I let it go. I wasn't here to squabble over that. "When are you heading back to Switzerland?" I asked.

Han-bae smiled and managed to look angry while he did it. "Soon," he said. "When are you going to go back to California?" he asked.

"When Ji-hee is ready to go with me," I said.

Han-bae's face hardened and he looked at her. "It's a no go, then. If you leave with him, I'm not making any deals."

Ji-hee held up a hand. "I'm not leaving with anyone. And Han-bae you just sat here and told me not to worry that since the prenuptial agreement is only in your name and not your mother's you won't pursue it. Are you really going to make me fight you in court?"

Han-bae's face fell, and all of the fight seemed to drain out of him. "No, but I might if you leave with Harrison. You've never even given me a chance to prove myself. I helped you with my mother and that's going to cost me. I at least want a fair shot, and I can't have that if you leave with him." Han-bae said with a not-so-subtle sneer in my direction.

"What if I did give you a chance?" Ji-hee asked.

My spine stiffened, and I slanted Ji-hee a look. She couldn't really be considering this guy.

"How would that work?" Han-bae asked.

"I'll give you two weeks. We spend time together, go on dates and—"

I didn't realize I'd made a rude noise until Ji-hee's hand landed on my knee and she squeezed, not gently.

"We go on dates," she repeated. "And get to know each other."

Han-bae started grinning and I leaned in his direction.

Ji-hee cocked an eyebrow. "Settle down both of you. It will be nothing physical. I won't be intimate with you. But if at the end of two weeks we decide we're right for each other then we stay married. If not, then you give me an annulment without seeking retribution with the prenuptial."

"Three months," Han-bae said.

Ji-hee shook her head. "The most I will do is one. I'll know by then. We both will."

"I'll agree if Harrison goes home."

"I'm not leaving her here with you," I snapped.

Han-bae scowled. "I've proven that I'm not out to force Ji-hee, and if you're here she won't have a fair shot of getting to know me." He stood up and began pacing in front of the fireplace. "You owe me this, Harrison. She wouldn't have made it out of my mother's house if I hadn't been there."

"I don't owe you anything," I snarled.

Ji-hee held up a hand and spoke with command. "Knock it off, Harrison. Han-bae, sit down." She waited until Han-bae returned to his seat and then glared at me until I leaned back in mine. Finally, she said, "No single person can take credit for me breaking out of there, and I'm not a prize to win."

I tried to nod, but it made my head spin, so I stopped. "Ji-hee's right," I said. "It was a miracle we got out at all. But I'm still not leaving you here alone with him."

Han-bae leaned back in his seat. "Then there's no deal. I guess I'll see you in court, dear wife."

I was going to murder Han-bae.

Ji-hee spoke quickly. "I agree."

"What?" I turned to her. "You want me to leave you here with him?"

Her eyes softened. "He's a victim in all of this too. He deserves at least a chance."

"He doesn't deserve a single thing from you." I lunged toward Han-bae, but my movements were stiff. My vision swam right before I toppled to the floor, hurting myself instead of him.

He just scooted past me and stood. "I'm going to go now." He looked down at me with disgust. "I'll text you later after he calms down."

My ribs burned with each shallow breath but I shouted, "You're a coward. Do the honorable thing and let her go."

Han-bae walked away before I could say more, but he wasn't counting on Garrett waiting outside the library door, apparently listening in. I watched as Garrett clamped one hand down on Han-bae's shoulder. He snarled something I couldn't hear, but Han-bae practically ran down the hall to get away. I was starting to like Garrett.

Ji-hee kneeled down next to me. "You're already hurt and then you do this. I can handle Han-bae."

I tried to get up but searing pain kept me down.

"Come on," she said. "Let's get you back to bed." She had one hand under my shoulder and was trying to lift me off the ground.

"Wait, listen to me," I said. "If you reject him, he'll probably turn around and try to force you anyway. You can't trust a guy like him."

"I don't trust him, not at all, but he won't force this."

"How do you know that?"

She continued to try and lift my arm up, but it was like a mouse trying to carry a bulldozer. I gritted my teeth and made myself stand. Ji-hee grabbed my arm when I swayed and helped me sit. I collapsed down onto the sofa.

"How do you know he's not lying or trying to trick you. He could even send Chan-woo after you."

She sighed. "I know because Han-bae is like me. He's been in an unhappy home most of his life and had to deal with a manipulative mother. The last thing he wants is an unhappy marriage. I might not know him well, but I know that much."

I looked down at the floor and felt sick. How could Ji-hee risk so much for this guy? "I can't Ji-hee. I can't let you do this."

Ji-hee took my hand in her own. "I need you to let me handle this. Go home and wait for me. I'll follow you."

My eyes started to burn with tears, and I swallowed hard. I tried to nod again but my skull throbbed with each heartbeat. I couldn't solve this, and I couldn't make decisions for Ji-hee. If I really loved her the way I thought I did, the only thing left for me to do was put all my chips on the table and bet it all. "Okay. I'll go," I said.

JI-HEE

It took three more days before Harrison was well enough to fly, and I got a special pass so I could wait with him at his gate. Garrett was tactful enough to go get coffee and leave us in peace.

I reached up and brushed some hair out of his eye but realized too late, he'd styled it down to cover a massive purple goose egg on the left side of his forehead. "Ouch," I said. "I bet you still hurt all over."

Harrison shrugged. "I don't really hurt anymore."

"You wince like every five seconds," I said.

Harrison sighed. "I think that might just be my heart and not my body wincing."

That was the most he'd said to me since our argument over Han-bae. I leaned close and whispered, "Tell your heart to cheer up. It's safe with me."

Harrison nodded but didn't say more.

Han-bae agreed to put our "dating" on hold until Harrison left, but every attempt I'd made to get Harrison to be his old self hadn't worked. The guy was like a fortress. He'd answer my questions or even talk when pressed, but it felt like he couldn't to talk to me, like the right words were lost to him now. Under normal circumstances I'd be mad, but I was acutely aware that what I asked of Harrison wasn't normal. "I'm going to be with you again in four weeks," I said. "What's the next dance they have at school? Is it prom? I can't wait to go with you."

"It's winter formal, then prom," he said.

"Will you take me to both?" I whispered.

Harrison nodded yes and tried to smile. It just came out sad, and that only made him quieter.

Garrett walked past where we sat in the hard seats and stood next to the gate. An attendant's voice came over the speaker. "Flight 887 to Los Angeles is now boarding." She spoke the announcement in Korean, followed by English.

Harrison looked down at the dirty airport carpet and sighed. "I guess I'll text you when we land."

I cocked an eyebrow. "You guess?" Harrison didn't even look at me. I placed a hand flat against his chest. I could feel his beating heart, steady and strong and so alive. This doubting wasn't him, but I didn't know how to tell him any of the things I knew. I wanted to show him how much faith I had in us, that we were stronger than some guy and four weeks. "I wish you could just trust me," I said.

His head shot up, and I didn't hesitate. I leaned forward and captured his mouth with my own. We'd already kissed a lot in the short time that we'd been dating. And what we lacked in time, we made up in passion. Only this kiss wasn't about passion. This was the kind of kiss that spoke its own language. When words failed and all my big ideas seemed small, this said the things my heart wanted to say. It was my own personal vow that I would not leave Harrison, that I would return to California. He gripped me harder and pulled me close. I moved with him and let my kiss beg him to believe in us.

He broke away first and then cupped my face softly. "I do trust you," he said. "Hurry back."

37

HARRISON

Even though Mom took me to our doctor, who assured her that I was healing great, my parents worried. But I still went back to school and had my grades back up within a week. I didn't have much more to do, anyways. The bowling alley fired me, and I didn't want to hang out with anyone, not even Calvin. That left homework and talking to Ji-hee.

Being away from her was the hardest, but she called me every day like clockwork, after I ate dinner and mornings before I went to school. I didn't have to think. I only had to wait.

So why was I so mad? I knew why. I was afraid that she'd fall for the richest guy in South Korea, a man that on paper she was still married to, a guy that might be easy to fall for. And I was afraid that after loving Ji-hee, I couldn't love anyone else the same.

I didn't ask her about it. I couldn't. If I asked about Han-bae, I would sound jealous. And I was jealous.

She did all the right things to soothe me, to build my ego. She kept up a constant flow of ideas for dates once we were together again. She wanted to go to a planetarium, a bunch of museums I'd never even heard of, the theater, and an escape room. She wanted to try bowling, go to the batting cages, and she really wanted me to show her how to spear fish. She even had a big night set where she'd teach me Korean dance moves. Ji-hee had enough planned that we'd be middle aged before we could do it all. And that was fine with me. I'd grow old with Ji-hee.

Last night when she called, I realized I'd be down with pretty much any date as long as she was here with me.

"Do you want to know what I'm planning for our first date when I get back?" she asked.

"Hmm. What?"

"I want to sit in calculus and just hold your hand."

"For a date?" I asked.

"Yep. That's our first date once I'm in California," she said.

"Why calculus? Wouldn't you rather go to Venice beach?"

"No," she said. "It's got to be holding hands in calculus."

I flopped on my bed with my phone to my ear. "Why?"

"Because it's ordinary," she said. "It's like those everyday things you do together that mean you have all the time in the world. People go on big dates when they want to impress the other person or think their time is limited."

"But I do want to impress you," I said.

"You beat up Chan-woo. You're like superhero status to me and my brother. We're impressed for life."

I laughed. "Still, it doesn't mean I can't take you on cool dates." Part of me worried that maybe she thought I didn't have the money to date her. I couldn't fly her to Paris, but I could take her to all the cool places in California. I still wondered how rich she really was. She said that Han-bae had way more money than she ever would. I held on to that. "Sitting in school isn't exactly romantic, though," I said.

"Being together is romantic."

"And for you that's sitting in calculus?" I asked, shaking my head.

"Think about it. How would you feel if I was there with you tomorrow?"

It would mean she was done with Han-bae and that she'd chosen me. "I get what you're saying, but I'm still taking you to the beach for our first date when you get back. Count on it."

"We'll see." She giggled. "I'll be there very soon, and our first date will be us holding hands and solving polynomials."

I groaned. She had three weeks left with stupid Han-bae. That wasn't soon. I felt like a whiney kid in the backseat asking if we were there yet. Maybe I was a kid because a month without Ji-hee felt like years. And a month knowing another guy was sniffing around felt like a lifetime.

The next day Calvin picked me up before school. He'd broken up with Tiffany while I was in Korea and then they made-up again last night. It was the third breakup since homecoming. Now this morning he was so happy that I was surprised the car wasn't just floating us to school. Full-swoon Calvin mode was semi-annoying. But it was a weird annoying, entertaining enough that you couldn't look away, like watching someone walk backward into a swimming pool.

He was bouncing in his seat a little as he gave me a play-by-play recap of their date last night. "And we went to get ice cream, and she said that she was fat, but I said she wasn't, so she ordered, guess what flavor?"

I yawned. "Chocolate."

"No, chocolate swirl and she got hot fudge on top."

"Yeah, that's cool."

Calvin looked over at me. "Are you just saying *that's cool* to everything? Are you actually listening?"

"I'm listening," I said. "And I think it's totally cool that you're back together and getting ice cream and stuff. You know I like Tiff. You guys are good together. Don't break up anymore."

Calvin frowned. "You should at least be happy for me and not talk about us breaking up."

I raked my hands through my hair. "Sorry, man. I didn't mean it that way. I am happy for you."

"No, you're not. You're over there all mopey like you've been since you got back. Look, Ji-hee dumped you for Han-bae, but there are more fish in the sea."

I gritted my teeth. "She didn't dump me."

Calvin snorted. "She's in Korea with some rich guy who followed her halfway around the world. She totally dumped you. Just get over it and ask someone else out."

"I'm good," I snarled.

"You're not, though," Calvin snarled right back. "You're still moping."

"Stop the car."

"No, you'll hit me."

"I'm not going to hit you," I said. "Pull over."

Calvin eased the car to the curb and stared straight ahead, tense.

"I'm not going to hit you, Cal."

He turned and looked at me with one eye closed, still afraid I'd deck him. But I'd had enough of fighting. The bruises on my face weren't even fully healed, and I didn't think my nose was ever going to be the same. Plus, Calvin was my best friend. "I am happy for you," I said. "But I'm hurting, and when you hurt, I let you. I didn't tell you to give up, or that it was your fault you broke up in the first place, even though you flirted with another girl." I sighed. "And I think you're wrong about Ji-hee. I think she'll still come back to me." I grabbed my backpack from the floor and got out.

"Where are you going? Look, I'm a jerk. Sorry. Get back in."

"I need to clear my head." I slung my backpack over my shoulder. "Go without me. I'm gonna walk."

"You'll be late," he said.

I nodded. "I'll be there for the important stuff." I closed the door without slamming it and walked away.

I almost had my head wrapped around surviving another day by the time I made it to class. I was more than thirty minutes late, but I didn't care.

Ms. Smars looked up from her computer and said, "I'll mark you tardy. Take a seat, Harrison."

I moved down the aisle and wondered if I should have just skipped today. *He's here. Does he know? Why's he late? Is he mad?* The whispers followed as I passed each desk. It got to me. Just like everything got to me these days. I stared at the floor, refusing to look up, and even brushed Calvin off when he frantically tried to grab my arm.

I dropped into the middle seat of the back row, the only one left in the room. It wasn't like being late was that big of a deal.

Suddenly the attention shifted, and I felt the eyes of the class move to the kid next to me. I'd seen someone in my peripheral, in the chair to my right. I turned my head and looked over.

Ji-hee smiled at me.

I blinked. She was here, just like someone had waved a magic wand and teleported her right next to me. She looked exactly the same as when I left her a week ago, perfect skin and long silky hair.

My mouth hung open. I tried to stand but forgot that I was in one of those L shaped desks. When I stood up without swinging my legs out first, I almost toppled the whole thing over. I steadied the desk and tried again. This time, rising carefully to move to her side. She was still seated, so it seemed like the most natural move for me to drop to my knees next to her. "Ji-hee," I breathed.

She leaned close and cupped my face in both of her hands. "There you are," she whispered.

38

THE ENDING

Dear Reader,

This is where I would stop writing. The action is over, they suffered, endured, and now they get that happily-ever-after. I love that it's full circle. They're right where they met. For me, this is the perfect ending.

But many of you voiced that in *Falling for Korea,* the ending was too fast. I had one dear friend explain it to me with this:

"It's like I just watched someone do a cannonball into the pool, and then you didn't let me see the splash."

I'm an imperfect writer, but I am a good listener. So, keep reading if you want that splash!

39

JI-HEE

Harrison admitted that I'd been right. Our first date *was* in calculus. We'd held hands and he'd cried just enough to get teased for the rest of the school year. Then he kissed me until Ms. Smars yelled. But neither of us cared.

When school got out, I went home with Harrison to be greeted by his entire family. I guess he texted them, and everyone had a party ready for me when I walked in the front door, complete with a cake his mother baked herself. The only mothers I'd ever known of that baked cakes were in the movies.

Both of Harrison's parents and even his grandparents hugged me. I got to meet Ozzy, my failed date. He blushed and looked away when I shook his hand. Becca hugged me tight and made me promise to braid her hair sometime.

When Garrett offered to let us borrow his BMW for a trip to Venice beach, Harrison got this look like someone had just offered him a flight to the moon.

It sounds strange, but all of it hurt some part of my heart. There couldn't be a more perfect family than this one, and I worried that I'd never measure up to that. But when they waved to us from the porch as we drove away, that part of my heart eased a little. And by the time we were on the freeway, I had this faint fluttering hope that one day, I could be a picture on their wall.

"I want to ask something," Harrison said. There was a crease between his eyebrows, and his mouth was turned down. "But you don't have to answer, if you don't want to."

I already knew what he was going to ask. I'd seen him almost speak a few times during lunch. Only he'd snapped his mouth down over the unspoken words and seemed to want to think more. "You want to know what happened with Han-bae." I said. "Why I'm here three weeks early."

He stared at the road. "You're like a mind reader now?"

"Not really," I said. "I would want to know the same thing, if I were in your shoes."

"I do want to know, but I'm not going to push you to talk about this. If you need time—"

"You're going to like my answer," I said.

"Okay, now I can't wait. Why are you back three weeks early? I'm thrilled, by the way."

I sighed. "Han-bae and I lasted only a day, less actually. We went on one horrible date."

Harrison gripped the wheel more tightly and the leather made a squeaking noise. "What happened?" he asked.

"I was actually trying to give him a shot at winning my heart." I laughed. "Even though I knew he'd lose. But I couldn't be fair. Everything he said, every move he made, I compared him to you, and even though I didn't say it out loud. Han-bae could tell."

"Did he get mad at you, or threaten you?"

"No," I said. "Despite what you think, he isn't all bad. He asked me what was so special about you that I couldn't give him even a sliver of attention."

"What did you say?"

"I can't tell you that." I looked at my lap and grinned. "Maybe someday I will, but not yet."

"And what you told him is tied to you coming back early?"

"Yes, Han-bae called his lawyer that night. It took five more days to finalize the annulment, and then he personally put me on his private jet chartered for LA."

Harrison took a deep breath. I loved watching the rise and fall of his chest.

"But you won't tell me this amazing answer that had Han-bae rushing to set you free?"

I shook my head.

"Will you tell me the day we get married?"

I drew in a breath. "Do you want to marry me?"

Harrison's voice dropped lower. "Yes. Absolutely." He blushed. "I know we're in high school, so not today, but eventually I want to marry you." He looked over at me, worried. "Is that weird?"

With Harrison, nothing was weird. "No," I said and reached over to touch his arm. "It's kind of perfect." If someone would have asked me that six months ago, my answer would have been: *it's weird because I'm never getting married*. But things were different now. My life had always felt like this library where all the books were on the wrong shelves. Some of them had missing pages and some were scarred. Only now, my books were orderly. I still had damaged ones, but it felt like Harrison built new shelves or something, maybe even a new library. Every part of me, even the bad parts, had a space where I could belong. "Okay, it's a deal. I'll tell you what I said to Han-bae the day we get married."

"You're going to make me wait that long?"

I nodded. I wasn't going to spill. I'd hold off on telling him for as long as I could because I just couldn't look Harrison in the eye and say such nauseatingly embarrassing stuff. I'd told Han-bae in all my lovey-dovey seriousness that Harrison was my soulmate, that I wasn't counting the days until I could leave, but the hours. That our love was written in the stars. That last part had done it. He'd sighed with resignation and turned the car around. That night his lawyer called me to start the annulment.

When we were close to the beach Harrison pulled off the highway to fill up the car with gas. His grandmother had lectured him about not getting any scratches or dents before Garrett gave him the keys, so he very carefully inched toward the gas pump. It surprised me. Not that he was being careful, just that they'd made such a big deal about it. I mean, it was the three series for crying out loud. If Garrett wanted, I could buy him a new one every week.

Before we got out, Harrison checked his bank balance on his phone.

"Do you want me to get the gas this time?" I asked.

His eyes flashed up and he frowned. "I can get it."

"I know, but I should pay some of the time."

"No. I'll pay for gas." He got out still frowning and put his card in the reader.

I followed him and walked around the car to lean against the driver's door. "If it was Calvin, you'd have him pay half."

"If you start paying for everything, I'll get a complex." He turned and started filling the tank.

I leaned forward and tried to look sexy. I don't usually do that kind of thing, but it seemed to work because he let go of the pump and moved closer.

I smiled sweetly. "So, you want to pay for all the gas, but what about when we take my car? Which one of us is paying then?"

Harrison's eyebrows shot up. "You have a car?"

"It's not here yet, but my brother wanted me to buy one." I pulled out my phone so he could see the picture of the limited-edition Aston Martin Valhalla I'd ordered. "What do you think?"

He took it and scrolled through the pictures of the satin carbon finish and diamond turned hubs, then coughed like he was choking. "You actually bought this? Like you paid for it?"

"Do you like it?" I asked.

He nodded enthusiastically but seemed to sputter.

"I'm paying the gas on this car," I said. "That's fair, right?"

Harrison's face had a slight deer-in-headlights daze. Finally, he said, "How about . . . uh." He shook his head. "When you drive, you pay for gas, and when I drive, I pay."

"But I can't drive."

Harrison balked. "You don't know how or you don't have a license?"

"Both," I said. "I'm taking driver's ed next semester."

"But you're getting a car now?" he asked.

"I told you. My brother wanted me to. He said that I could just insure you as the primary driver and let you drive me places." I smiled. "Unless you don't want to."

If I'd told Harrison that the sun was about to consume the earth, I don't think he would have looked any more shocked. He held up a hand. "Let me get this straight. You're buying an Aston Martin, and you want me to drive it?"

I knew he liked Aston Martins. On the second day of school, I'd overheard him arguing with Calvin about which car was the best, and he'd talked about how cool it would be to even test drive one. It was the single reason I'd picked this car. I wrapped my arms around him and leaned against his chest. "I could hire a driver, I guess."

Harrison shook his head and started laughing.

"What?"

He laughed harder. "I can't believe you just up and bought my dream car, and you want *me* to drive it."

I stepped away from him. "Would you rather I buy something less luxurious, like a Mercedes or Audi? I can look at those too."

Harrison grabbed me, pulling me back to him. "No, I'm just surprised."

"That I have good taste?" I was playing dumb on purpose, and he knew it.

He cocked his head. "I knew you were rich, but I didn't know you were Aston-Martin-rich."

"I am, but the cost of my money is a crazy mother."

Harrison nodded. "I'm not gonna lie. She is crazy."

"Wait until you actually meet her," I said. "She's worse in person."

Harrison winced. "I hope it's not soon."

"It won't be." Before I left South Korea, I sat down with Mother and three of our lawyers. She grudgingly agreed that in light of her egregious errors I should maybe be given the freedom to live where and how I wanted. That meant turning over my share of the stocks.

Since Gun had been running our business, it was doing a lot better than when Mother had been in charge. Now I had the freedom *and* means to live exactly how I wanted for the rest of my life, if I managed it well. Part of that management would be gently easing Harrison into the idea of how much money that actually was. The car was just the beginning. I knew I'd still have to curb things and stay inconspicuous. Harrison wasn't ready for the kind of cashflow I could produce. It would completely freak him out. "She's still kind of licking her wounds. She won't show her face in California," I said.

He let out a breath. "I'm mad at your mom, and I don't think I'd hide it well if I met her."

I held up both hands. "See, if anyone should get a complex it's me. You have a mom that bakes cakes. I have a mother that tried to marry me off to the highest bidder."

Harrison tilted my chin up and brushed his lips across mine. "We have each other and that's all we need."

I kissed him back, more eager than his light caress. When I pulled away, we were both breathless. "I'll remember that I don't need a perfect family, if you remember that money doesn't matter. Only us. Only we matter."

Harrison nodded. "Only us and Aston Martins." He grinned. "They matter."

The End

ACKNOWLEDGMENTS

I couldn't have written this book without my writer's group. My deepest thanks to Cindy, Keri, Alene, and Brenda. I love writing with you guys. I'd like to thank my editor, Liz Richards. I learned so much working with you and look forward to the next project. Kevin Thompson, you did an amazing job with the cover. Thank you for being so patient and helpful. A big thank you to Heidi and Caitlin Penrod. Your ideas and sharp eyes are again appreciated. Also, your friendship. I miss watching Kdramas with you guys. I'd also like to thank my sensitivity readers, Eunbin Whittaker and Ezekiel Lee. Both of you provided valuable feedback and friendship. An unending thank you to Janean. Your constant friendship helped me breathe life into just the idea that I could be a writer. I'll always cherish you. A big shout out to Mary Ringo who read my manuscript more than once, and to all my beta readers. You helped me polish the rough spots. Thank you to the many readers that reached out to encourage me to finish this sequel. I had a lot of fear, but you guys pushed me around the corners.

I used to follow my children around, writing at swim meets and music lessons, waiting in parking lots with my computer on the steering wheel. It was hard. Only now I miss those times and realize you will always be the stories that really matter. Thank you for the honor of parenting you.

And lastly, the biggest thank you to Peter. Your love makes me brave, and everything seems possible when I'm with you. I married up!

www.ingramcontent.com/pod-product-compliance
Lightning Source LLC
Chambersburg PA
CBHW020316200626
46814CB00006BA/2276